*A Gentleman in
Charleston and the
Manner of His Death*

A Gentleman in Charleston and the Manner of His Death

WILLIAM BALDWIN

University of South Carolina Press

© 2005 William P. Baldwin

Published in Columbia, South Carolina,
by the University of South Carolina Press

Manufactured in the United States of America

09 08 07 06 05   5 4 3 2 1

Library of Congress Cataloging-in-Publication Data

Baldwin, William P.
  A gentleman in Charleston and the manner of his death : a novel / William
Baldwin.
      p. cm.
  ISBN 1-57003-602-0 (cloth : alk. paper)
  1. Dawson, Francis Warrington, 1840–1889—Fiction. 2. Dawson, Sarah
Morgan, 1842–1909—Fiction. 3. Journalists—Crimes against—Fiction.
4. Charleston (S.C.)—Fiction. 5. McDow, Thomas B.—Fiction. 6. Murder
victims—Fiction. 7. Murderers—Fiction. I. Title.
  PS3552.A4518G46 2005
  813'.54—dc22

                                                2005014137

PREFACE

The Dawson murder trial that lies at this novel's core was front-page news across the nation. Charleston newspaperman Frank Dawson had once been the most influential editor in the South, and in 1889 he was still expressing himself with a strong and surprisingly liberal voice. His senseless death at the hands of a neighbor was viewed with outrage, and his contribution to Southern journalism was roundly applauded. Dawson's wife, Sarah, had also written for his paper, but the extent of her literary ability would be known only with the posthumous publication of her diaries. (Literary critic Edmund Wilson considered Sarah one of the best of the Civil War diarists.) There was much to draw on, and, like my fictional narrator, I have made extensive use of Frank and Sarah Dawson's lives and the lives of their friends and of their enemies as well. And, except for shortening, the written record they left behind occasionally finds its way into *A Gentleman in Charleston and the Manner of His Death* almost unchanged.

It was difficult to improve on the drama of that turbulent age—on characters that lived so large—but like the narrator I, too, did not hesitate to draw on my own imagination, and at times this was an unreined imagination. For that reason I have changed the names of those involved. Do not let that detract from the fact that what follows is a true story. After all, isn't that the best kind?

*A Gentleman in
Charleston and the
Manner of His Death*

Straightway I was 'ware,
So weeping, how a mystic Shape did move
Behind me, and drew me backward by the hair;
And a voice said in mastery, while I strove . . .
"Guess now who holds thee?"—"Death," I said. But, there,
The silver answer rang . . . "Not Death, but Love."

—Sonnets from the Portuguese
Elizabeth Barrett Browning

AN INTRODUCTION

PARIS, AUGUST 1907

I know the power of language to destroy. I have witnessed that, and I have felt anger, loss, and longing. I do know something of love. But not enough. Can one ever know enough of love, love open or illicit, confessed and unconfessed? *Twixt Love and Law?* No, that title has been used before, and besides, we have more to contend with than the love of lovers. In what is to come I am certain we will also find the love of husband and wife, the love of parent and child, and of sisters and brothers—all are snared by love. Should I include you? All right, Reader, you as well. All are linked by this devise. You, I, Rebecca . . . especially Rebecca.

Because I have grown stout and bearded, she did not know me, nor did her son. And having gone undiscovered, I am now entrusted with a great task. It seems they require a biographer, and having served both Poe and Lanier in that capacity, I am the one chosen. And because I once lived in Charleston I am the one chosen. They, too, are exiles. Like me, Rebecca and her son have abandoned Charleston and come to Paris, where the wisteria blooms late in the spring and confines itself with Old World propriety. In Charleston those vines grow thick as arms and twist with wild abandon to the very roofs. Isn't America still the land of opportunity? Odd then that Paris should remain their city of dreams, their receptacle of shimmering promise. Should I say "mine" as well?

They assume that the story is to be of the man—her husband, his father. "The most powerful man in the South!" That was said of him on more than one occasion. Yet seventeen years have passed since his death and no monument to him stands in Charleston. "An insult! He had enemies. He has them still." So says the wife, the small woman with rich auburn hair now silvered—

but whose violet eyes still gleam with a challenging intensity. "A vain and silly child" her son calls her, and he means this. But he dotes on her. And together they tend the memory of the man. Or rather they have passed that burden on to me. Yes, what monument there is to David Lawton can only be found in Paris, and it was entrusted to me. What have I been given? The family's papers. No more, no less. A small mountain of letters, diaries, and memoirs both published and unpublished. The relevant newspaper articles, the essays and editorials have already been clipped and pasted. I have both his views and those of his opponents. I am assured that all is included. I have before me both the censored and uncensored. All will be revealed.

Private matters? Yes, they are. For this reason and because I will, when necessary, fall back on imagination, I have decided to change the names. Still, these people of whom you will read did and even do exist. Rebecca is not Rebecca, nor is Abbie Abbie, but flesh and blood goes on unchanged. Rebecca did marry David, who was also called by another name—two other names, in fact. And he was, in fact, the editor of a Charleston paper—but not one called the *News and Independent*. And he was killed. In the course of this story he will die. That we can be sure of. Am I responsible for his death? I wonder this myself.

But again, enough. I have read, sifted, stacked, read, sifted, and stacked again. I will start with Abbie. In the late summer of 1886 she wrote a lengthy letter to her sister Rebecca and described in detail the great events that had just enfolded the Southern city of Charleston. Of course, she does not tell all. The truth is for us alone to know.

CHAPTER ONE

CHARLESTON, S.C., AUGUST 1886

Awake. Abbie Dubose lay abed and watched the odd patch of sunlight broaden across the bleached pine floor. Like a crooked finger, it seemed to beckon, to nudge at languor, for Abbie's day was filled with promise. Her daughter Catherine would be up by now, dressed and gone off down the beach to see Mrs. Griffen or find a companion her own age. And Abbie was left behind to lounge away another morning, to lie on the soft down mattress and speculate on what a certain man might be doing at that very moment.

David. David in Charleston. She imagined him across the harbor—in the city. She saw him journey towards his business. At that very moment he was stepping from the trolley. She saw how he dressed in soft gray linens and how he raised his cane and tipped his boater, for he had reached such and such a corner and stopped to greet a strolling couple. They parted with smiles, and then he went two doors further and entered the stately building with the broad cornices. She imagined him speaking to people in his office. Then he would have his lunch and continue to do his work, bend across his desk, and call out for such and such to be done, and then he would come across on the ferry to the island—to her—well, not that very afternoon but soon. And then he would invite the two of them, mother and daughter, to his nearby house. At fourteen Catherine had interests of her own and would make her excuse, and Abbie and this man would go on alone to the dwelling. He would sit with her while they waited for that boiling August sun to set, and they would drink iced juleps. He would roll a cigarette for himself and another for her. Here on the island a woman might smoke a cigarette if she stayed well back in the shadows of the porch and made sure that her daughter was not about.

And then they would talk and talk and talk. They would have supper, her daughter now arriving and helping to prepare and serve the meal and taking part in the conversation—as if this were the familiar order of their lives and not the feeding of a drunken, sad, and unemployed husband, a husband who let his ravings pass for conversation. Then her daughter would be off to nap in some higher recess of the house, and this woman and this man could split a second bottle of wine and talk until midnight. She would wake Catherine and they would walk to the boardinghouse—after both receiving from him a chaste hug and the promise of a swim in the morning, and with the implied promise of more talk and more wine and more of . . . what should she call it?

Love! How long had it been since Abbie had felt this way about a man? Since before she was married? Yes, perhaps so. Well, here she was separated at last from Mr. André Dubose, free thanks entirely to the generosity of this man, her brother-in-law, David Lawton. Yes, David had taken on the support of both her and her daughter. He had moved them from New Orleans to Ohio and enrolled Catherine in the Conservatory. He had even provided for this summer idle. And now here was Abbie walking through green meadows, idly, unthinkingly in love. No, not green meadows exactly but a grand wide sandy beach with an ocean of blue water in front and an ocean of rolling dunes behind, and not unthinkingly either, for she did consider to a degree her current course.

The boardinghouse was a great clapboard construction, sealed no better than a barn but comfortable with its surrounding porch and its convenient and well-provisioned dining room. Yet David and Rebecca's beach house was almost as large. From either window of Abbie's room she could glimpse the end of their wide, breeze-filled front porch—another house for Rebecca, but at least there was little in the spare vacation furnishings to remind Abbie of her sister. During these brief weeks, she might pretend it was her own.

Oh, she did miss Rebecca with a second part of her heart, for despite her current infatuation with David Lawton, Abbie knew her sister to be the true intimate of her life. Of the two, Rebecca had the gifts, the intellectual power to construct delightful essays and fine poetry. This sister, who she assumed would never marry, had made a match for herself that many would envy—though Abbie knew better than to assume any marriage was truly made in heaven. After all, David was a man like any other—vain, demanding, petulant as a child, and always in need of attention. And he was a Catholic. While Abbie had not opposed the marriage on that or any other grounds and had joined with their brother Asa in nudging Rebecca towards the altar, still David had finally come to make demands of a religious nature which might be construed by some as unreasonable.

In January of that year he had taken his family off to Paris, enrolled both children in good Catholic schools, and left Rebecca behind to supervise. Their progress to date (approaching eight months) was rocky. Thomerson had been ill and was withdrawn from school. Then feeling unwell herself and finding it impossible to cope with their lodgings, Rebecca took Anna from her classes and began to drift across the Continent in a rather aimless fashion. All this David had confided to Abbie with many shakes of the head and requests that she use her powers of persuasion to settle the "Gypsies."

Abbie had written as instructed, for she might, in truth, still have some control over her sister. When they wrote they opened their hearts to a degree, and when they met they still fell into each other's arms. But those years since they had gone their separate ways seemed more and more to stretch endlessly, to have passed almost as a dream. Abbie's own fine dancer, her philandering, decadent husband was sinking his family further and further into debt as she struggled to provide for her daughter some remnant of security and home, while Rebecca was enjoying the opposite—the mirrored image. How nice to wake for at least this brief moment, to suffer but in a different cause, to exchange the old pain for a new. Happy difference.

The old was old indeed. At twenty Abbie had begun to feel at times a melancholy folding about her, a grim, gray shroud. Even before the death of their brother Hamp, those periods of despondency possessed her. Only Rebecca could tease them away, but not always, and that was long ago. In recent years these "blues" returned with a vengeance. And as Abbie fought to rise from this deep pit, she realized that there was nothing she would not do to have her own way, to be for one last time the spoiled belle, the center of attention in that trampling that was called "life's dance."

No, wait: "nothing she would not do" was far too strong a phrasing. Her intent was not that serious. After all, Rebecca was in Switzerland, or France perhaps, and she might understand how Abbie and David—how her sister and her husband could innocently enjoy themselves. She might. Only a summer flirtation, that was all Abbie was asking. Dignity? Common sense? These were not allowed when the temperature rose above ninety. She had observed this even here. A formerly prudish soul could take a simple ferry ride across the harbor, and once enthroned in her island cabin, all notions of proper deportment vanished. Good-bye to church and society and hello to a skimpy bathing costume and mixed drinks in the middle of the afternoon.

Flirtations were a standard requirement. Yes, if fortune favored her, a married woman could become a temporary widow for those short, hot months. She could look down and sigh and perhaps go so far as to whisper "if we had only met sooner," and she knew that at the summer's end she (and he) were free to leave—without tears or reckless promises—to simply end the game, to call a draw and smile and part. David understood this.

At least she hoped he did. Abbie had risen from the bed and with the leisure of a well-kept woman completed her toilet, returned only once to the mirror to examine herself. Hair of rich mahogany red piled high, eyes of deepest violet, her refined features were unmarred by any wrinkle. But exposure to the sun had darkened that usual ivory complexion, and along the ridge of that classical nose she spotted several freckles. She hadn't seen those since her honeymoon.

Abbie tied upon her too-thin body a cool muslin shift, a white shift with a tracing of vertical brown lines and a linen collar, and thus attired she went downstairs to claim her breakfast of melon and coffee. She was always the last down and did feel guilty that the staff might suffer on her account—but just barely guilty. The maid entered and met her with a smiling nod. Abbie sat at the sturdy plank table and sipped from the white china cup.

The morning edition of the *News and Independent* lay folded at her right hand. She opened to the front page. "THE TRADE OF THE YEAR" read the headline, and below was the yearly economic report for the state of South Carolina. No, not a subject for which she cared. But that newspaper was not David Lawton. Or rather David was more than a paper. On the previous weekend hadn't he confessed that to her? Against all better judgment, the *News and Independent* would soon include serialized novels. "Silly fictions," he called them. "Love-laced fodder," he called them. Could she forgive him, his all-too-human need to have subscribers and hence to show a profit?

"Yes," she had laughed. "David, you must make room for romance."

"Do men and women actually speak so to each other?" he teased. "God forbid."

God forbid that he discover her secret vice. On rare occasions she read those same romances. In fact, she faithfully followed those serialized in her Ohio paper.

Abbie finished the melon and carried a second cup of coffee out onto the porch. In the distance the rippling ocean, the glint of an already harsh sun—the night before a cool and silver moon and breeze to match—now the gust of hot breeze. Abbie sat in the wicker rocker and touched her free hand to her throat. What did David understand?

David. The perfectly tailored clothing rested easily upon this man of above-average height and sturdy build, he with the broad mustache of rich brown and joy-filled eyes of matching hue. He was still the soldier. He moved with grace, but his manner was touched with a formal almost military bearing that suggested both the past war and perhaps, too, some connection with the courts of the Old World. His habit of demonstrating with his hands was decidedly French. He was educated in that country. And yet he remained thoroughly unaffected, speaking in a light baritone often edged with laughter and shaped with the cultured accents of an English gentleman. He was a gentleman. Gentle to her in all ways. This was her David.

But on the previous Saturday, well into the night, she had attempted to tell his fortune. She had taken his broad palm between her two small hands. With steady forefinger and an authority which she felt she did not possess, she had begun to trace the heart line, a line which she saw at once was disturbingly divided. "There are mysteries in this world beyond the knowing of many," she began.

"No!" he said quite suddenly. "No, there are not, and it is ridiculous for you and your sister to believe such nonsense." Of course, she had released his hand. But he did not remove it. The hand lay there, untouchable, naked and red, like a skinned animal. Not knowing what else to do, she had again taken it between her own and held it.

"Well, I only meant to help," she said in a quiet voice.

"Yes, yes. I know," he answered. "But Rebecca has quite taken leave of her senses. Since baby Stephen's death nothing will do but that she be off twice a week to see the fortune-teller."

"When we were girls . . ." Abbie began, but he cut her off.

"You are not girls now," he said.

She had never known her brother-in-law to be so curt. Indeed, she had never heard him raise his voice to another human being. But she had heard he had a temper. A famous temper where his work was concerned. Of course, she had withdrawn her hands from his, but still his hand remained on the table, palm up. "I have been ill," he said quietly. "Please forgive me." So Abbie took his hand in hers again and held it until they parted, which was before the next chime of the clock.

Could Rebecca hold that against her? How many of her beaux had Abbie shared with her sister? "All," she said aloud to no one but a passing seagull. Scores of poor men, men often made ridiculous by their attention to the Wright sisters. There in the midst of bloody war they had rushed to pay homage to the Wright sisters. Flirtations. Rebecca would not even kiss them. Just pitted one against the other. But the sisters had paid. They had paid the price of two brothers. She knew that Rebecca felt the same. God had taken both. Two young men of infinite promise were fated to die so that two silly girls might see and understand that love was not a game, that war was not a gallant pageant, a chivalrous masquerade, but the awful and bloody product of that pretended romance. Shelby and Miles both dead. Hamp, too. Rebecca's

Hamp. Since the death of her baby Stephen, it was Hamp whom Rebecca searched out in the séances, for if contacted he would watch over her infant. Another chore for the departed. "If Hamp had lived . . ." was a preface oft used by her sister.

Though not a victim of war, Hamp was victim, nonetheless. A victim of love? Victims. Weren't they all? And yet, Abbie still yearned to feel the ground move beneath her own feet one last time—but that poor choice of words, even unspoken ones, caused her to bend low and rap the wooden floor for luck. Five days earlier a small earthquake had tumbled dozens of chimneys in Summerville, a community just north of the city, and she did not wish to invite such a catastrophe.

As for David, on the coming Saturday she would ask him to take her dancing at the Pavilion. He had begged off twice before, but she would plead this time on bended knee. And how could he refuse to lead her at least twice around the floor? They would take her daughter, of course. David would dance with her as a father would, and all three would enjoy something resembling a domestic outing.

On that Sunday night, before he left her, she would stand behind him as he sat at his kitchen table, and she would with her fingertips caress his temples as she and her sister had done for their brother Asa so many times and so many years before. But she would not tickle the bottoms of his feet. She could hear herself saying that to David. "I will not tickle the bottom of your feet." And despite the heat it did seem to her to be the most perfect of summer days.

As the sun was sinking that evening, Abbie walked alone on the beach. She was going to the Griffens to retrieve her daughter. Jonathan Griffen was David's personal lawyer. More importantly, the Griffens were friends of David, and, as Abbie was a visitor, they were her best friends on the island. Though a young couple, at times they seemed older than Abbie—especially the woman, who would, in fact, tease and look after Abbie like a mother. So on the way to the Griffens the whole sky was the strangest blaze of glory ever beheld, and Abbie said to herself that if the earth had to die she would wrap herself in just such gorgeous robes. It looked so wonderful that she hurried on to share the event with the Griffens. At dark she and Catherine returned to the boarding-house, not taking their usual circumventing path and not knowing quite why they should hurry. The usual breeze of evening did not rise. After supper, which she did not touch, Abbie sat on the piazza with Mr. Howard, who had long-fingered gambler's hands reminiscent of her husband André's. She sat with Mr. Howard not because she enjoyed his company—though he was bearable—but to avoid the stifling heat of her room. Catherine and several others were playing cards in the hall.

Abbie said, "This is just the weather for an earthquake."

Her companion answered, "You are only nervous because of that rumble last week."

Again Abbie rapped the floor. "Yes," she had answered. "Yes. I know that is true." Then the two of them sat, not speaking for another five minutes.

"I wonder . . . ," began Mr. Howard, but a hollow roar like train cars passing over a bridge drowned out the rest. Then the house pitched to and fro like a ship. They sprang to their feet and, clutching each other, staggered to the steps, where her daughter took the place of the gentleman.

Clinging to each other, Abbie and Catherine went together down the reeling treads, climbed the ten feet of drifted sand beside the dwelling, and stood isolated and together while the earth rocked and the very stars swayed. What was solid was now adrift.

Oh the horror! Before them the ocean lay in glassy calm, but at any moment a tidal wave might form! Yet others did not perceive this threat, for screaming women and children were rushing madly to the shore. Abbie wondered if she should call after them, call out: "Beware of the tidal wave!" But she did not.

Still, it was far more sensible to have found this high ground among the trembling grasses. Others had. On all sides came the groans and prayers of those who had also taken refuge in the dunes. A couple from the house next door (the two of them playing cards with her daughter) had rushed home, grabbed up their three sleeping children, and brought them to stand beside Abbie and her daughter. And Catherine herself had rushed back into the rooming house to retrieve her violin, which she now clutched with one hand as she held her mother with the other. So now their meager refuge held six and the violin. There in the starlight they stood waiting. Another shock! They clung to each other in silence, and for the first time Abbie thought of David, powerless to help them. She looked to the distant city and saw a blazing fire leap to the skies, then another, then two more! Would the entire city burn? Or had it collapsed already into formless rubble? Earthquake and fire and threatening sea, as well, and the entire harbor separating them from David. God only could help!

But what if David was beyond that help? Dead? No. Not him. But what if he were trapped beneath some roof beam or pinned by a fallen wall and yet alive? She imagined his pale hand rising above the debris. If he needed saving, she must save him. And . . . and if the world were indeed ending, at least this small portion of the world—a remote possibility but who could say—then she wished to be at David's side. Abbie said to her daughter, "We must get to him. Let us go to the Griffens and then to the boat, if boat there be."

It was dark and the Griffens were half a mile off, but Abbie took the lead, and when she grew faint-hearted, Catherine insisted, "We must go to David! Mother, we must go to him." At the Griffens' fence they found others, most terror stricken and all anxious to return to the city. Though standing, the Griffens' two small boys were barely awake, and. Mr. Griffen held each by the hand. Mrs. Griffen alone thought to tease and said to Abby, "How many years since you have felt the earth move under your feet?" And Abbie wondered how much of her recent behavior had been remarked on. What could it matter? If David died then nothing mattered. "Dear God, let him live," she whispered. "Let him live."

Now lanterns were brought, swinging lights that showed ghastly white faces. And as they walked towards the landing, dark faces showed as well, for the Negroes were rushing back and forth and praying and singing out "God have mercy!" with each new quiver. Abbie felt nausea rising in her throat, and others spoke of this sensation. As a body they moved along, reaching the balcony of the grocery and that of the saloon, but none dared to enter these buildings while the shocks continued. "For the best," said Mr. Griffen. "Alcohol will not calm them. Neither black nor white."

At the landing a boat had just arrived with news that the office of the newspaper had collapsed but David was safe. Still, they would go to him. She and her daughter belonged at David's side. She saw herself there, holding David and being held. But for now, Mrs. Griffen sent him a note by two young men, who set off rowing. David would know they were safe. How many hours passed after that Abbie could not tell, or how they passed them either. At early dawn she went back to the boardinghouse with Catherine, packed a trunk, and before returning to the landing begged the Griffens to accompany them, which they reluctantly did—bundling up the two boys and a single small case of belongings.

Finally they began to cross the harbor, the city before them bleeding smoke. Again Abbie feared a tidal wave might come, come to lift their cockle shell up into eternity. She imagined a great black wall of water rising over the silhouetted fort. Laughable. As girls she and Rebecca in far-off Louisiana had looked upon the possession of this Fort Sumter as somehow vital to their personal well-being. Now that little fort, so dark and squat, was certainly without value to her, unless such masonry might magically act as breakwater and shield them from the approaching wave. But no wave came, only a gentle breeze rising with the sun, but this enough to whip the spray across the occupants of the small craft.

By the time they reached the wharf, all aboard were drenched, clothing matted, hair disheveled and streaking down the sides of faces. Happy they were to go scrambling unladylike up the ladder. How odd to have the solid wharf pitch beneath their feet. Not because of tremor, though. No. On disembarking, the gentle pitching of the little boat was still attached to them. Abbie swayed and was held up once more by her brave daughter, who repeated, "We must go to David." And immediately on leaving the wharf, they were met with a morning edition of the *News and Independent*. Only David Lawton could have accomplished that in the midst of burning ruins—a fact Mrs. Griffen remarked on as they stood surveying the partially collapsed newspaper office. David's pride, the massive Venetian cornices had broken from the roof and were scattered in fragments across the width of the street. They followed the trolley tracks. Though broken and splaying forth in spots, the blue line would still lead them faithfully to David and Rebecca's home. Each and every afternoon it carried David there. And so huddling together and hardly pausing to listen to the many shouted warnings, they moved forward.

On all sides were more houses and shops reduced to ruin. To the right the half-crumbled spire of Saint Philip's hung high in the sky as if dangled by an immense but hidden thread. And on the corners and open space of little Washington Square, they came upon more Negroes, shouting and singing together, pleading in their raw emotional way that "God have mercy!"—while beyond them on all sides, the smoke of fires continued to spread.

Mr. Griffen did pause at the police station and placed a hand upon his forehead. The building's five massive columns now suggested a Greek temple in ruin. "They'll take that one down," he said. But why? Abbie wondered. To their right still stood the ghostly ruins of the Catholic cathedral, and that had burned in '61. Why not leave them all as ruins? Why not leave them as a warning? But Mr. Griffen had spoken with such certainty. A slight man with thinning hair, he spoke with an odd authority on all matters—as men often did.

"A carriage!" Mrs. Griffen shouted. As ever, she had a clear vision of the necessary, and fortunate they were to secure this conveyance. Especially fortunate for Catherine, who in protecting her violin case, had slipped and stumbled several times and was exhausted. They piled in and followed the blue line track up into the smoldering, rubble-strewn city. Past "the pond" they traveled. The calm waters of the elegant rectangle now appeared gray and troubled, and, of course, the promenade was abandoned. Gone were the goat carts and children and their nannies and the young ladies who might stroll in search of a husband and the young men who might stroll in search of a wife.

Overlooking that somber lake, the stately hospital still stood but with arched interiors open to sky. In the far distance patients lay on mattresses in the street, where white-coated attendants moved among them as ghosts in a graveyard ruin. "Can't be repaired," said Mr. Griffen. The rest just shook their heads. From somewhere undetermined came the familiar sound of Negroes in fearful praise and song, and the carriage lurched forward, rocking them as a trolley might.

The house that they approached? While out riding three summers before, Rebecca had come upon this dwelling, not a mansion but very close and in a more orderly and suburban neighborhood than they had then enjoyed. The trolley stopped practically at the door. To reach David's office was a twenty minute trip—at the very most. Not a mansion? The house was quite grand. Why hedge on that account? A traditional arrangement of four major rooms over four over four, with storage and kitchen on the ground level, living spaces next, and then bedrooms above. Oh, but such high-ceilinged and airy rooms, and a grand curving staircase sweeping through the middle. David had bought an organ. As Rebecca boasted, such a house could accommodate the rich deep basses of the instrument and her husband's accompanying and quite operatic baritone. Oh, this house meant much to Rebecca. As girls she and Abbie had seen their own, in Baton Rouge, destroyed. Enemy soldiers had overrun the city, burning, looting, destroying, or carrying away all that they valued. It was a loss not unlike what she saw before her now.

At the entry of the home, Abbie thought her legs would fail. The portico was ruined, collapsed completely. They entered through the rear. On all sides the walls were cracked. Mortar and dust and fragments of broken chandeliers littered the floors. The books of that well-ordered library were tossed in disarray, the pages flapping as angry waves. Along the walls were sheets of water and great puddles on some floors. And puddles on the stairs, which she managed to cover in a most unladylike haste—only glancing as she passed into the hall mirror, which in all improbability still hung and reflected back her quite haggard self. Ah, vanity. As she rushed higher, she smoothed back the locks of salt-laden hair. There was David asleep in his bed. He was beneath the sheet. The incongruity of it made her smile. She thought to find him—well, not dead — but in some state of disrepair. Yet he slept like a babe. "David," she whispered. "David." When he did not stir she advanced through the room and gently nudged his shoulder. How odd. For a moment she had seen them there as in a tableau, she a second self observing from a far corner. The three tall windows stood like broad columns of light, and she, an upright figure bathed in this same light, was moving toward the bed and then bending to touch the man she wished so much to love.

"David" she whispered for a third time. "David!" she called out louder, for she did wonder at his deathlike stillness. But he opened his eyes, and he was glad to see her. He sat up. Clothed only in his undergarments, he seemed to be half-man, half-bed.

Abbie needed to weep but did not. She needed to hold him in her arms but did not. She needed to be held but was not. Instead she placed both her hands around his forearm, but this simple gesture did contain more honest affection than any previously managed. Indeed, this seemed a moment of perfect intimacy. "You are alive," she whispered. "You are alive."

"Of course," he laughed.

Then, given his privacy, David dressed and came down to see Catherine and the Griffens. On the back lawn they found the cook, Elsa, a sturdy German woman of advancing age, a previously reasonable woman who now seemed to have completely lost her senses. But all of them took refuge beside her, for addled or not, hers seemed the most sensible place to be. The shocks had not ceased. No, these continued to be felt and even heard.

Still, they refugeed in style. Chairs were brought out from the house and an old carpet spread on the lawn and pillows secured for those ready to collapse. Mrs. Griffen settled her two boys, and then she and Abbie made Elsa lie down between them, and they soothed the sobbing cook, who, once comforted, managed to cook them a dinner on an open fire. This was eaten picnic fashion and only abandoned once and that for a particularly violent convulsion of the lawn beneath them. Just before dark Mr. Griffen returned with an immense tent, which was hung between two trees. Abbie had four mattresses thrown down from the top story and these spread upon the floor of their canvas abode, and Elsa supplied her quilts, which were bright and many. The two small boys were put to bed, and the adults sat in the easy chairs that had found their way onto the carpet. There, with only the stars above, they sat and waited for the next awful roar.

David seemed calm enough. She expected nothing less, but how amazing that he could awake in the midst of a collapsing house, find his way to a collapsing office, put out an edition of the paper, then return to his bed in that same collapsing house and go to sleep while others were still in a state of helpless shock. Studying his profile in the semidarkness, she imagined him staggering down the reeling stair and out the door. All the great masonry of portico and columns now lay a mass of broken marble, brick, and wood, but in the dark he had not understood this and fell ten feet to the ground. Yet, God had preserved David. He had only torn his trousers and wrenched a leg, which now caused him to limp slightly and rely on his cane. She had not lost him. But was he hers to lose?

Considering that, Abbie had apparently fallen asleep. Then nudged awake by Mrs. Griffen and guided by that same friend, she called good night to her brother-in-law, entered the tent, and slipped into a profound and dreamless slumber.

On rising the following morning, Abbie was pleased to discover a bathing stall in place—a tin laundry tub filled with water and surrounded on four sides with draped blankets. For their honeymoon, she and André had stayed in a clapboard shanty on the Gulf Shore, and in the center of the main room was just such a tub. But that was twenty years before and under entirely different circumstances. Abbie stripped down to her shift and tucking that between her knees had made a glorious ablution, all in total privacy—unless someone was inhabiting the neighbor's house and looking down upon her. But those houses were all empty, and her only audience was Nellie, David's old setter, who stuck her nose between the hanging blankets and viewed Abbie's semi-naked form with large, sad eyes.

Soon dressed in her sister's garments, Abbie spent the remainder of the morning judging the damage and tidying the house, at least to the extent of helping Elsa sweep away some plaster. Then in the afternoon she and Mrs. Griffen managed by hook or crook to find provisions. No servants returned, so she had only the faithful Elsa to instruct. All this David left to her, for he had returned to his office and to surveying the town. So Abbie's dream had come true. She had secretly imagined that she might someday be mistress of this house, knowing this consideration to be the most awful of sins—and God in His wisdom had granted her that wish.

Odd how Rebecca's possessions fared. The marble backs of her washstand and that of David's, too, were wrenched from the wall but unbroken. Great sections of plaster were collapsing, every window pane was broken, and the organ badly splintered. Yet in the midst of all that rubble, not a single piece of her sister's china had even cracked, both the cupids in the entry stood untouched, the gilt mirror still hung, the rosewood dressing table was merely dusted, the mahogany rocker unimpaired. Inconceivable that these would have escaped when the entire front of the house had sheared away. Most fortunate. For Rebecca to lose her possessions a second time would have been perhaps unbearable.

That evening David came home exhausted but surprisingly cheerful and told them what they already suspected: the city had suffered a cruel reversal—but one that the citizens would rise above. "The world will not, as some are insisting, come to an end," he laughed.

"There are such rumors," Abbie laughed.

"And much prayer," he answered.

They ate standing in the kitchen. Ham, bread, and cheese, with coffee. That night, with all retired to the tent and lying on the mattresses, David sang a song, a gentle French lullaby. And, not to be outdone, Catherine played on her violin a piece by Chopin of such sentiment and mournful beauty that Abbie openly wept, and finally to halt the entertainments, Mrs. Griffen laughingly declared, "Oh, please let us get some rest!"

So they all slept until midnight, when such a roaring convulsion sounded that they bounded to their feet. After that Abbie could not sleep again but lay on the mattress enduring every hour or so slight vibrations and the low mutterings of a discontented earth. She would write to her sister and tell her of the earthquake. At first light she would write.

An end to summer's intimacies had come, an end to David's laughing as he trotted off into the surf with Catherine and her close behind. Through the wrenched collar of his bathing costume, she saw the rippling white scar just above the collarbone. A similar mark upon his calf. These were the distinct markings on the shape that was David, the shape of a man, a man aging; but the connectedness of those parts still held for her a pleasure. Of course, she thought of André, the thin, muscled hardness of her estranged husband. But that was long years before when they had shared an ocean, and André, too, had gained weight—as she had lost it. The thought of André then. The thought of André now. Such an impossible breach. Unfathomable.

"Come deeper!" Catherine shouted. "Come deeper! What are you afraid of?"

The pleasant sting of the salt, the plying press of water, the immense sky extending blue forever. "Not one single thing, daughter! Not one single thing!" The swirling tide pulling at the three of them. David, frolicking as a boy might, and she and her daughter now clutching each other in a laughing embrace. A sister-like embrace.

Oh, she had held her sister so. Many times. She and Rebecca. So far the two of them had come from those dark times of war, from those days of flight. Two sisters, not knowing their home was even then plundered by Yankee vandals, hand in hand they had wandered the grounds of the Baton Rouge Asylum and hugged each other and waited for the sun to rise and talked of the kind of man each would marry—and, in Rebecca's case, whether she would marry at all. Both of them had been so willful, inflicting pain on those poor men who came courting, taking secret delight in the most calamitous of situations.

Yet God had not completely turned his back on the two sisters. He took their brothers, took Hamp first—oh, if Hamp had lived. She, too, used that preface. But in place of brothers God had granted them children, and Abbie was proud of her daughter for behaving so bravely—for being young and strong and not frightened by earthquakes or what the morrow might bring. She knew that the years ahead would be difficult. She could not allow her brother-in-law to support them forever. They should leave Ohio, perhaps

15

move to New York. In that great, distant city of opportunity Catherine could continue her music lessons and Abbie would find work.

"God have mercy," she whispered, but no one heard her. Elsa gave a gentle mutter—perhaps lost in a cook's dream of roasting chickens or chocolate sauces. The children, too, were asleep. And David and the Griffens had gone into the house to sit around the dining room table, drink wine, and talk and talk and talk.

They would talk until the sun rose.

The house was a wreck. The great cistern in the attic had ruptured, pouring its contents onto the rooms below. The plaster from all the ceilings lay upon the floors. The east wall of the house was pulling away from the rest, and across the front piazza, columns, portico, and steps were collapsed into a pile of rubble. The newspaper office was in worse shape, its massive cornices now rubble resting in the street and both floors trembling when walked upon. But this could all be patched. Five thousand dollars? Perhaps. Already David had upon him the cost of Rebecca and the children and Abbie and her daughter, including the expenses of the Cincinnati Conservatory; plus his ailing brother was being nursed in London, and his brother-in-law, Asa Wright, expected David to support his youngest daughter. Yet, with the exception of Asa, who could easily afford to pay, he begrudged none of them. The uncertainties of his own childhood had fostered in the adult a more-than-ready willingness to look after those around him—within reason.

Still, David wondered even then if he might be finished. Of course, in his editorials he spoke only of rebuilding and the present enthusiasm of Charleston's citizenry. And he was a member of that citizenry. But the quake was as bad as any bombardment and farther-reaching than the Union guns. The largest of the rice mills was roofless, the city's hospital would have to be abandoned, the police station, too. Train tracks were twisted and the trains themselves derailed. Many of the "Greek temples" had lost their porticos, and other artful buildings were similarly defaced. Just three doors down, the tobacco shop's handsome façade had slipped away to reveal four naked cubicles. The bricks of that façade mingled in the street with those of his own office. And the parks were filled with homeless Negroes. Much work for the poor, both black and white. A silver lining? Already hucksters were busy selling souvenirs.

Thank God Rebecca and his children were abroad. How easily they could have been killed, and how difficult his wife would have found their present conditions. But Abbie was managing well enough. She was quite taken with his bravery, with his putting out an edition of the paper and then coming home to bed. Indeed the entire town was—the nation even, for the story had taken wing. It seemed odd to be made a hero over such a little thing. Over the years he had done much more that went unnoticed.

Oh, yes, David had done great good in the city of Charleston, and for that he was usually cursed as the "ringleader," the manipulator. They claimed he ran the party and chose the mayor to suit himself—or at least chose who would *not* be mayor. But in Mayor Courtney's case, he had managed to do neither. This present mayor was his mortal enemy, but he had others, other foes who meant to do him in. What would the future bring? Only more.

He pulled back the flap of the tent. Abbie still slept. The children were up and gathered at the kitchen, but his sister-in-law lay half-curled across a mattress with no covering, her nightdress pulled high on one knee. That summer at the beach had done her good. Still thin, but at least she seemed alive again, assertive in a way that he wished his wife could manage. Abbie was her old self again.

Yes, David had had thoughts of Abbie. More than once. . . . No, often he had imagined the two of them together. But such a wish required him to be a widower. God forgive him for such thoughts, for such profound selfishness. Why, in centuries past the Church had even deemed such unions unnatural. Of course, that had changed. Still he asked forgiveness for his imagined transgressions. Hadn't venerable Dr. Johnson defined the novel as "a small tale, generally of love"? Yes. That was it. He and Abbie. The two of them. What a strange summer they had shared.

CHAPTER TWO

The neighborhood was neither the best in Paris nor the worst. Slate-wrapped garrets atop houses that tumbled together, and the street was narrow and sometimes crossed by people of questionable virtue. Artists favored the place. On occasion one might be seen painting in the park, his easel propped open on a sunny rise, his dabbing gestures broad. Close by were the smaller theaters, those presenting the more radical entertainments. "Bohemian," Madame called their surroundings, and made it clear that her own home in Charleston was finer—though since the great earthquake of the previous autumn, she could not say to what degree finer. Madame could now manage a slight smile when mentioning that catastrophe, and in part, she credited this improving outlook to Hélène's own presence.

Morning. A dog barks. The hour chimes. Grass grows, and the world turns. With a child on each hand, Hélène exited by the front door. The door was ancient and sagged heavily upon the hinges. Long, long ago it was painted blue. The color changes from gold to blue to purple—depending on the sun's mood. The door. The faint and ragged flakes of paint. Blue now. The sky above was bluer still.

Held on the left, the dark-haired Thomerson was large and healthy, yet oddly frail in manner. He was a cautious child. But on the right hand, the golden-headed Anna lightly yet steadily tugged. This was allowed. A smiling Hélène let herself be gently pulled towards the park at the narrow street's end. Hélène sang, but just a scrap of verse, just enough to tease. Madame called Hélène "her nightingale."

Yes, the governess felt herself the most blessed of God's creatures, for almost by accident she had been employed by Rebecca Lawton, a woman whom she had gradually come to view as both instructor and guardian and to love as a mother. Not that Rebecca was similar to Hélène's mother in any way, for that peasant woman could barely sign her name and Rebecca could write an entire book if it pleased her. Her husband had written a book. Even their children wrote. Each night both the boy and girl made entries in their little leather-bound diaries. They told what they had seen and done that day. Childish still, but not without insight, especially the boy. Each night Hélène would read the entries, comment in some favorable manner, and correct the punctuation.

Books did matter. Hélène, following the ambitions of her kind father, was a great reader, and she had been told she would have free access to her employer's library. Also she would be allowed to play the piano and have the run of the house in ways often denied to a governess. She would be—no, already she was—a member of this family, and her two charges not unlike siblings. Both spoiled, of course: Anna had an awful temper, and her little brother was a timid, nervous soul, but both minded her and learned quickly, extremely so. She was proud of both and already felt that she loved them.

Of course, no family was without its difficulties, but Madame had been quite frank in reciting those of the Lawtons. In that way she was more like an older sister than an employer. Indeed, Madame had an older sister, Abbie, who had recently moved to New York City and gained employment as a secretary. Madame sorely missed this sister and lifelong confidante and wrote to her often. On two occasions, Madame had by accident addressed Hélène as "Abbie." Hélène was like this sister now and hence privy to private thoughts. By confiding in this manner, did her employer not indicate an extraordinary trust?

As Madame admitted, the death of her baby Stephen four years before had complicated the Lawtons' life together, for it left her melancholy and more concerned than ever with death's looming possibility. But God had given her two to cherish. Oh, she knew her living children were not perfect little beings. Anna had her father's temper and would hurl herself about in tantrums, which David advised her to ignore. Anna must not be taken seriously. She must not be made a criminal.

"Perhaps," her husband had told his wife, "perhaps that temper is preferable to our son's womanly softness. And you push the boy much too hard, my dear. Perhaps it is not so wonderful that he write me letters at the age of four. I do not doubt his potential and yet to push him so is to court disappointment."

Madame had delivered the speech just so, and, of course, Hélène had agreed with the wisdom voiced there.

"Yes. Yes." Madame replied, "But there is such magic in the written word!" At barely four Thomerson Lawton had learned to write. A visitor gave him a box of anagrams and teased him. She said with these he could learn to spell. "Hélène, I was resting on the bed and he was playing on the carpet. He asked me how to spell each word, and I answered rather automatically without noticing what he attempted. He spelled out a letter to his father that extended a yard square."

This discovery of learning had occurred not in South Carolina but five years earlier on a summer retreat in Massachusetts—a place which the parents felt could perhaps offer greater cultural advantages. They hoped the same of Europe. Of course, Thomerson's father was not there in Paris, and yet Madame assured her he was present in spirit, and that Thomerson, though separated from his father, understood that the harmonious pattern of all their lives revolved around pleasing the father—which actually was not so difficult to do.

"In the Lawton family," Madame went on to explain, "no sharp words are spoken between the parents, and David does not scold his children directly, but will say to me, 'My dear, will you please tell, Anna, or will you please tell Thomerson, that I never wish to see that done again.' That will suffice, for both children feel for their father a fear which is a tribute alone, the fear of displeasing, the fear of compromising his love for them."

Hélène understood and thought this a proper course. And she understood that her employer, Captain Lawton, was a man of much influence and no little bravery. He had left England as a young man and served through three years of bitter fighting on the side of the Confederate States of America. All this was written in his recollections of the War. Sharpsburg, Gettysburg, Petersburg—the names of the battles seemed more fitting to a Prussian campaign, but such places were in America. The Captain had fought these battles and many others. Twice wounded and once taken prisoner, he had distinguished himself and continued in this brave manner even after the War's end, for it was then that he created a great newspaper, the most influential in the American South. As editor and owner he campaigned against drunkenness, gambling, and prostitution, and most successfully, he single-handedly brought a halt to dueling in the American South. For this last act he was knighted by the Pope. He journeyed to Rome on that occasion.

But Hélène was not to expect such events on a daily basis. "Knighthoods are few and far between," Rebecca said. But neither would Hélène be in danger from the rougher elements, which Captain Lawton did not hesitate to confront. Such kept their distance. No, they would lead a most ordinary and regulated life. But first they must wait. The Captain was occupied now with a further act of heroism. Following the great earthquake, he was leading the city's efforts to rebuild. And also repairing the home they would eventually share.

For now Hélène must content herself with this park. A quite delightful place. The girl had already strayed from her, but only to the distance agreed upon by them both in some secret, undiscussed manner. Thus tethered, Anna stood at the rise of the crest watching a group of boys race to and fro. "Wild Indians," Hélène called them. Thomerson agreed. He leaned against her, and over his shoulder Hélène suddenly spied a large cat slipping though the shadows of the flowering vines. A domestic cat of mustard color, but large and living wild perhaps, it stalked the pigeons—which now flushed upward in a whirl of shimmering purples and left the frustrated animal still crouched beneath its cover.

"If he grows up to be the person we wish and is successful that is fine, but if he leads a quiet life and is happy then perhaps that is even better. Our responsibility should be that Thomerson becomes in the end simply a good man." Those were the Captain's words to his wife. And now that responsibility had fallen upon Hélène's shoulders, as well. Let her charge grow into "a good man." Hélène had two brothers, one older, one younger. They were quite self-sufficient. Both now worked in London. Thomerson was not at all like them. Still, at nine he was a mere boy, and as such, subject to a universal need. She patted the top of his head, tossed the thick brown hair, and then with care, smoothed it back.

For an entire unhappy year the children's mother had led them across Europe, jumping from doctor to doctor and from school to school. Though Thomerson did not dare to speak out, his sister, Anna, had been quite vocal concerning her unhappiness, and finally salvation did arrive. Their mother had engaged Hélène to be their governess. She was Swiss. She had joined them in Geneva when their mother, hoping to relieve the pain in her back, was shuffling them between spas. Now it seemed likely that the new governess would return with them to America. The boy stayed close to her. Especially in the park. As she sat upon the bench, her carriage erect, palms folded, he leaned against her and spoke eagerly of his father:

"He reads to us and yet he does not appear to read at all, but to tell the story with only a glance at the page, and, Hélène, he reads funny stories to us in this manner and gives the parts each a different voice. He laughs when we laugh. Hélène, he, himself, is very funny. Once . . . once, he told us of a little boy who overturned the dinner bowl because the contents were labeled 'Gravy.'"

"Gravy? *Oui. Gravité!*" Hélène smiled. She raised a palm to his forehead and ruffled his dark hair, which his mother would never do. Never. And then she smoothed it down. "This poor boy, he spills out the gravy for he reads in French."

"And once, Hélène, once we played a joke on Father. At home—in our Charleston home—to one side of the marble steps leading into the garden is a large century plant. We thought it a rather barren tree, for there were only long needle-sharp leaves that would poke us in painful manner and no blossoms at all. But Father explained this plant of ours was the 'century plant' and was so named because once every hundred years blooms burst forth. He said we must be patient.

"Hélène, we considered this, and then after some time had passed we went into the vegetable garden and stripped the red pepper plants of their fruit and placed on the spiked tip of each century plant leaf a bright red pepper. Then we waited for Father's return and greeted him at the gate calling out: 'Oh, Father, Father, come and see—the century plant is flowering!' 'Can it be?' he shouted, and we led him straight back to the garden and revealed our discovery. Hélène, he knelt down and studied the century plant and shook his head back and forth."

"What can he say? Your father? What does he say?"

"'You have caught me!'"

"Yes! You have caught him!"

"Father laughed and laughed. We have only to mention our century plant and he laughs."

There were other stories Thomerson could tell her. But he must be careful not to give the wrong impression. To say too much was far worse than to say too little, and he was desperate that she return with them to Charleston—for he doubted his mother would return without this governess or someone equally talented and responsible to accompany them. And he was quite fond of Hélène. He must be cautious. No. He would not tell her of the Minton china, though adults often found the story amusing.

Thomerson remembered well the arrival of the beautiful Celebration china, china with graceful corners that would harmonize with their Minton dinner service. His father was delighted. The butler arranged a plate at each of the four places while his father warned the children not to spoil the set by breaking one—warned them using a phrase that came to haunt the boy. "For the person who drops one, it will be Death on a Pale Horse!"

Thomerson felt certain the admonition was from the Bible, but beyond that he was left struggling. Would a vengeful skeleton ride the horse, or did a particular person actually die while on horseback? What horrible fate awaited?

Fortunately, a practical application came not long after. His father would request certain books be brought from the library, an errand his older sister Anna had mastered long before. His father would say "I want such-and-such volume of *Appleton's Encyclopedia*," or he might even call from the office and say, "Little Daughter, run down like a good girl to the library and get me the third book from the left on the second shelf of the tall mahogany bookcase and turn to page 217, and read to me the opening sentence of the second paragraph." And Anna could do exactly that.

Well, on this monumental day, his father sent the Negro butler instead, saying, "Bring such-and-such book, which is lying on the library table." The butler did this, but then a mishap occurred. Perhaps his father was playing a trick, pretending to be clumsy, for he was not a man to drop things. Indeed the boy had never witnessed him drop anything, much less a valuable book. But on accepting the book from the butler, his father lost his grip, and the heavy, rounded leather volume crashed down and one of the corners snapped clean off. Thomerson sat stunned and waited to see what form this "Death on a Pale Horse" would take. Surely, his father would go into a rage. But instead his father only laughed. The joke was on him, and the boy saw, and also his sister saw, it was permissible to laugh—but their father got the most fun from the incident. Still, Thomerson thought best not to share this tale with the governess, for it reflected poorly on someone in his father's service.

Oh, surely they would be headed home now. Their father was making repairs to the house. Surely they were done. The Minton china had survived. Only two plates cracked and one cup missing.

That night in his diary Thomerson wrote: "I have long since tired of these foreign cities." Hélène smiled and nodded in appreciation.

Had she said too much? Rebecca thought perhaps she had. So anxious to impress Hélène, to have the girl return with them to Charleston, she had used confidences to coax. She had told some, but of course, not all. She did not tell Hélène why they had settled in this particular neighborhood. Had not mentioned that it was here her brother Hamp had stayed—what?—a quarter of a century past, that time of great innocence before the War. And now on the bridge where she strolled alone, she imagines her brother, a young man, forever a young man abroad. Hamp upon the boulevards. Hamp, here, gazing down upon the whispering Seine. What a couple they would have made. Her brother beside her now.

Oh, Hamp was not a handsome man. Yet in his countenance was a gentle benevolence, one lit by bright and laughing eyes. Of course, he was intelligent. He read everything and was capable of sparkling conversation, but around strangers he was often silent. Yet with her he was carelessly open. Open and devoted. He had been her teacher, her guide. From him she gained her happy knowledge of all that mattered, of Shakespeare and the others—that grand hoard of genius. As soon as she could read, he took responsibility for her learning. And with a complete intensity the two of them explored the loftiest achievements of civilization. Such a passion they had, especially for plays and novels. They often read to each other, acted out the parts, laughed and even wept, for Hamp did insist that these imagined people were created out of the deepest instincts of man. Hence, whatever had been imagined for those mouths to speak was the nearest they might come to the truth. *King Lear.* Rebecca did not play the good daughter, nor even a thankless one, but spoke as the old blind king himself, with Hamp as the fool to keep her company on that dark, dark plain. Them both howling and chattering away—and not always in private.

Of course, in the beginning his enthusiasms were hers, but in time the opposite was also true. For though five years her senior and a doctor, he did listen to her. While others thought she was a baby, Hamp declared she had a soul.

In those last three weeks brother and sister were as close as ever. Hamp returned from Paris, and if he felt troubled he came to Rebecca. And if he was happy?—why, he still came to her. He made her laugh. Once more they read aloud. He drove her in the buggy. He had called her pretty. "These people cannot appreciate you," he said. "When I get rich we will at least visit France. You will pass for a beauty there."

"But you have told me that French women are ugly!" she laughed. "What compliment is that if I am to be only better than the worst?"

"No. No. You are the best looking here as well!"

Such laughter between them.

Could he ever have imagined her taking such an initiative? Leasing a flat in that handsome five-story building and now out on all the promenades? Surely the park and these prospects of the river were the best for miles. Not the most fashionable neighborhood. No. Simply the best. And she upon her way, dressed in black muslin flounced to the waist, a cape too! Recently purchased, the satin cape had the longed-for fitch collar, that triangular collar of gleaming black fur from which her slender neck rose with the iridescence of alabaster, unless, of course, she was given cause to blush. Rebecca paused upon the height of the great stone bridge and watched the French women pass. Her own figure was still trim, quite well proportioned to her small statue, and her complexion was creamy white (for she wore her veil), her eyes a perfect violet and her hair still tumbling to her waist when released from its bun, a rich auburn. She had aged, of course. But she was not so very changed from youth. Was she more beautiful than these foreign women? Hamp had said it. Should she ask him?

Hamp? Why, Hamp was beside her now, there on the bridge, he stood beyond the edge of her vision. She felt him there. Had she willed his presence? No. Since the baby's death, he often came. As the seventh child of a seventh child, Rebecca possessed an entry into that other world, and at the War's beginning he had often visited her thus, and now he came again. At first she would turn quickly in the hope somehow to catch him. No longer. Best not to see. Would it be the laughing Hamp of old or the Hamp with bleeding bullet hole in sleeve and side? She shook her head, raised a hand to shield herself from this ghost of a brother.

"Know yourself," her brother Hamp had teased. Her brother, the doctor, teased first and then insisted, "Look inside yourself." That was the modern way, she must get to the bottom of every little pit, sump, or indentation. Yet when the young Rebecca did look, what good did it do? She had no self-esteem. That was her problem. Yet knowing this proved no solution. If people said, "You sing, I believe?" Rebecca responded, "Only for the family. But Abbie sings." And she would answer in the same manner for dancing. The guitar that sweet Hamp had bought for Rebecca alone, why Abbie mastered that instrument in a mere week. Was Abbie prettier? She was only an inch taller than Rebecca, perhaps five foot three, they were shaped much the same, and the complexion and features of both were clearly those of sisters. Yet Abbie's mouth was a trifle wider and more pleasing (didn't the men find it so?), and the eyebrows arched in a peculiarly graceful way. There was something catlike about her sister, something that suggested the animal, and of course, men responded to what they might mistakenly perceive as . . . well . . . not wantonness. Certainly not.

And the new governess, Hélène, with the golden curls and crystal-blue eyes, the slight gap between the front teeth, surely a sign . . . but she could not fault the girl her attractiveness, which was no more than God's gift. Hélène was modest enough, but the desires of men. . . .

Below ran a river, deep and strong, hypnotic swirls, bridged over by gothic ornament mounted upon bold arches. Seen from this angle, did it not suggest that wall of water her sister had feared on the night of the Great Quake? Might not the river suddenly forget its course and come crashing up toward her? Rising vertically, a tidal wave of dark French origins? How many women flung themselves over this rail? Surely the French kept some yearly record. How many chose "a watery grave"? Of course, she could not. She had children to tend, a husband to tend. She, who had begun with nothing, had ended with a full and . . . could she say happy? . . . life. She was at the center of so much.

Rebecca turned slowly toward the shape that might be her brother. She thought to find there some citizen of Paris, some living human form that had suggested these memories. No. Nothing. Wait . . . there, practically at her feet, stood a dog. A setter not unlike her husband's bitch, dappled like that distant dog. But this animal was smaller and the fur thinned and touched by mange, and the eyes were dull and watched her with a frightening steadiness. Rabid! Of course, that thought came first, but no foam dripped from the mouth. Rebecca slowly raised her parasol and with some fierceness thrust the point at the animal and shouted "Shoo!" The dog shied to the side and with only a glance over its ragged shoulder, loped unsteadily away. There. Now she was truly alone.

No one on the bridge beside her, not beast or man. No one at all. No one to approach, grab by the sleeve, and whisper "I have sinned." No one there to grant her forgiveness.

And no one here to forgive me.

CHAPTER THREE

In these lodgings of the Lawtons' papers, it is easy enough to recall that other place and time—tropical, shambling Charleston in the fall of 1888. Here in fabled Paris I enjoy only one window, and that looks out on a wall of meagerly laid brick. But the library building itself is quite substantial. I simply inhabit a negligent garret, an archival space secured for me by Thomerson. He came five months ago when the papers were delivered. (No, I realize it is coming on seven months.) He pronounced my space "comfortable" and was confident enough in the institutions of the French and in my honesty to leave behind the thousands of letters and tumbling sheets of unbound script and volumes of script and print that tell his family's story. They are spread out across every available surface of this attic room. I am now reading many for the third time. Stacks are forming within stacks. Layers of meaning have begun to occur. Nuances are forming. Of particular interest are the diaries Rebecca kept in the first years of the War. Three books, actually—over seven hundred pages penned in a firm if girlish hand. In these I have begun to suspect there is much of value, and I am quite alone in my meditations. Rebecca does not come here, and her son, Thomerson, has gone with Teddy Roosevelt on an African safari. Thomerson was the only reporter invited. Quite a coup.

And I, left behind with only my voluminous reading and note taking, my precipitous storytelling, I have begun to think on fear. What is the source of that grand fear that comes upon us at the moment of birth and lingers until that last breath is drawn? Is it the certainty that we do not belong? The fear that we are somehow to be "found out"? Is that what keeps us confined to the narrow spaces of our rooms or the even narrower confines of a city's streets?

I give you Charleston.

David Lawton wore a hat of light gray felt and gloves of calfskin. He carried a majorica cane. Nodding farewell to a companion, he boarded the trolley. He took the blue line—the second blue line, not the one running out to the cemetery. An "excursion car" this was called, for it traveled the length of Broad Street, the street of lawyers and banks, and then turned up Rutledge Avenue away from the harbor and towards the newer residential districts, to the distant three-story town house that he shared once more with his wife and children and numerous servants. The second blue line ran there and then beyond to the renegade outer wards—the strongholds of political heretics—before reaching the broad grasses of the city's picnic and parade grounds. In the outer ward the houses of assignation occurred. These, too, these places of rendez-vous, could be reached in this same open horse-drawn car, the one trimmed in the lighter blue.

Here by his office, here on Broad Street, above the creak and clunk of passage, the editor could hear the familiar sounds of a port city—a tranquil Southern port city—the screech of gulls, the call of street vendors, the rumble of approaching wagons. No matter. David Lawton had no ear for these noises of an ordinary day. A pistol shot still drew his attention, but those were rarely heard. A good ten years since the city had enjoyed open gunfights and even murder in broad daylight and on respectable street corners. Then the violence of this place had seemed endemic, but even in these peaceable times, the rate of manslaughter was running ten times that of the New England states. Plentiful guns and whiskey. Easy enough to diagnosis. Or was it? And wasn't it that unending possibility of violence and hence adventure that had drawn him to the city in the first place? He gazed out on the wide and not-so-busy street.

Twenty years he had been here, been witness to great upheavals, both man- and God-made, seen the city rebound against amazing odds, rally, and move forward. Yet for all that, Charleston was amazingly unchanged. She still seemed no more than an exotic little town, an eccentric, misplaced community, one floated by mistake from some Caribbean anchorage of the previous century. A place of thin polished surfaces and deeper, violent intents, a place of endless quiet traditions and sudden noisy confusions.

The majority of the people were still poor and probably would remain so. No, David did not think the South, and particularly his corner of it, capable of the economic glory thundering across the rest of the continent. Even with Reconstruction ended, wealth would not come. As he feared, the earthquake was a final blow. Now there was only pretense.

Many in the lower classes could dress with happy casualness, but for those Charlestonians long on bloodlines but reduced to credit, externals had an ever increasing value. No matter how impoverished, a white woman of station could not present herself on Broad Street without a voluminous layering of clothes and upon her children pinafores and starched calico. And nurses in attendance. A gentleman would dress as David, perhaps not quite so refined and with a darker palette, but tailored nonetheless.

Elsewhere in the city most of the quake-damaged mansions had been "stood back up" and glazed with stucco. Those and the fabled "single houses," the narrow buildings with twin piazzas facing to the breeze, were by hook or crook kept upright. Carriages might be garaged in collapsing stables, but they were pulled by fine horses and driven by black coachmen in green livery. This was Broad Street on an ordinary afternoon. Colored nurses passed by in crisp white aprons and other Negroes passed, too—street vendors, fishermen, laborers, and washerwomen, each going his or her way at a leisurely pace. A presentable white boy lingered here or there, and two or three might bunch together for some errand of mischief. An accountant strolled with ledger in hand.

But just a block over on either side lurked the forces of squalor, endless bands of ragged urchins, foreign sailors, toughs, prostitutes, barkeeps, and faro dealers—an underworld waiting just around the corner. Black and white and all the shades of tan had filled up every nook. At the market buzzards perched upon the rooftop. In the river floated great rafts of logs (but fewer rafts). At the harbor's edge waited ships driven by both sail and steam (but fewer ships). And in the harbor center was Fort Sumter, a low block of gray masonry anchored on the silver-gray expanse and fired on by the city of Charleston when it attacked the United States of America—dragging a willing enough Southland along for the ride. To the landward lay a countryside of increasingly abandoned fields, a backland that continued to bleed impoverished rural immigrants into a city with few sewers and only the most rudimentary health care. Two races, separate and mixed, and all classes and creeds living cheek to jowl in what should have been an unmanageable jumble. Cows, horses, goats, dogs and cats, monkeys and parrots, all spoke out in a variety of calls. And yet this tree-lined, lawyer-lined Broad Street conveyed at least a suggestion of disciplined calm. The shops along this avenue still served a respectable clientele—and on adjoining King Street evidence of an even bolder economy was to be seen. And for all of this David Lawton did deserve some credit.

Pride. In the two years since the Great Earthquake, it was he, editor Lawton, who led the rebuilding. Hardly surprising, for since his arrival in Charleston, David had been a relentless advocate of improvement. Telephones—now many had them. Electricity was on the near horizon. A deeper harbor mouth. Northern investors. The softly whispered promise of reform and betterment could still be heard. And yet change did not come, at least not quickly enough. His partner, Colonel Latimer, was right: Charleston was to be eclipsed. Atlanta would flourish. Richmond. New Orleans. Perhaps even Jacksonville and the new cities of North Carolina. Despite all, David Lawton managed to study the street with satisfaction. This was his home. The *News and Independent* editor clung to the leather strap and felt the blue line car gently lurch to and fro.

Behind him was the old Exchange Building, whose cool dungeon had housed martyrs of the American Revolution—the revolution of 1776. And just here, on one of those final violent days in the Southern Redemption of 1876, he had crossed on horseback and been shot in the leg by a member of an angry mob. A shot fired perhaps by a Negro. Perhaps not. He had ignored that wound and stayed in the saddle until he reached home. To the left, the curved brownstone face of the Charleston Bank, the bank of his partner Latimer who, though a friend, could not be counted on for further credit. And to the right, the patched French roof and hooded windows of the Home for the Confederate Widows and Orphans. The South, as ever, the South. Captain Lawton of the Confederate Army. From the blue-line car he saw his world.

Here at the crossing of the two main thoroughfares were found the principal institutions of his community. God's house on the left—one of them, at least, the grand white steepled St. Michael's Church, an Episcopal haven for many of his Broad Street allies. Lawton heard its bells chime the quarter-hour. To the left, the town hall—that, too, a venerable building and one now occupied by a mayor who was known as "Lawton's man" and was a close friend as well. "The Broad Street Ring" his enemies wailed, and they were right. David Lawton did run—at least he had once run—the city and most of the state from behind the desk of his newspaper office. More than ever, though, he was beset by these same accusing enemies, these traitors, malcontents, and contenders, men who had felt the lash of his editor's pen and others who simply hated him for reasons unknown. These, too, were legion. And how many of this multitude had threatened to "kill David Lawton!" or at least wished to see him in the grave? A staggering number, colossal. He laughed to himself. He had wished the same for them, hadn't he? On this pleasant day, it was easy enough to shrug off such concerns. He waved and called back to a street-bound well-wisher.

To the far left was a bastion of the restored nation's law. On the site of the old police station a tremendous granite post office was nearing completion. At this federal level the ground was even less firm. Being a member of the Democratic National Committee and the first editor in the South to endorse Cleveland four years before now meant little. His man Cleveland had not been reelected, and soon the reviled Republicans would once again take over the White House.

On the right, however, the other house of law, the County Courthouse, remained relatively secure. A stately but simple structure, quite plain and over a century old, in its courtrooms Lawton had triumphed over the seemingly endless array of villainous and often murderous scalawags and carpetbaggers. Now, with the Union occupation ended and the power in Democratic hands —well, the spoils were simply grounds for further combat.

Finally, just beyond that crossroads, lay the sad ruins of the Catholic Cathedral. It had burned back in '61, but with considerable support from the editor, a new soaring Gothic building was about to be erected. Though he made a studied effort to keep religious commentary off the editorial page, he saw himself, above all else, as a Catholic lay worker and hoped his children would follow him in this faith. Each Sunday he carried them to worship. Who in that city would not know that for halting the practice of dueling in South Carolina, David Lawton traveled to Italy and was knighted by the Pope? And now for his own bishop, he had made a sacrificial promise, one he prayed that he might keep.

The trolley swung north on Rutledge Avenue and preceded at a walking pace past the gentle ripples of a newly impounded salt marsh lake. Ten acres square and with a promenade, the attraction was close enough to the Lawton house for the governess Hélène to bring his children. They are there now. Their new Newfoundland puppy is splashing after ducks. Two young men are standing beside Hélène. Both nod their heads and laugh in the agreeable manner of young men who cannot be trusted. These are not the first young men to pay her notice. He must speak to the governess. But first he must speak to Decatur. Though his own home was four blocks on, David stepped from the car.

The house before him was small, three narrow stories stacked precariously high, for the uppermost tilted to the left and slightly out. But the neighborhood was fashionable enough to satisfy the doctor's wife, who was satisfied by little else. And the address was convenient to the man's clients. In the side yard, a carriage house had been converted into an office containing both examination room and small library. There he would find the doctor—the expert in all matters of love, the man whose wife had cuckolded him countless times.

Of course, this was not the sort of professional that David would have chosen, but Decatur had been the physician of his first wife, Virginia. And so David had come to rely on the man. When Virginia developed more fully the consumption that would eventually take her, he relied heavily. Watching the doctor watch over his wife had made the two friends—well, had made them more than acquaintances. And soon after, when David began to court his new wife (a mere four weeks later), it had been the good doctor who quietly encouraged the bereaved widower to seek a new companion. Thus the consultant for "the old love" had come to look after "the new love." David paused before the office door and knocked.

Thomerson and his sister had a new puppy, a Newfoundland called Bruno, which they took to "the pond," and despite the cold, the dog would leap straight in to fetch sticks. The dog's fetching often attracted a crowd. Young men, especially, were drawn to the spectacle of the happily floundering puppy, and they would come close and ask Hélène questions concerning the animal and tease her in a pleasant way about the odd English in which she answered.

That was occurring now. In the underhanded way of women, Hélène had pitched with a high arc into the water. Shouting as if some great distance had been covered, the two young men made much of this. They were quite taken with Hélène. But she was not taken with them. "They are boys," she would say when they could not hear. "How can I care for such boys?"

They were "men" not "boys." Often they smoked cigars. Thomerson had smelled liquor on the breath of one. She said, "They are not acting the grown-up. That is how you act." Thomerson could tell she meant this. She could be trusted.

Home. Hélène Burdayron had indeed been their salvation. When their father had finally written insisting that they return home—Anna had peeked into the letter—Hélène happily agreed to accompany them. And as their mother now had both helpmate and confidante, the European adventure was brought to an end.

Thomerson rejoiced. The old order was restored. Their father read to them. He took them to his church and to the opera and to the theater. Thomerson was now ten and Anna twelve, and both were better able to appreciate all three. Hélène walked them back and forth to school, a school which, as his mother put it, "did not fully exercise his capabilities," but still an institution fittingly close to home. Hélène also walked them here to "the pond" which was, in fact, not a pond but a great square lake as big as two city blocks. The irony of that description was not lost on Thomerson, for he paid close attention to language. No. Nothing was lost on Thomerson. His sister might call him "poor little Thomerson," but he was not poor. Their father was rich. And the boy was large for his age. Anna said "poor and little" to be mean, and when Hélène heard, she would censure his sister in French. Conversations with Hélène were often carried out in French.

The new puppy scrambled out of the pond, and from his sopping coat he shook a wide circle of icy water. This caused the two young men to shout in alarm, but the boy did not think them truly disturbed. They acted for the benefit of Hélène, that was all.

Home.

"I have found no significant shift in the womb," Dr. Decatur declared.

"Her monthlies?" Captain Lawton asked.

"She tells me all is as it should be."

"Ah."

"Captain, I am quite certain the problem is elsewhere."

"And where might that be?"

Before them on the desk was an unrolled chart showing the internal organs of the female, a rather simplified arrangement in this case and one established in conveniently distinctive colors. Reality, the doctor had found, was something else again. No, it would do no good for the husband to examine these diagrams as if he were Caesar planning his military campaign. The human body, at least the female body, was something else again.

"Mrs. Lawton is an exceptional woman," the doctor said. "A brilliant woman, I might venture to say. She is a woman of remarkable gifts, but as is often the case, she possesses a high-strung nature."

"Yes. That is certainly the case. All you say is true. But that is not an answer."

"There was a brother. That is my understanding. And some incident involving a cane. The brother struck another young man, was challenged to a duel, and then killed. And for this your wife blames herself."

"Yes. Needlessly, of course."

"Needlessly. Yes."

David Lawton gave the unrolled chart a significant tap. "You find nothing physical? Nothing at all?"

"Nothing of this nature . . . Captain, I think . . ."

"What, then? Say it, Man."

"There are reasons in the heart that reason does not understand."

"Yes. Very pretty words. Next you'll declare there are mysteries in this world. Decatur, my wife is not haunted."

"No. She is not."

"Good. I hear that enough at home."

By inclination, Dr. Decatur was not a talkative man. In fact, with all patients and their relatives, he tended to take a wait-and-see attitude. On David's previous visit, however, he had volunteered the fact that Rebecca was seen in public talking to herself. The editor had turned on him in a momentary rage, and the doctor had decided that in the future he would answer only direct questions. And he knew Lawton could not bring himself to ask, "Is my wife insane?"

The doctor would have said, "No." But while abroad Rebecca's condition had seriously worsened. Gone was the fire, the concise wit, and the masculine rationality that had attracted him to the woman in the first place. Yes, those essays had caused the doctor to fall in love. Well, at least, to strongly admire his patient.

Of course, there were theories in print suggesting that the energies taken up by writing were necessary for the functioning of the womb, and hence the task was harmful to women. The doctor thought that ridiculous, but the true and multitudinous causes of hysteria were certainly beyond his meager abilities to understand. As a young student in Baltimore, he had spent several years working in the asylum, and on returning here, he gave ten hours a week to the Charleston institution. In all that time he had cured no one. Rebecca? The thought of her in such dismal surroundings caused him to flinch. Not likely, really, for in a place like Charleston, eccentricity was well tolerated. A woman might live on in her house for years and be as mad as a hatter. No one seemed to notice.

Insanity?

While defending a state house politico, Rebecca's brother Asa had been shot in the back and given up for dead. Rushing to his friend's side, David Lawton met Rebecca Wright. Of course, Asa was indestructible. By constantly sipping champagne for six weeks he cured himself—or so he claimed. David, it seemed, was the one stricken, the one driven to distraction. Yes, through desperate love-struck determination, David had convinced Rebecca to train as an essayist, for he felt success in such a field would give her a sense of self-worth. And having gained that, she would marry him. "Was ever a woman in such a way wooed?" Apparently so.

Decatur held in his hand a sheath of Rebecca Wright's writings. Between March and December of 1873 she had composed eighty-nine articles for the *News and Independent*. She touched on everything—battles in Russia, the trust of the sewing-machine makers—society, politics, war, death and life, and child-rearing and marriage—especially marriage. To the doctor's amusement she most often directed her remarks straight at David, who with amazing good grace bore the brunt of her sharp wit and printed her challenges. She had no training in journalism, only the tutoring of her older brother, Hamp, who fortunately had stressed the English essayists of the previous century.

Maternal love, the vaunted, is pure selfishness, if traced to its source. The fiercest animals possess it in a greater degree than woman. While the idealized Mother is glorified by poets for tending her puny babes in her self-inflicted nursery, it is Old Maids like Miss Dix, Miss Nightingale, and Miss Faithful who go about bringing God's sunshine into darkened places, raising the fallen, loosing the prisoner's bonds, and preaching Hope and Charity to men.

All women cannot marry. Witness, the seventy thousand majority of nature's "last best gifts to man" in Massachusetts alone! For them . . . no male stick presents itself to drape themselves around . . .

"No male stick presents itself to wrap around?" poor David had paraphrased in dismay.

"Yes," the doctor had replied. "Not totally encouraging. But, Captain, I shall tell you this much. Women do not always say what they mean."

"Yes. But it is her health that concerns me most. She must build up not only mind but body."

"Blood tonic," the doctor prescribed.

And so it went. Rebecca had begun the very next essay with, "Marriage is the sole end for which woman was created." Yes, fine that sounded, but then the reader was told, that is, her suitor was told:

The grand climacteric and the period of teething are not as dangerous to man as the transition from the lover state into that of husband and wife. Ignoring the fact that union is strength, they are content with its conventional semblance. After the brief period during which lovemaking is endurable, instead of uniting their aims and efforts for one definite object, they find themselves growing only farther apart. She contracts to the size of the nursery, while he expands in a larger life. At last, no common interest binds them, save household expenses and the welfare of children. Many have reason to sympathize with the French Lady who said: "The first year of my marriage I adored my husband! I could have eaten him! The second year—I regretted that I had not."

Again Decatur consoled the suitor.

Flirtation is murder.

Again he consoled.

Comfort me with apples, for I am sick of love.

And again.

Captain Lawton had endured six months of such assaults, until with a final sigh, Rebecca admitted in print that though man by his very nature was a tyrant, woman was made for him. Decatur's efforts as matchmaker had succeeded The groom said as much. David Lawton had won his bride, and Decatur had gained a patient.

Though she had returned to Charleston three months before, Rebecca Lawton still used the map, the one showing the routes of the city's streetcars, those little horse-drawn trolleys that were forever moving one way or another, webbing together all points of the compass with twin ribbons of steel. A map was needed, for now two rival companies were running similar operations. Though the lines were known by colors and the cars traveling on that particular line were painted the appropriate color, both companies had blue, yellow, red and green lines and the shades varied little. Yes, travel by trolley could be confusing.

Indeed, Charleston itself was still confusing—confusing and lonely. In Baton Rouge her family, the Wrights, counted themselves among the first rank, and even in New Orleans they were not embarrassed by the friends they kept —even after the War. But in this city the aristocracy girded itself around to an astonishing degree and shut the doors to all newcomers and some not-so-new, no matter their merit—or their wealth. The St. Cecilia ball had once been open only to those whose ancestors had inhabited this narrow peninsula for at least a hundred years. Of course, with its reorganization, she and David had been included, but Rebecca knew they were not true members, and that single ball, or rather series of balls, placed its restricted stamp on all the year's events. Oh, yes, such a surprise to arrive here and discover that even Colonel Latimer, one of the wealthiest and most accomplished men in the country, North or South, was not always invited to the best of homes. Of course, the man's wife was hateful in the extreme, but that was not the cause of this ostracism.

These first families had married into one another long, long before and were quite content with their past achievements—often long past. The Germans, the Irish, the Jews, all the portions that her husband took such care not to offend without reason, these owned the businesses and held the bulk of the political power, and yet they, too, were excluded. And the vast Negro majority, though still expecting much from their Republican Party, was also content to let that narrow white aristocracy live on as if nothing had changed in the city. Inhabitants? Why even the buildings and streets seemed somehow joined in dark conspiracy to lock out the rest of them, the Lawtons, even the Latimers, from any true sense of belonging. Was this what had kept her wandering through Europe with the children? David sent them, but it was she who refused to return. Loneliness—ah, there was the rub.

Yet, she had planned for loneliness, had planned not to marry anyone at all—only to marry and marry well. And she had managed here in this city. At least until that bitter hot summer of '83. Much to David's satisfaction she had remained healthy and grown big bellied, and then at the end of July, delivered a child who appeared robust. But fever was everywhere in the city, and within ten days that third child, a boy, was taken from them. David blamed himself—at least, blamed himself for keeping them in such an unhealthy spot.

She and the children spent the following summers in New England and finally went off to Europe. Alone for over two years, her husband had continued to publish his newspaper in this place of pestilence and quarrelsome enemies. But David did have friends here, friends aplenty, while Rebecca did not. In all of Charleston, South Carolina, there was not a single woman in whom she could confide. The exception, of course, was Madame Chazzar, but she was not what was normally considered a friend.

Those were the thoughts of Rebecca Lawton as she rested on the hard bench of the blue line trolley, the blue line that passed before the grand columns of the Charleston Hotel and ended its run at the Magnolia Crossing turn-around. Not the blue line that began on King and ran the length of Broad and up past that grand square lake they called "the pond."

The vehicle swayed like a cradle. Even the watering troughs that served the teams had the shape of babies' bathtubs. On the seat directly across from her a colored woman cradled an infant, a dark-skinned infant of her own. Two seats ahead sat a young man. She could not see his face, but he wore a black coat buttoned high on his chest, a frock coat of the old-fashioned cut. Her brother Hamp had worn just such a coat. But this young man was adorned with a cravat, a neckpiece of canary yellow, which her brother would have never worn.

The trolley halted. The colored woman with her infant abandoned them at a lonely crossroads that promised no immediate habitation. They proceeded to the last stop—just two remaining passengers, the young man in the black coat and Rebecca in the gray of extended mourning. They reached Magnolia Crossing. The horses, a fine pair matched in steadiness, halted and drawing air into their great chests let out identical bellows.

The young man descended first, then extended a hand to Rebecca. She saw him clearly now. He was no taller than Hamp and of a similar sturdy build. And the forehead was high. But his face had a dark coloring, rather coarse features, ink-black sideburns cut on the rake and a definite wildness about the eyes. Only the antique cut of the black coat had suggested a similarity to her brother.

Rebecca took the proffered hand and descended from the car. They nodded to each other and then, side by side, continued down Magnolia Street. Though starting together by accident, she could not bring herself to change the pace and either step ahead or fall behind. Neither, it seemed, could the young man. Not speaking, they went in tandem, she raising her skirts as they broached the abandoned railroad tracks and continuing on together until Rebecca turned right into the Catholic cemetery and the young man in the black coat crossed the lane and entered the garden-like grounds of the city's Protestant majority.

The way in was familiar enough. Down narrowing paths she went, turning and twisting among the graves, until she knelt beside the little stone. With fingertips she brushed aside the litter of dried leaves and twigs. She had brought no flowers, but the sesanquas were in bloom, and she picked two pale red blossoms and laid them in offering. She wondered that she did not feel more pain. She had attached herself to this child so fiercely. Even more than to the other two. Was that possible? It had seemed so. And now she felt nothing beyond an ordinary grief. The trip abroad had changed her. Cured her? No. Not that.

She prayed for the soul of little Stephen and asked God to protect all still living and to forgive her many sins. Then after several more dutiful minutes spent upon her knees, she rose, dusted off her skirt. The next car was not due until four. She would be early. She decided to walk by way of the adjoining cemetery.

Laid out in the modern mode, the Protestant enclosure was as much park as graveyard. Ornamental ponds spread across the interior and finger like coves of salt water intruded upon the borders. A tropical paradise, thick with greenery. The live oaks, they said, were natural to this garden and were centuries older. Yet, the tree-like camellias seemed as ageless. Even the stones, none dating earlier than midcentury, had an appropriate moss-grown patina. Beautiful, this garden crowded thick with memorials to the Confederate dead—giant obelisks, and smaller rectangles and squared and rounded stone.

Crossing the bridge designed in the Chinese manner and painted bright white, she spotted the young man. He traveled in the opposite direction. This time she did not mistake him for Hamp. No. His motion was of a different nature. And he was younger than her Hamp—six, seven years or more. But then, she wondered as she often did, there in heaven had Hamp aged? She thought not, for the corporeal was denied that realm.

In her dreams her brother did not age. Certainly not. No more than the face presented in the locket she wore against her skin. And herself? In reference to her brother did Rebecca age? No. In dreams she stayed a blushing seventeen forever. But none of these were dreams of heaven. Even the best of them (these very few) were of this world.

She turned towards the river, a favorite walk for it reminded her of Baton Rouge's cemetery, the place of Hamp's interment. But that was long ago and far away. She was in Charleston now with husband and children. She paused to admire the vista. She raised her veil and for a vital moment let the bright November sun spill upon her face. She had done right to abandon her foreign adventure.

She might bring Hélène to this very spot, share this with the girl. A generous thought, but one answered by a sudden darkening. A cloud had obscured the sun, and in accompaniment, a sharp breeze pulled from the land to water, rustling dead leaves, creaking the branches of the palmettos. In an instant Rebecca sensed she was being watched, wrapped her arms tight about herself, and waited for the sun's presence—or to be taken from there.

Since she had returned to Charleston, Hamp visited the house with increasing frequency—not actually appearing, but nonetheless being with her. This graveyard disturbance, however, was not the benign aura of her deceased brother, but some force of threatening darkness. "Deliver me," she prayed. "Deliver me. Hear me. Hear me, dear Lord." Thus reassured, she risked a quick glance over her shoulder and was struck as if by some hidden hand. She blinked or briefly close her eyes in terror. There had been a face among the azaleas. Most certainly, she had seen brooding features, lips twisted into a sinister smile. The young man? But he had been walking away. No doubt, others were here. She was not completely alone. She took a nervous step towards the Catholic cemetery. Then a second and a third. She glanced back. Saw no one. She went quickly into the other grounds, and from there she walked with purpose straight toward the distant trolley stand.

Despite herself, Rebecca recalled the lines, "The grave is a fine and hallowed space, but none, I fear, do there embrace." Oh, David. Oh, her husband who still held himself responsible for the death of the child that lay sleeping in this garden cemetery. For ten days she had held that infant to her breasts and each day that infant grew weaker, burned with fever, clutched. . . .

Rebecca quickened her pace.

She must give consideration to news that came by the morning post. Abbie had written to say her husband, André, had asked for reconciliation. He had declared, "Yes, I am a scoundrel." Yes, and admitting it changed nothing.

André wished Abbie to return to him. And if not that, he would go to her in New York or they might pick some neutral spot to settle. Perhaps Charleston. "What do you make of that?" her sister wrote.

"What indeed!" Rebecca was tempted to scream. Who would hear in this unlistening graveyard? Well, the young man in the black coat, for one. She saw him now across the low hedge, standing before the rows of Confederate dead, head bowed in homage. He would hear such a howl. Best to bottle that up. That Abbie would even consider reuniting with such a man! No matter the promises of sobriety, thrift, and labor—for none would be kept, and even if they were, André would still be André. And certainly this should not occur in Charleston, for André Dubose hated her husband.

Until Abbie found work in New York, David had supported both the fleeing mother and her child, Catherine, and as a drunkard would, André saw this as the total cause of his troubles. He had made threats against David's life. Even before the separation he had done that. The two men had met only once, and that on the occasion of Rebecca's marriage to David. Tonight, after dinner, she would tell her husband. Together they would formulate some response, one which was certain to discourage Abbie from making such a disastrous mistake—from making it for a second time.

Rebecca reached the stop and took a seat upon the bench. Not long after the trolley arrived, and as this stop was also the end of the line, a circling was made. From the stable two fresh horses were harnessed, and watching this pleased her. She did not realize that the young man had returned. He took the bench opposite. Rebecca nodded. The young man nodded in return and added a spoken acknowledgment.

"Mrs. Lawton," the young man said. How odd Rebecca found it to hear her name announced by this complete stranger. As wife of the city's leading newspaper man—leading citizen some might say—she was no stranger to such unsolicited salutations. But the matching of her stride in the walk from trolley to graveyard had not been completely welcome, and now something in the stranger's countenance suggested a familiarity which she found unsettling. "David," he added, still staring. She thought at first he meant a reference to her husband and then realized this was an introduction. "David," he repeated. "David Spencer."

Rebecca nodded slightly and turned her face from him, and for the remainder of long trip home considered again the multiple questions of her day. When she reached the Market and rose to switch over to the second blue line she finally looked up. The young man, this David Spencer, was gone. With no word of farewell, he had left her. Would she mention him to David? Not at dinner, but later when they were alone? Resettled in the second car, she looked out on the city's sights. But she knew them all too well. The damage done by the Great Earthquake was still evident. How quickly she'd come to take that breakage as always so. The car was running on schedule. She would be home before the dinner hour. She fixed her gaze on some intermediate distance beyond the window and formed in her mind various responses to her sister Abbie's question, "What should I do?"

The girl was under his protection. Surely she understood that. With her own father in Switzerland, it was David's place to protect the young governess—his and Rebecca's duty, theirs together. Though she was not their daughter in flesh, still she must be treated so, and as their daughter, he could not stand by idly and see her set upon by every young Charleston layabout. These would-be Don Juans must be put on notice. The two he had seen that afternoon at the pond were exactly the sort whose attentions should not be encouraged. He meant to tell her so this very night. He would begin by saying, "Hélène, you are like a daughter to my wife and me." For this reason he had asked Hélène to remain with them after dinner. The cook had taken temporary custody of the children, and here he was seated between the two women of the house—wife and governess. He had not told Rebecca the purpose of this gathering, for he made the decision as they ate. But he knew she would approve.

He poured a cognac. The women chose coffee. The dining room was furnished with fine brocade drapery reaching from floor to ceiling and flickering gaslights handsomely dressed in silver sconces. The stage was set. The tableau could begin.

"Hélène," he began, "I wish to speak to you on several matters of mild scandal. Not true scandal, not at all, but you may hear talk." He nodded to Rebecca.

"Charleston is a great place for 'talk,'" she seconded. "A hotbed of gossip."

David Lawton smiled in approval. He thought it best to start with a tale of his own trials, make her see that he, too, had been young and capable of innocent actions which could easily be misread. And, in fact, he did need to warn her of the occasional slanders made against him. Those pertaining to his war years he found particularly annoying, for despite some youthful misadventures, he was quite proud of his Confederate service. No harm in saying that. Simply telling the truth.

David spread his hands in an expansive manner and declared: "As a young man I came to the South to be a soldier, and I did find my sought-for adventure. Like you, Hélène, I had been in this country but a short time, and while I am certain you find your surroundings strange, war added an even grander degree of uncertainty. Fate had seen that I enroll in the Confederate Navy, and

41

since that navy was already in the process of disintegration, I was stationed on the outskirts of Richmond, Virginia, my ship a derelict hull which passed for a floating battery." David paused to laugh and sip his cognac.

"He is far braver than he will tell you, Hélène," Rebecca volunteered.

"No, my dear." David nodded to his wife. "I think that barge was in every way equal to my seafaring abilities. I had talents, though. Richmond was an armed camp. Streets were clogged with marching soldiers, and hurrying clerks, and men and officers seeking rest and play. Tobacco warehouses were hospitals, churches were hospitals. And, in places, the city was a barnyard filled with bellowing cattle, squealing pigs, and the commotion of recalcitrant mules and prancing thoroughbreds. But each afternoon carriages paraded their contents of respectable ladies up and down. Up and down. Oh, yes, for the young and young at heart there were still pleasures untainted by the stress of war. I mean picnics, dances, concerts, dinner parties, and parlor charades, tableaux, and all manner of amateur and professional entertainments.

"These I had the skills for. I played the piano, a rare thing in a man, and sang—quite well. After all, I had trained for the London theater. I danced with some grace and performed in the charades as only a professional might. I was quartered quite respectably, boarding in a house and avoiding my post as often as possible."

"David! You must tell something resembling the truth."

"Rebecca, I am simply being honest. I was a great boon to hostesses, but to the navy—" he finished the thought with another laugh. "The boatswain mate, Patrick I believe he was called, this Patrick had taken an instant dislike to me. A hard little man, the kind who saw the world through the narrow prism of his own experience. I mention him because I am certain the charge of desertion can be traced to there.

"Now, this hulk seemed but a farce, a mockery of the Southern nation's bright new ironclad hope. Not a happy situation, especially as we were fastened hard to the bank while the fight was happening a good eight miles to the north. All that day came the dull and brief rumble of cannon. A distant battle. I, as master mate, was nominally in charge and watched over the scrubbing of the deck and the wheeling in and out of the single gun. I recall on that final night I sang a ballad for the men, one I had composed myself. They were simple country boys. 'No vandal's hand shall e'er command / The land that gave us birth.' Pretty words, was all.

"In response the boatswain said nothing beyond a deprecating grunt. He stood up and, facing the river, brought one huge fist down into the equal's palm. You see, that was his review of the music, and with that single gesture he returned the crew to his control. A grunt—that was Mr. Patrick's appraisal of the music.

"The evening had brought the threat of rain. At some undetermined point the shelling had ended. Conversation, too, was at an end. The gangway, a single plank, was drawn on board. The men curled into blankets on the well-scrubbed deck. Just one left awake, a guard with a smooth-bore musket to face the empty black night and hear only the whisper of river.

"It was then that I leaped into the water and swam towards the opposite shore.

"'The Brit's gone over!' I heard the shout and, looking back, saw the muzzle flash followed by a thunderous report. I saw the boatswain lurching forward raising a suspender and shouting to all: 'He's gone to the Yanks! He's gone to the Yanks! A spy! Didn't I tell you? A spy!'

"The watch was pointing into the blackness and he too shouted. 'I might have got him! I seen the head bobbing, just there, just there!'

"'A spy!' the boatswain shouted. 'I told you. A spy!'

"Floating well out in the current, I listened with rising disbelief and even glee to all these shouts of 'Spy!' and 'Going to the Yankees!' My father would have approved. Just four short months and his prophecy that I would hang was being fulfilled. But, you see, in my pocket was the approved transfer from the Navy to the Army. Soggy and illegible, of course, but a legal document nonetheless. Just a matter of time for this paperwork to filter down to that barge. I could not wait. I was swimming toward the army so that I might fight the enemy.

"But to be hanged in the process? To be hung as a spy!" David laughed.

"Oh, explain yourself, David," Rebecca insisted. "Don't tease Hélène so."

"Yes, my dear. Yes, yes," he laughed again and with a nod continued. "When I announced at the family dinner table how I intended to leave England, to run the blockade, and enter the American South to fight for that new country's liberty, my father responded with outrage. If captured, a person crossing the Atlantic in such a manner and for such a purpose could be hanged as a traitor. 'To risk death is no matter!' my father roared, and he rose to grip the table's edges. 'But you will not dishonor this family's name with such a tactic. No Reeks will be hanged! Do you understand?'

"And I, young John Austin Reeks, stood and declared 'Very well. I shall be hanged under a name of my own.'"

"And *David Thomerson Lawton* was his choice," said Rebecca. "*David* from young David of the Samson contest, *Thomerson* for a noble ancestor, and *Lawton* for his beloved uncle, a soldier martyred in India."

"Which," David said, "is why you may hear a rumor that your employer is base-born—that he is a bastard, a man who does not know his father's name."

"Completely absurd! All of it," Rebecca added. "He was wounded in battle two days later. The Richmond papers made much of his valor."

"My commander was the true hero," said David. "'How can man die better?' That was his directive."

"My husband was wounded twice more. He was present at all the major battles of the east, and yet his enemies—and I do not mean the Yankee Republican, but a handful of his fellow Democrats—spread the rumor that he was a deserter from the Confederate Navy and suspected of spying."

"And no doubt you will hear that at some point. All going back to Patrick, the boatswain."

"Lesser hate-filled men," Rebecca said. "The world is filled with them."

"Did not matter," David laughed again. "A fine farewell to my naval career. But you see, Hélène, it was only a fondness for seagoing novels that led me there. I had read Marryatt. Reading those adventures, that alone enticed me. Yet, all along, I had secret dreams of the cavalry and saw myself galloping along on a Kentucky thoroughbred with a saber held high, rifle in my scabbard, pistol in my holster. And the fearsome Rebel Yell upon my lips." He paused and pretended to prepare for this fabled yell.

"Don't David," his wife laughed. "You'll startle the children and every cat and dog for blocks."

"Some other time, then. In any event that was my dream. To have a Bowie knife, an old Arkansas pig-sticker, to plunge into the very heart of a Yankee Colonel intent upon the violation of a Southern maid." Using a dinner knife for a prop, David rose from the chair to pantomime this final act. "You see, a thin rawhide cord would keep the fearsome weapon connected to my wrist, so that it might be yanked free and thrown into the breast of the next offending invader from the North."

Rebecca applauded and Hélène joined in. David beamed his appreciation and then, still standing and with arms braced to the table, he finished his tale.

"Of course, I did not find it quite so, not on water or on land either, but there was glory enough if a fellow could simply put himself in the proper place. A man can make his way in this new country. And let me add, a young woman might, as well." He made a slight bow to the ladies.

Rebecca, thinking that the evening's discussion had ended, rose clapping and came towards him still clapping. Hélène, too, abandoned her chair. At that point he could not wave them back, saying, "There is more." Could not start again with "Hélène, you are like a daughter to us." But perhaps that speech was not required—at least not on this night. Rebecca had long before made their feelings clear to the young woman. Before she engaged their employee in Switzerland and again here in Charleston, Rebecca had emphatically warned Hélène of the dangers lurking on street corners and even on the edge of suburban lakes.

David bowed again and accepted their thanks.

The smell of cigar smoke permeated his clothing. Hélène had lived so long in the company of Madame and the children she had forgotten for a time the continual smell of a man's smoke—and the continual sound of a man's voice. She returned her employer's smile, murmured her thanks for the evening's entertainment. She found him charming.

Oh, Hélène was quite taken with Charleston. Most exotic, these narrow streets echoing with the odd cries of the Negro vendors, the thick and tropical gardens, the blanketing wild rains, and the fresh smell of the salt sea, which was so foreign to the governess's Swiss mountain upbringing. On Sundays she attended the Cathedral chapel with only Captain Lawton and the children. She was sharing the pew with a gentleman who had been knighted by the Pope. No matter that she had been raised a Protestant. On Sundays she felt herself to be most fortunate of all.

On a weekday, the children did not see their father in the morning. He worked well into the night and then slept late. Madame and he would breakfast at nine, and then Madame would drive with him to the office and, after doing her errands, return home with the carriage. At half past three in the afternoon (and he was very particular in his hours), he would return home and go straight to his room and then reappear with Madame at four, which was an hour later than Charleston's fashionable three o'clock dinner. The children were free to join in the dinner conversation, but usually they wanted only to listen. Though generally addressed to Madame, Hélène saw that the children found their father's remarks absorbing, and any questions they asked were answered immediately. Madame was equally entertained by this process, and Hélène, too, enjoyed mealtimes. On occasion they might go to the theater or opera, but most evenings were spent at home with the children in Hélène's care. They attended to their studies and were in bed by eight. Except on this evening, for cook had taken over the children so that her employer might warn her of the lies sometimes told about him. But she understood this and would not be easily fooled. She was not so naive as they thought. The Captain was a brave man. He had been a brave young man, as well. The cook, Cecilia, was a young Negro woman. Elsa, the German cook, had left the previous year, so now all the servants were Negroes. The house had new steps and entry and was freshly painted throughout. In this house, at least, there was little sign of earth-swaying collapse.

As she should, Hélène found Anna in her room bent over a schoolbook and humming softly. Hélène voiced her approval and wished her a good night.

She found Thomerson in his room and in a similar attitude—only he worked away at his diary. "What secrets?" Hélène teased. "What secrets does he enter there?"

Surely, his wife was in some discomfort, for she still wore her corset and the rest. Dr. Decatur warned that such warping apparel could only do her harm. But she would not leave home in a "naked" condition, nor could he blame her. At least the dining room had been exchanged for the parlor and hence the straight chair for the lounge.

Each night they did this, came here to discuss in private the occurrences of that day and perhaps touch on the composition of the next day's paper. That finished, Rebecca would retire to her bedroom to read and David would sit in his small study across the hall and write until two or three in the morning. Then both would go to sleep, wake in the morning, and begin again.

Quite naturally, the after-dinner conversation was touched on first.

"Such adventures you have enjoyed," began Rebecca.

"Your own tales of war are more than a match, my dear."

"No. No. I have never been so brave as you."

"Nonsense. That is not what Abbie says."

"Well, perhaps. A time or two," his wife conceded with a smile. "But, David, in all seriousness, even in a sport like this evening's, I do wish you would confess more to your successes."

"Modesty forbids," he laughed.

"Truly—no, do not laugh. Men such as you often turn aside the accolades they deserve."

"Yes. Yes. Aren't you tired my dear?"

"I am, but I must tell you of Abbie's letter. David, I speak here of a quite opposite problem. A husband who deserves the curses so roundly placed upon him."

"André, of course."

"Abbie writes that he wishes to reunite with her. Does André get a second chance? That is the question."

"Ridiculous," David said. "That man is beyond redemption."

"I agree with my whole heart, husband."

"Listen to us," David laughed easily. "It is Christ who is supposed to decide that, isn't it?"

"Yes, of course."

"You know, when the Yankee lawyers rewrote this state's laws, they allowed divorces."

"And when they went, those laws went with them," Rebecca said.

"No choice really. Laws must arise, at least in part, from the customs of a place. And the customs of this place, while they exalt women, do not grant them many liberties."

"Happy Abbie, to be residing in New York."

"Yes, as a Catholic I must at least have misgivings, but in Abbie's case they are few—no, they are nonexistent. The sooner she is free of Dubose, the better."

"Oh, I do feel for Abbie. That marriage is like a shadow hanging over her."

"I have the impression that New York has done much to lift her spirits."

"I am hardly surprised. A place such as that Ohio town . . . a place like this same Charleston, where all is gossip . . . indeed a most difficult place to belong. So many cliques, so much backbiting. New York is certainly preferable."

Across the width of the parlor, David saw a frown cloud his wife's delicate face and her doll-like posture stiffened. He knew the difficulties of Charleston were not a row that needed further plowing. She claimed to have no friends here, and yet she did. Some. Some few. When visitors called she could still be quite charming. Only beyond the walls of this house, the fences of this yard, did problems arise. He should point that out to Decatur—emphasize the fact. Within this house she was graciousness embodied, quite ordinary, even inviting in her conduct.

Rebecca smiled once more, smiled prettily, and he considered the possibility of making love to her that night. She would be dressing for bed soon, and he could with a brief word announce his intention to join her. Except she did appear so tired, and in addition, Decatur's charts had left their impression. Though the doctor said otherwise, the female organs might attach somehow to a woman's fragile mental state. Once that was suspected, what pleasure could he hope to find there?

On Rebecca's return from France, they had enjoyed something of a honeymoon. Several nights of enjoyment. But only twice since. Though she did not openly complain, he knew that injury to her back from a long-ago carriage accident continued to give her pain, and the birth of children had aggravated this further . . . a child's death and a miscarriage, beside. No, his visits upon her person could not be entirely happy enterprises, and yet he longed. . . .

"Perhaps," he declared, "I should make that my next crusade. Divorce on demand in the state of South Carolina. I shouldn't think there'd be a knighthood coming from the Pope, however." He raised a rolled newspaper above his head and shook it with a flourish.

"In that poise you appear a knight ready for battle," his wife teased.

"Not Don Quixote, I hope."

"No, no," she smiled, "a true and perfect knight and even more."

David rose, bowed, and happily kissed her on the forehead.

"Yes, Hélène sees me exactly so. Knighted by the Pope. She expects me to walk upon the water at any moment."

Rebecca laughed. "You have made quite an impression. I think she is quite happy to be with us. It was a great leap on her part and speaks highly of her faith in us."

"Oh, you treat her well enough." He thought to mention the warning he had meant to give the young woman but only added, "We must watch after her."

"Yes," Rebecca agreed. "Whether city or children, governing can be a thankless task. One you could not force on me for love or money."

David laughed. The warning speech could wait. And as for his wife's so-called lapses, they were only that. This wife of his was quite rational. To a fault, some might say. Again he kissed Rebecca on the forehead and let his hand linger for a moment on her shoulder. There was no fire in that touch. Yet, he loved her so. She was his. She was everything.

"Should Dorthea marry?" he teased from the doorway. This was a private joke of theirs, one of several. While courting her he had read from *Middlemarch,* making George Eliot's pleas his own, and to simply recite that line could still bring either or both up from the doldrums.

"Yes, my dear husband, she should."

They parted with smiles.

Perhaps David meant to seek her out that night. Rebecca hoped that would not be the case. He was such a large man. Oh, so very handsome but nearly a foot taller than she and easily a hundred pounds heavier, and no matter his gentleness, she felt smothered, driven deep into the mattress. Her light frame could hardly stand the stress of such encounters—especially when the condition of her painful back was factored in—and if she were to whisper to herself the truth as she exchanged the strictures of formal dress for the comforts of her nightgown, she had never taken pleasure in the act. Not once. She wondered, despite herself, what her sister Abbie might feel when penetrated in that manner and whether that supposed pleasure alone might explain her marriage to a scoundrel like André Dubose. Despite herself, Rebecca did have a momentary vision of those two people locked in an embrace, limbs intertwined. And suddenly it was Hélène whom she pictured, Hélène of the golden curls and broad smile, and between her two pearly white front teeth, there was a crack —but some men took that flaw as a sign of lustiness. Her breasts . . . yes, men paid great attention to such. Hélène was well endowed and she stood erect, moved with shoulders back . . . but could such deportment be taken as invitation? Men and women, how odd the business was.

Such a heaving, such a grunting, such a silliness, and she wondered at God's wisdom in placing all of humanity in that thoroughly awkward and revealing position—in tying procreation to such an unsettling device. Rebecca stood beside her bed and with great relief began to pull off the thick, pleated corset. The long trolley trip to the cemetery would have been bearable if not for this clothing, this great and torturous wrapping that one needed in order to venture out beyond the confines of this house—no, beyond this bedroom. Oh, yes, Dr. Decatur had cautioned her. Corset and heaping pounds of constricting clothing, they were crippling, worse than childbirth, but Rebecca did not complain to her doctor—or to her husband.

For a brief moment she was naked, saw the black triangle of her most private part, saw her thighs, knees, shins, and tiny feet—still girlish but not so thin as she had once been, which was certainly for the best. Then she circled the gown about her, cinched it tight, and sat at the dressing table and began to apply her nightly unguents.

No, that wretched coupling could not be the true basis of a marriage, at least not marriage as she and David experienced it. Indeed, Rebecca had no complaints of marriage other than that one—the physical embrace. The companionship of her husband, raising her son and daughter, managing the house, those portions of marriage were delights beyond her wildest expectations—or her worse fears. But, of course, all these listed actions were confined to the perimeters of their handsome house.

She, Rebecca, in handsome house shared with handsome husband; she, who had sworn never to marry; she, who had sinned so grievously; she, Rebecca, whose brother Hamp might at any moment show his face in the mirror above her shoulder. She had come to expect this. Not a true reproduction of that face but a presence reflected in the gleaming surface. No, even on those nights he appeared, she could expect only a hint. A flicker upon the glass.

There was another apparition, though, who showed more fully. Downstairs she had once glanced in the wall mirror and seen another and totally unknown face staring back at her. Another woman. Not someone she knew, not herself, but a strange woman dressed in black satin and wild about the eyes and with the saddest down-turned mouth, and though she only saw this vision for a flashing instant, Rebecca knew that it must be the wife of the patriot Isaac Hayne. Her ghost was known to haunt the city. Rebecca had been warned.

Hayne was hanged by the British during the Revolution, supposedly because he broke parole but principally to send a message to the patriots. Hayne was marched from the dungeon of the Exchange, a building not a single block from her husband's office. Hayne was hanged on the town square, and his wife spent the brief remainder of her life roaming the streets, crazed by grief. And their son was a third martyr to the cause, for not long after the hanging, the boy shot himself. Rebecca did not see the boy, only the woman.

Oh, yes, easy enough for Rebecca to associate herself with poor Mrs. Hayne, for each time her husband David left their home, he took a similar risk —not to be hanged but certainly to be shot, and for the same reason—that he was a champion of freedom. Yes, the thought of losing him was a melancholy consideration that she could not drive from her mind. But she could not speak to him of this, for though he was a patient and loving man in all else, he would not listen on this single subject of his sudden death at the hands of his enemies.

Rebecca touched the cool surface of the dressing mirror with the fingertips of her left hand and pulled the brush through her hair with the right. Oh, yes, and on one other subject he would not listen. She could not tell him of the ghost that now shared her bedroom, for David's tolerance of her supernatural experiences had long since reached its limit. "Please," he would beg. "Put those things from your mind."

Best that she had not mentioned the young man at the cemetery, and certainly for the best that she had not mentioned the apparition, the face in the azaleas, and certainly not the black frock coat or anything else suggestive of her brother Hamp.

Rebecca rose, dressed for bed, slipped beneath the covers, and adjusted the flame of her bedside lamp. The previous evening she had begun to read a recently published novel, *Crimes Which the Law Does Not Reach*. Of course, such a commonplace romance was not her usual choice in fiction, but Hélène had expressed interest in the book and so an inspection was required. Rebecca began to read as censor and, despite herself, became engrossed. At chapter's end John Edgerton, the heartless wastrel, had announced that he was leaving his wife, the lovely but high-strung Fanny, for a Sicilian opera singer. He planned to live on Malta with his wanton mistress and under no conditions would he give poor Fanny a divorce. And now. . . .

"So"—Fanny spoke with withering scorn—"you see no degradation to your-self, no breach of honor, in this wanton business? You would not dare cun-ningly to delude a man into trusting you—to make him risk his last dollar, his credit, his hopes, his all, in some wild scheme—and then when the poor idiot, forgetting his past failures and blasted fortunes, looks for a future of rest and peace, withdraw yourself from the connection, and scatter the ven-ture to the winds? but I am raving—I am wild—I am foolish; my brain turns —I do not know what to say—I cannot tell what I feel. Heaven, earth, right, wrong, justice, honor, love, faith, truth, all is one cruel chaos. Help me! Save me! There are strange lights before my eyes—dark phantoms chase me with their sneering wicked faces! John, I love you—I love you so wildly and so deeply, that—I think—I fear. . . ."

She fell to the floor. He caught her up with eager haste, and rang for assistance. Physicians came and exchanged grave looks. Mrs. Vernon, with streaming eyes, asked their opinion, their fears. "The brain," was all they said.

Rebecca paused and laid the open book on the spread. There were such men in the world. The faithless defaulters. Perhaps they were the majority, these men who might bring such a heroine to a state of madness. Yes, André Dubose, the thin-lipped André, Abbie's mighty dancer of a husband was one. She recalled that clean-shaven and sneering upper lip, the hollow cheeks and burning eyes. Surely this was the countenance of a villain, a man incapable of loving—a betrayer—a man clearly intent on breaking her sister's heart.

Tucking the pillow behind her head, she raised the novel and once more began to read. *Crimes Which the Law Does Not Reach*. She could not imagine a better title.

Though it was accessed through Thomerson's room, Hélène's own quarters were far grander than she could have imagined. Her two previous employers had consigned her to closets. Here she had space to spare and a great window that looked out across the garden—where the century plant did not bloom but so much else did. The scent reached her on the night breeze—a rich sweet notion. Though narrow, her bed was comfortable and crowned with a head stead of gleaming, rolling brass. Above it hung an elegant canopy of netting, one folded away now that the bothersome mosquitoes of summer were in retreat. Beneath her feet was a carpet of elaborate Turkish design, before her was a small scrolled desk with silver ink well, and beside her a bookshelf, brim-ming with titles. Downstairs the piano was hers to use as she chose. The library as well.

Weekdays, such as this one, passed with a pleasant ease, but Hélène enjoyed Sundays best. On Sunday mornings the Captain took them to nine o'clock Mass at the Cathedral Chapel. Hélène was free to go with Madame to the Episcopal church or to find a church of her own, but she chose to attend with the Captain and his children the Latin service with the strange pictures, glass, and statues on every side. "Popish" some called them. A bright-robed Jesus rent his garments and then his very chest to expose a bleeding heart, in the window frame close by he cradled a becalmed lamb, and on the cross that towered above them he died in great pain. The beatific Virgin Mother, though positioned in the lower shadows, did she not seem to reign mysteriously over all? Ah, Sunday.

For Thomerson and Anna, Sunday afternoons were times of sheer delight, and for Hélène as well. Captain Lawton gathered the children in the drawing room, and often Hélène attended, too, sitting with them beside a blazing grate fire. But when she had first arrived, the windows were still being thrown open to the garden and the lawn beyond. A magical room, and here their father read to the children from *Tanglewood Tales* by Mr. Hawthorne, the *Wonder Book*, and many others..

There was such familiarity in that voice. As Thomerson had promised, his father could make the text seem not read but spoken to them. Indeed, at times the Captain had appeared to recite from memory, but Hélène soon realized he could scan the words ahead even as he read and then, looking up, simply talk. This magical rendition was always letter perfect. And always magical.

Magic! When an opera troop came to the Academy of Music, Captain Lawton took them all to the evening performance, and then returning home, he selected from his vast collection the musical scores they had just heard. And accompanying himself on the piano, he sang in his perfect baritone all the most famous arias and duets and choruses so that his children should remember them. But, of course, this lesson of the Captain's was also a fine entertainment, one which Hélène, but not always Rebecca, cherished. Rebecca, most often, would retire to her room when they returned, for such nights out exhausted her.

But the music was hardly confined to those occasions. Hélène was engulfed. Thomerson's father had given him a solid introduction to operatic conceptions, and the boy could sing with some skill and often did. He did not sing in public, though, nor did his father. This passion for music and the ability to perform it were not a side of the Captain that the people of Charleston had ever known. "It is not considered manly," Hélène was warned. The ability to sing and play the piano was best kept a secret. But not a secret from her. Of course, women were allowed such expressions of beauty. She and Madame often sang with him and with the children, and also without them. She was encouraged to sing, to be the "nightingale."

Hélène was still pampered by her mistress. Spoiled, some might say. Yes, and the Captain, too, was quite solicitous of her well-being. Quite.

Oh, Hélène did not consider herself to be a coquette in any extreme sense. She understood that her mistress had no tolerance of flirtation. Yet Hélène understood, as well, the reality of David Lawton's attentions. In her first month he had, on several occasions, offered her quite tender if awkward assurances of affection. In that strange little museum, beneath the whale's skeleton that dangled from the ceiling, he had placed his hand upon her waist. He had done something similar on the stair landing, and raising her into the carriage, his hands had lingered upon her. Twice that had happened. But that was all. These flattering touches were his only demands, and even those had halted. Rebecca had shown some signs of jealousy. Perhaps she distanced herself from Hélène —withdrew at least a portion of the love granted so freely while they stayed in Paris, lessened that motherly affection which Hélène had come to lean on. But the governess did not fault herself for that.

Still, Hélène did wonder at the physical aspects of her employers' marriage. She was aware of Rebecca's illnesses and back pains and knew of her determination not to have more children—due, of course, to the death of little Stephen. But wasn't marriage often a complex arrangement? Indeed, the Lawtons were apart for long periods and had apparently come to expect estrangement as a part of their union. What else might they endure for the sake of harmony?

She sensed that despite his attempt at constant good humor, the Captain was having financial difficulties. She read the sadness on his face. And she witnessed his exasperation with Thomerson when the boy would not defend himself against his sister's torments. She heard the anger in the man's voice when he spoke to his wife of her obsession with the spirit world. It did seem that since returning to America, Madame's concerns with that world had grown. At times she spoke to herself at length. Also she could become lost in deep thought—to the exclusion of her children and Hélène and her husband.

But Madame had suffered greatly. No family was perfect, and judging by the tales of the other nurses and governesses and the books she read, Hélène had fared far better than most. Indeed, it was the overriding attractiveness of David Lawton and his entire household that put her in mind to find a husband of her own in this very city.

On her day off Hélène would put on the prettiest of her wardrobe and ride the trolley cars to visit the fashionable promenades and parks, either alone or in the company of other young governesses. She particularly favored the Battery, the high, paved walk, which like a dike, separated the city street from the rolling waves of the harbor. In the nearby drains one might listen for and even see the rise and fall of waves. Here the sea breeze came wafting, an antidote to the city fevers, "a healthful tonic." Here blackened cannons pointed toward passing ships, ships which might take a passenger off into the wide world, across the ocean to Paris or even Geneva. These departures were overseen by the dark cannons, cannons which now served only as decoration. The shelling had ended some years before and been replaced with promenading, which some referred to as "a more serious business."

Yes, while strolling on this walkway or on others, she would encounter young men and smile at the bows and compliments that came her way. But, in this city of caste, she suspected that an actual suitor would not come from the ranks of these idling boys. She would do better to marry a shopkeeper. At night she often read American romances, some purchased and others passed on to her by her mistress. These books were sent to the Captain's newspaper in hopes of some favorable comment—which was seldom granted. Of course, she did not see all the books that came. Her mistress condemned the majority, declaring them to be products of the gutter and certainly not fit reading for the young and impressionable. "Such base desires, the very thought of such desires," said her mistress, "belong not in print, but in the sewers. Yes. I must use that word, The sewers!"

For this night, however, Hélène pursued a purely English work, one she had taken from her employers' library.

"But go on, go on," exclaimed Mary. "Tell me more. Does Fanny Brice know her own happiness?"

"No," Henry declared.

"What are you waiting for?"

"For—for very little more than opportunity. Mary, she is not like her cousins; but I think I shall not ask in vain."

"Oh! No, you cannot. Were you even less pleasing—supposing her not in love with you already (of which, however, I can have little doubt), you should be safe. The gentleness and gratitude of her disposition would secure you just as well. From my soul I do not think she would marry you without love: that is, if there is a girl in the world capable of being uninfluenced by ambition, I can suppose it her, but ask her to love you, and she will never have the heart to refuse."

Hélène lowered the book upon her bosom and placed her palms along the spine. There seemed no end to this Jane Austen. The English. So confusing. What did they mean by love?

In a distant corner of the city, in a neighborhood not so genteel, in a room of similar size but with grimmer furnishings, sat a young man. He was Hélène's age—well, slightly older. He was twenty-four and some months, and thus her elder by three years and some months. They had not met, these two young people. Not yet, at least. David Spencer, the young man in the black coat of an old-fashioned cut and the canary yellow cravat, sat in his meager lodging and considered for the uncounted time, his fortuitous meeting with Rebecca Lawton, the trolley trip to the cemetery and all that it entailed.

Though neither knew the leanings of the other, he shared Rebecca's dismal assessment of Charleston's healthfulness and openness. But he had found the cemetery to be a place of great beauty, and a poet needed beauty. He intended to be a poet, or if not a poet, then a novelist who wrote with a poetic bent. Perhaps that was his mother's doing, for she was a great devourer of novels, read them by the stack—masterpieces, often enough, but she read popular romances, as well, miserable, poorly bound pastimes that blathered on about love and love and love and made him want to rip them from her hands and say, "This is this, and this is this." Instead, he smiled and nodded and when free from the pharmacy ran errands for her, which was what he had done that afternoon.

Picking his way among the cemetery stones, he finally had come upon the one indicated by his mother's little sketch of a map. There he had paused and taking the rosary from his pocket muttered the incantation required by his mother. There, in that Protestant cemetery, he spoke over the mortal remains of a man whom neither his mother nor he had ever laid eyes on—but because of her occupation it was necessary to bless. Her "gift" she called it, though she was more likely to summon up the past than speak with any confidence of the future. "There be no difference," she had assured him more than once. What did she see for David Lawton? "What of David Lawton, Mama? What see you there?"

"Why do you hate that man so?"

"Why do you not hate him more?"

"I hate him not at all."

"Then I will do it for both."

David Spencer did hate the newspaper editor David Lawton, hated him with an unrelenting, malicious anger, hated that opinionated, pompous stridency, hated that finely tailored, hale-fellow-well-met manner, hated that beaming countenance that spoke only of deceit, deceit, deceit. He knew David Lawton to be his father. He knew it with a certainty unchallenged by his mother's insistence that the man was not, for her denial always ended with the remark, "I am your mother, let that be enough."

He hated the newspaper almost as much as the man. He read it every day, cover to cover. The *News and Independent* was his only reading matter. He edited each issue and made comments in the narrow margins—tirades that went on in narrow strips for thousands of words. He wrote letters to the editorial page that he did not mail. And he wrote other letters, anonymous letters, that he did mail. The most recent one had gone to the Catholic Bishop and concerned Captain Lawton's moral rectitude—a lapse of which had been unknowingly reported in the editor's own newspaper. David Spencer underlined the passage and sent it along to the Bishop. He had decided to leave no word of the illustrious *News and Independent* unread. He would know the man who betrayed his mother.

Yes, happening upon Rebecca Lawton was the grandest of luck. Since her return with the children from Europe, the poet had spotted her twice on the street, and on one of these occasions he followed her into a millinery shop and pretended to make a purchase. He had spied on her. He meant to spy on them all. He had left Hartford for Charleston and taken the job as pharmacist's clerk for just that purpose. He had arranged his life for that purpose alone.

But on this day he had not set out to follow Rebecca Lawton. He often visited that graveyard in his spare moments, enjoyed wandering among the stones, reflecting on matters of weight—immortality and the unfairness of the Almighty's meandering and man's tumultuous strivings. Charleston. City of tumultuous strivings. City of Secession.

Yet wasn't the graveyard, at least, a place of communal concord, for within those quiet bounds all citizens were finally quiet. But as metaphor this entire surrendered city already seemed as silent as a grave—or a battle ended. Though born in Richmond in the final year of the War, David Spencer saw himself as the last Union soldier standing on the field, the true avenging angel and defender of the Negroes. But, in fact, he had little contact with the Negroes. Beyond the pharmacy he had none. Still, he meant to strike a blow against these Charleston people, who prided themselves on how many of their fellow men they had once owned or how many years they had fought (on the battlefield and after) against the legal enforcement of the Constitution—that is he would strike a blow against his father.

Such were the considerations of the young poet and perhaps novelist stuck away in a dreary room whose only view afforded the slaughtering pens of a large butcher and the more distant glory of a roaring phosphate furnace.

Fine lodgings for the new American Adam, the young man chosen by God to do the unenviable task of renaming the American South, of sifting through the rubble of a dead culture and naming each animal anew, each stone and raindrop specified aright. Yes, he would deal with animate and inanimate, give voice to every new emotion, each honest complex emotion that would now arise with the abolition of not only slavery but the entire feudal order that had maintained it. The modern South. He would write about that. He would write a new literature, one fearlessly in defense of the downtrodden—those who were ignored by the editor David Lawton and his like.

His intention: To avoid at all cost the sentimentality of the English and to ignore most especially the so-called "Romance" so popular not just in the South but across the entire civilized world. He would not bow to the cynicism of the French, but neither would he blather on endlessly about love. He would address only important issues, those dealing with "good" and "evil" and clearly detailing the iron forces of history at work in this world. Yes, love might have its place—but not in any work of his. Here he drew the line. Here he marked the end of love—the end of man and woman coming together in some final eternal embrace, some expression of a devotion so complete only God might truly understand it. Soon he would start this novel of his. Soon. Very soon.

David Lawton waited for sleep to come. He was exhausted. Plain and simple, he could no longer keep the hours of wild youth. He had spent that youth—recklessly. He smiled to himself. Abandoning the ship? No, he had not told Hélène the entire story—had never told it all, not even to his wife. David had almost drowned that night, for in truth his experience of watercourses had been no broader than his knowledge of all else practical. He had traveled upon his share of rivers but never before been submerged in one in the pitch of night. Yet there David was, carried along in a muddy turbulence, weighted beneath the surface by a heavy gilt-edged uniform, and his brain pointlessly filled with visions of his drunken, irresponsible father. That man had spent away a fortune and left his wife and children alone at home with neither food nor coal. His wife—her rich auburn hair dulled by want, her matronly fullness turned sallow thin, she spent her days in sad quietness. And David and his brother? They had been reduced to beggars—sent off to plead with relatives and even neighbors for life's simple necessities.

Black, black water, his river of escape. How quickly David found himself benumbed. How quickly he forgot even his father and all that had passed. They said there was a peace to drowning, and he did enter a state of irresponsible calm. He thought to pull his rosary from beneath the tunic. This gift from the nuns was his talisman, his infallible blessing—but the collar button fought his charmless fingers. He raised a leaden arm to make a stroke and found it would not move. Indeed, which way was the shore? He had made it there, but wasn't he still wondering? Still a man in search of the shore? What else could he do, but pray to God, submit himself to the endless waves, and then by the exertions of his own hands and feet, make the deep, deep waters keep him up. River? Had it been an ocean?

In those days of the War, rather in those nights, he often dreamed that he was not in America, but living happily at home with his parents—though he had not been happy before. Then word of a morning advance would reach him, and he found himself separated from his unit by an entire ocean. A true nightmare, this was, where despite his frantic efforts, he failed at the impossible task of arriving for battle. But that was only a dream. He was here in America and committed to the course.

Committed. After reciting his glorious wartime adventure, he had not gone on to speak to Hélène of the young men—the unwanted suitors. He had meant to lead gradually into the subject of scandal, and instead, he had done nothing but brag of his exploits. Of course he had. The bleaker the future looked the more he turned to the past. That, too, was a part of aging, to see behind and not before, to ignore the blight and relive the valorous. He wanted her to think well of him, wanted the admiration of the young girl, and felt it necessary to fuel those fires from time to time. Ah, vanity. So sayeth the Preacher. Worse, though. David knew more than vanity was involved.

On the girl's second week in the city, he had taken them, her and the children, to view the whale, the grand skeleton that hung high in the College's museum. Almost fifty feet long, the insect-like apparition was suspended from the ceiling, a grand hollow construction of whitened bone, which glistened oddly along the ribs and down the sliver-thin edges of the mouth's baleen.

But other exhibits fared the same, for the museum's main room was a dusty cavern filled with dark shadows and startling shafts of light. "You see," he had pontificated, "we have on all sides the curiosities of the natural world. Yes, comparative osteology is still the basis for all knowledge in the zoological branches and thus the skeleton, the organizer of creative investigation." He pointed above, and his three listeners craned their necks. "But the museum hall offers so much more. There are stuffed birds, the adjutant bird of India, the spoonbill and the flamingo and the secretary bird of South Africa. There are phosphates holding fossil traces not only from native riverbeds but from Europe as well. They fill three cases." His final gesture sent the two children off to explore, though, they had seen it many times before.

"Oh, Captain," said Hélène, "This is quite exceptional."

"Yes," he agreed, "for a city such as this, it is." And then he had placed a hand gently at her waist and, in the pretense of guiding her, eased down the narrow aisle. His children's backs were turned. Through his fingertips he felt a shock, a mild jolt, a tingling of electricity that he had last felt long years before when he had courted Rebecca. No. In honesty, he had felt the same when touching Abbie.

"The baleen!" Thomerson had shouted. "Do you see? Set in the jaws of the animal!" The boy had turned his head briefly in their direction, and David felt, at once, a tremendous anger with himself, a sad anger, and pulled his hand away. The young woman had paid no notice—neither to the hand's placement or its removal. She went on and began to speak to the children of the bony cage of baleen and other wonders before them.

The whale had been captured while David was off in Rome being knighted by the Pope. The poor animal had wandered into the harbor and been hunted down by a flotilla of bloodthirsty citizens. And when the carcass began to stink, the college president, one of his bitterest enemies, had stepped in to scour the bones and have them reassembled and hung in this place of honor. With its bars of rib, the skeleton did suggest a colossal cage. What had Latimer called it, "the remnants of a missing God"? How wrong the man was. Very real this God of his, very real, those admonitions.

Is God missing? As both participant in and teller of this tale, let me second David Lawton's assertion. For better and for worse, God is with us always. That is my single certainty. General Robert E. Lee also believed in God. He, too, believed absolutely—but he did not read novels. He felt they weakened the mind.

What does it truly mean to love someone? Or to be loved in return? Even now I wonder.

CHAPTER FOUR

Dreary Saturday. The wind moans. Struck by a freezing rain, the window panes rattle. A fire burns in the small parlor of the modest flat she shares with her daughter here in the distant Northern climes. Abbie is snug enough. Happy enough? Are we ever?

On first arriving in New York, Abbie Dubose did secretarial work and then became the receptionist for a doctor who was quite famous, a man who for both wealthy and poor managed remarkable cures. Strange to say, the second job proved no more interesting than the first, but she did not mind. She enjoyed living in the city—the press of anonymous humanity as she window-shopped for fashions she did not need and could not afford—the notion of being alone in the midst of many.

Not alone exactly. Her daughter, Catherine, was still with her, but Catherine had her musical studies and new friends, and Abbie wanted her daughter to enjoy a modern life with all its modern freedoms. Of course, she drew the line at the more outlandish excesses of the suffragettes, the fashion of bloomer-wearing and the like. She simply wanted something for her daughter that she had been denied: the freedom to step beyond the fated roles, to choose—within reason, of course.

Also Abbie prayed less. Perhaps she had less need to. Perhaps not.

Rebecca's letter had arrived that morning. Such a missive. Abbie must not under any circumstances return to her husband. Not if he is living in New Orleans, or New York City, or Timbuktu, and certainly not if the scoundrel should appear in Charleston. David would contact Asa, who would contact friends in that Louisiana city of decadence and inquire into the "condition of

André," but no matter what the reply—which would certainly be negative—Abbie was not to go back to her husband. The end. Well, she had not intended to, but she was not sure how she felt about such sisterly commands. This was her choice to make, not Rebecca's. Rebecca should tend to Rebecca.

On their arrival from Europe, Rebecca and the children had stayed a night in New York, and Abbie met them at the boat and shared a supper. The children were overjoyed to be coming home and held their governess, this Hélène, in high esteem, since they believed it was her presence which allowed them to return. Perhaps that was true, but Abbie did not think it wise of Rebecca to interject such a nubile young woman under her husband's roof. This one had a figure—breasts that men would die for. Wasn't that the expression? Abbie had thought her own breasts quite adequate, but no man had died for them, and at this late date, none was likely to. Yes, the governess had those lethal breasts, and even though the features of the woman's face were rather broad, reflecting a peasant background, some men might find her pretty. It was difficult to say what men truly found attractive.

She knew David to be a man of honor, but he was a man nonetheless. Why invite trouble when there was plenty around already? But perhaps Abbie was jealous, jealous of the sisterly rapport shared by employer and employee—or jealous that Hélène would be in close proximity to Captain Lawton? She laughed aloud—at herself and at life's numerous absurdities.

Only twenty-one hours in New York to share with Rebecca. Two years they had been apart. So much to catch up on, but her sister kept insisting they attend a séance conducted by some table-thumper she had heard praised aboard the ship. A charlatan pure and simple. Abbie did not discount the abilities of some such performers, but the one mentioned was neither subtle nor sincere. Yet Rebecca, desperate for some word with Hamp, insisted. And Abbie insisted that she at least take that evening to rest, to sleep, which Rebecca finally did. At breakfast she'd recited the dream of the previous night.

"Abbie, I was seated beside Hamp's grave, plucking away the weeds until gradually I unburied him, first the corners of his black coat and then the rest of him. How distinct that seemed. He opened his eyes and said, 'I have waited for you so long! I am lonely here. Turn me in my grave. I am so weary.' I knelt and held him in my arms. I tried to comfort him. He spoke again, a mere breath of words. I bent even closer. 'The price is almost paid,' he whispered. 'What more is there, Brother?' I asked in the voice of a lullaby. And when he did not answer, I spoke out louder: 'Hamp, what else?' But he could not say, and he held out his left arm and in a last murmur asked that I warm it. So cold. Poor wounded arm! I counted three bullet holes. His naked arm was shattered. I cried over the red wounds and tried so hard to warm him into life. But he would not come back. He only wanted me by his grave. I laid him tenderly down and watched him as he slept."

"Best that you did, Sister," Abbie had whispered.

"Almost paid? Abbie, is there more to come?"

Catherine, who had shared this breakfast, said nothing at the time, only dutifully kissed her aunt goodbye. But once they were alone, Abbie's daughter, now a willful sixteen years old, had confided an obvious fact to her mother. "As to 'a price' to be paid, perhaps he refers to himself and not to those living at all. Perhaps he does not want to be bothered by those same living. Perhaps appearing in these dreams is the price Uncle Hamp pays. Perhaps, he wishes only to sleep."

Four months had passed since that unhappy meeting. Now a second discussion was taking place between mother and daughter, one again freighted with the easy give-and-take associated with the most "modern" of family arrangements.

"My aunt is quite insane." Catherine stood beside the warming grate. Palms extended, she looked across her shoulder as she spoke to her mother.

"Rebecca is happy."

The girl rolled her eyes and let out a deep sigh.

"Well, she is."

"Which is why she spends years separated from her husband and seeks out her dead brother at every chance?"

"Listen to me," Abbie said. "Sit here. I know you have heard pieces of this story, but I want to tell it to you now as one adult to another. I want to explain your aunt to you."

Catherine sighed again and then sat on the footstool in an attitude of resigned compliance.

"A cane," Abbie said. "A walking cane. That was the beginning."

"A walking cane," her daughter echoed. Her voice had a distinct lilt, a mocking lilt, an impatience which her mother now ignored.

"You see," Abbie continued, "a half-dozen men had been sitting around in the evening singing, and Hamp called on a friend to perform. He complied with a song that was not nice."

"What song?" her daughter asked.

"He sang 'Annie Laurie,'" answered Abbie, and after Catherine's dismissive laugh, continued, "Yes, hardly a tune to give offense, but it did. Old Mr. Sparks got up to leave, and Hamp said, 'I hope we are not disturbing you?' 'No,' he said. He was tired and would go home. As soon as he was gone, his son, who we have since heard was under the influence of opium—said it was

62

a shame to disturb his old father. Hamp answered, 'You heard what he said. We did not disturb him.' 'You are a liar!' the other cried. 'That is a name that none of our family has either merited or borne with,' shouted Hamp, and quick as thought he sprang to his feet and struck Mr. Sparks across the face with his walking-stick, a gutta-percha cane." Abbie, by this point, had abandoned her reserve and pantomimed the attack.

"Ah," Catherine said. "The cursed cane." But at least she did not laugh openly.

"Except!" Abbie declared, "Except the blow sent the lower part of the cane across the balcony and into the street, while the sword portion remained in his hand. You see, the gutta-percha had been hollowed out. It was my father's sword cane. I doubt that Hamp even knew the cane would separate. Certainly he did not perceive that it had done so until the other whined piteously that he was taking advantage of an unarmed man. Then, cursing him, Hamp threw the sword after the body of the cane, and said, 'Now we are equal.' The other's answer was to draw a Bowie knife, and he was about to plunge it into Hamp, who disdained to flinch, when an acquaintance threw himself on Mr. Sparks and dragged him off." Her voice lowered as this part of the recital dealt with a forlorn given—and she now had Catherine's honest attention.

"The following morning the younger Sparks offered a challenge to Hamp, but the family thought the matter patched up. Yet so many in the community were already aligned against Sparks or simply wanted to see a duel that the challenge was repeated. My brother chose for weapons double-barreled shotguns loaded with ball and to be fired at twenty paces. Asa was there. In the predawn hours he had climbed aboard the carriage as it left the house, but because being a relative, he had to remain at some distance. He said both shots sounded as one to him and that he ran straight to the scene. Mr. Sparks was obviously hit, blood running from a wound to his head, and our brother Hamp stood unmoving with the gun still to his shoulder. But in a moment it was discerned that Mr. Sparks was only grazed and the collapsing Hamp was fatally wounded. The ball had struck a bone in his right arm and, glancing, entered his body passing through the lungs."

Abbie rose and retreated to the window. Sleet had begun to peck lightly at the panes. She moved closer to the fire.

"May 1, 1861." Abbie said. "Oh, from that date on our family has never been the same. You see, Hamp was our happy center. That duel left my sister Rebecca only a little short of insane and my mother hardly better." Abbie hesitated, placed a hand upon her daughter's shoulder and went on. "That part I'm sure you know. What we don't speak of is Mr. Sparks. It was Mr. Sparks who must have the encore. He seemed to go mad and took to babbling

Hamp's name and weeping. He would visit Hamp's grave with great fistfuls of roses, throw himself upon the stone, and beg for forgiveness—claiming he had only fought the duel at his father's insistence. That was in the months just after. Then Mr. Sparks survived the war. Of course, he would. We had all settled in New Orleans. I had recently married. Your father and I had an apartment. Rebecca and our mother were staying with relatives.

"Here came Mr. Sparks once more. Only now he had added to his repertoire the notion that our brother Hamp had wished to die—that he, Sparks, was simply the innocent victim of our brother's will. Poor Sparks would stalk Rebecca, jump out at her from behind a corner, and babble all of this. He claimed that he had attempted twice to back out and Hamp had refused. He swore that Hamp had not even aimed in his direction—though a pellet had clipped his ear. A "stray pellet" he called that. And most contrary of all, he began to insist that all of this was in some way the fault of Rebecca. He had seen Rebecca and Hamp together at a dance, met them at twilight on the levee, passed a few remarks which he construed to be pleasant enough. It was these innocent words and not the incident of the sword cane that was at fault. The cane had been a deliberate insult on our brother's part, one meant to defend, in some perverse way, Rebecca's honor, and at the same time put an end to whatever misery lay at our brother's core."

"The man was mad," Catherine offered.

"Yes, most certainly. But Rebecca agreed with him. Though, of course, she would not say this to the piteous man. 'I forgive you,' was her only response to these accusations."

"And what happened to him?"

"Asa challenged him to a duel. In defense of Rebecca's honor, Asa meant to murder the poor lunatic. But we, your aunt and I, begged him to desist. In part, because we feared for Asa's life as well. In part, because it was a duel that had brought such sorrow to our family."

"And my father? What were his feelings on this matter?"

"I can't say. I don't recall."

"Really, Mother. That is not an answer."

"Those times . . . in New Orleans . . . we were happy. You need to believe that." Abbie shook her head. Catherine must believe on faith, for this was certainly not something she could share with her daughter.

"Mother! You are . . ." Catherine began to laugh. "You're actually considering returning to my father?"

"I did not say that," Abbie hastened to defend herself.

"He returns to you. I can hardly see the difference."

"I have memories of your father which you do not share."

"Next you will say you loved him."

"I did love him. Why else would I have married him?"

"I wonder if I shall ever marry. What is the point, really?"

"Rebecca said the same often enough."

"Yes. I have read the essays."

"Be warned, then," Abbie laughed.

"I wish he were dead," Catherine said.

"What?" Abbie caught hold of her daughter's shoulder. "What?" she asked.

"My father. I wish he were dead."

"Don't say that," Abbie screamed. "Don't ever wish such a thing."

"I am only being honest, Mother. He does nothing for us, which is quite forgivable. What can't be forgiven is he does nothing even for himself. He wallows in self-pity. He takes up space. Unnecessarily."

"Catherine! Stop!"

"He breathes the air that might give life to some approaching saint. How will we know until he halts the process?"

"Catherine!"

"Mother, don't you understand? He keeps you from living your own life."

"My own? What do you call this?"

"You might take a lover, Mother."

"What?"

"After all, this is New York City."

"Daughter. You do not understand. I have had a lover." Abbie felt the blush rising across her face but knew she must say the rest. "I was married to a lover!"

Beyond that she would not go. There were things that Abbie simply could not tell even the most modern of daughters. A great deal, in fact. How can you explain "the past"? There are no words, at least none fit to be heard by the innocent. The memories came upon Abbie with a curious sharpness—more vision than thought.

NEW ORLEANS, 1867. THE PAST.

Some sections of that city were meant to be viewed, if at all, only from the window of a closed carriage. Until her marriage, ten months before, Abbie had felt just so about the alley which was her current address—the "charming, narrow street" where she resided in a small garret apartment with her husband, André Louis Dubose. That which was solid was now adrift. "The morning of knowing." She still remembered it by that title. She had been standing at the one large window, and in fact, the light it gave was excellent. Each morning she stood there to brush out her auburn hair, which fell beneath the risen sun like a lapping flame towards her waist. No hair-brushing on that morning, though. She had pushed a wayward strand from her forehead and stepped closer to the open casement. Below, crossing cobblestones that gleamed with dew, stepped a young mulatto woman. She walked with an assurance—no, arrogance—white-turbaned, head high, and the thin cotton of her dress touched the contours of the body with a strong suggestion of the nakedness beneath. In truth, Abbie wore little more—less even, for she wore the muslin shift she slept in. Still, she was not out parading herself before the New Orleans public. In this city there was much to get used to.

For instance, her husband resting here on the bed, more or less dressed and ready for the day. One arm was cradled behind his head. Stockinged feet were crossed in idle repose. Of course, he was French, this new husband of hers, of French Huguenot ancestors, at least. But his parents had come here from South Carolina some thirty years previously—which hardly gave him a claim to this place. Still, he managed well enough in this "French" Quarter of the old city and lived with a relentless leisure in the Creole manner—which meant, as she realized at that moment (rather she accepted what she had long since known) that he kept a mistress, a dark-skinned woman he had maintained even as he was fighting his battles, and dancing his dances, and courting Abbie at the plantation and later here in the city at an elder relative's house. Sister Rebecca had been right. Sister Rebecca wept when she learned of the engagement to Mr. Dubose—to "the dancer"—and begged that Abbie save herself before it was too late.

Of course, now Rebecca was the one beleaguered—with a madman for a suitor. Mr. Sparks begging that she marry him and thus repair the damage done. And it was Abbie's turn to plead, but not with Rebecca, of course. It was brother Asa who pretended to take this proposal seriously. Asa who went about the streets, even the racetrack, shouting his demand of "Satisfaction!" Yes, a duel was to be fought. Asa Wright was to meet poor Mr. Sparks on the field of honor.

Abbie knew she must speak with her husband about this duel, which is what she had done then—rather than confront her husband over his infidelity, which would have done no good at all.

André Dubose had pulled a cigar from his vest pocket and begun to spin it between his palms. But he remained on the bed, dressed to go out except for riding boots, which stood ready. Though her back was turned, Abbie could see a hint of her husband reflected in the window glass.

"Rebecca says she forgives him and has actually said a prayer for his immortal soul—when she heard he was dead, she did that."

"But he is not dead," her husband laughed. "No, very much with us, your Mr. Sparks."

"Yes, and I would wish him to hell without a second thought."

"Which is why I married you and not your pious and lunatic sister," said André Dubose with a low chuckle. "It is difficult to say who is madder, she or Sparks."

Abbie had known better than to begin with a defense of Rebecca. No love lost between Rebecca and André. "What he is saying, André, that is the problem. He implies to any who will listen that our brother meant to kill himself through the vehicle of the duel."

"And did he? I have heard Mr. Sparks on occasion. He is a sad creature, but his rendition is quite dramatic. Perhaps he rants the truth."

"Truth? What do you insinuate by that remark?" Having heard what she half-expected, of course, she must now attack—for such was the pattern of their domestic discussions.

"Ah, 'tis a family trait, I see!" André teased, but before she could respond added, "Abbie, I meant nothing at all except that your peace-loving brother went parading with a sword disguised as cane and picked for the duel a weapon that was most certain to remove at least one party from this world."

"Which is the point of the duel, is it not?" said Abbie, for now, of course, she must support her family and a bloody practice she was asking her husband to halt.

"Exactly," said André, agreeing with what she had absolutely not intended. "I do not mean to find fault, not with your slain brother Hamp or your living brother, either. I have no argument with honorable men going about their business, which is why I am refusing you. If your brother Asa and his friend Mr. Sparks wish to shoot at each other, it is simply none of my concern. Perhaps your brother Hamp had tired of this world. Perhaps he had not. That, too, is none of my concern."

There was the answer to Catherine's question. What had her father done? Nothing—unless you count a lackadaisical defense of Sparks's accusation as an action. Only, in private, Hamp had told Abbie just that. If he survived the duel he would leave the country. She and Rebecca would never see him again. One way or another Hamp intended to leave them. Now, with his ruthless precision, her husband had struck at the matter's heart—that the demented Sparks did speak the truth.

But what is André's opinion to me? she had asked herself then. "I am tired of you," she said to her husband, and turning her back on him, she looked again upon the cobblestoned alley.

If Hamp had lived . . . was this fated to be, this current address and an unfaithful husband? At least she was certain of one thing. Yes, at that moment Abbie hated her husband more than ever. Absurd, his dismissal of her family. He pretended a cosmopolitan disdain which neither birth nor accomplishment gave him title to. André Louis Dubose. His father had been little better than a grocer, yet he mocked her family. And he ignored her, and she could not remember why she had married him except that he had danced with her a great deal and flattered her with his oily attentions.

Now reflected in window glass, she saw the man rise uninvited from the bed and heard his graceful footfall on the carpet. She felt his breath upon her neck and smelled the cigar and bourbon that announced his nearness. With the long and strangely tapering gambler's fingers he raised the muslin shift above her head. If someone were down on the street and looking up at the open garret window, they would have seen Mrs. Dubose standing quite naked. The proud, striding Creole woman or the ancient groundnut vender who sometimes stood at the corner, witchlike and babbling—if either had been present and glanced up, they would have seen André's hands circling her breasts. They would have seen Abbie raise a supporting palm to the window casing, arch her back, and tilt her head, seen the long auburn hair fall away like a dark flame. Seen, perhaps, but only Abbie could feel the silken touch of those rogue fingers along the tightening rims of her nipples. That had been her husband's answer to all problems.

CHAPTER FIVE

Colonel Latimer knew that to most citizens of Charleston he seemed a dry stick of a man. He was thin of face with crisp short beard and wispy white hair, which he combed straight back, accenting even further the broad forehead. When necessary he would perch a pince-nez on the bridge of his nose and peer out upon some delinquent debtor with the severe perusal of a hungry vulture. The banker had heard the comparison and only smiled. Of course, the black suits that hung shroud-like upon his frame did nothing but enhance this comparison. He knew the value of a dollar and did nothing to suggest otherwise.

Yet Colonel Latimer thought himself to be a man of some humor and good will and a man who, at this late date, was seldom surprised by any turn of events. The newspaper had been a sound enough investment—in the beginning, at least. Though he did not share in the usual Christian superstitions and expected no eternal rewards, he still felt a responsibility to his community. And in their decade together his partner, Lawton, had managed to keep their collective heads above water and still strike a blow or two for mankind's betterment. In evidence: the editor had attacked prostitution and gambling, cruelty to animals, cruelty to convicts, defended the starving Irish, defended the Negroes often enough, supported education for both races, argued for more industry and a better use of markets—and as the whole world knew, he had ended dueling in the South. Oh, a tricky business that, since from his arrival in Charleston on, Lawton had withstood the taunts of cowardice and used his Catholic faith as an excuse to decline all challenges. Well that he had. Challenges came weekly. Well that he had, for on every side wrongs required redressing. Yes, Lawton's views had been quite broad, but judging by the newsprint expended, pistols and whiskey were his chief concern. Pistols! He had printed the scientific view, the statistics. In one particular year, South Carolina had entertained more homicides than in the eight Northern states combined. Why? Because we preferred knives and pistols to fists and because whiskey was readily available and drunkenness tolerated.

In short, his partner David Lawton was, as editor, a fearless advocate of all that would make this city a contented place in which to live, and, apparently, two-thirds or more of the population did not wish to live that way. In the previous four years their political opponents had launched a pair of rival newspapers, whose main purpose was to drive them into bankruptcy. As near as Colonel Latimer could tell, these enemies had prevailed.

"Captain, only sad tidings from the accounts," he said. "I have been over it with Griffen, as well."

"The restructuring?" Lawton asked.

"The state must have their pound of flesh and the federal their half of the cow. Leaves us with a bit of gristle."

"I feared as much."

"You must go up to New York and see your friends. And you must succeed, or else we close the doors."

"You have come like that Dickens character."

"Yes. Scrooge. Christmas! Humbug!"

"God bless us, each and every one."

"You have often said as much. Still, I wonder."

David laughed. "I will go north next month. But I must tell you I see dim prospects in that direction."

"I see none in this one."

Colonel Latimer's bank could make no more loans to the newspaper. He and Lawton had reached the edge of that precipice. The *News and Independent* must find support elsewhere—and Lawton's personal debt must, at all cost, be kept separate from the business. Neither man could stand for the other. They were partners, not brothers. Of course, they were friends, as well. But remaining so? Would that be possible?

There was little thrift in Lawton's nature. He spent on everything without apparent thought, and his wife was perhaps worse. Approaching sixty-five, Colonel Latimer allowed himself a single luxury—a large emerald watch fob, which he ran through his fingers as he spoke. Each season his wife purchased a single dress and never tired of mentioning that Rebecca Lawton might buy a dozen. Yes, already the two women thought unkindly of each other, and now with Rebecca wandering the graveyard muttering to herself and riding the streetcars as in a trance, the banker's wife referred to her only as "the lunatic." The week before, they had even snubbed each other, passed within yards at the theater and spoke not a word, left it to their husbands to make greetings—and to the shapely governess to give a winning smile.

How far they had all come! David had courted poor Rebecca as a school-boy might. He wrote letters to Rebecca—three and four a day. She wrote back one. She refused to answer quicker, for at that rate what had she to say—other than to repeat her complaint that his wife was dead only those few weeks and such a display of affection was unseemly in a time of mourning and that she did not intend to ever marry anyone, not even him.

"Ah, Latimer. Rebecca is a belle, with both a beauty of the outward form and a beauty of the mind, petite in form, a china doll brought to life for not only my pleasure but the world's. That perfectly complexed face, those loving violet eyes, perfect dainty hands, and a crowning glory—for such it is, that great rich mass of glorious auburn hair, real auburn. Why it renders her as dreamers might imagine, but only I, I a man suddenly awake, a man quick to all. . . ." And so on in that vein until his partner would raise a hand and beg for peace, beg that a union of the two take place at once.

"David Lawton? Absurd!" On one occasion she had said exactly that to Latimer. In the absence of any others, she had spoken something of her mind to the business partner, and Latimer had murmured some assurance that "love would find a way." David he saw more often—very often, in fact. David, stranded in far off Charleston, came to the bank and, pacing the length of Latimer's office, recited to his partner:

"At our last meeting, there at the fallen tree, her voice held such melan-choly. There in the blaze of a setting sun she spoke of the lonely sadness which lay at her heart's core. Friend, I dared not touch her. To do so would have caused her to start and fall silent. But when I stood she did accept my hand and for a brief moment allowed our two hands to clasp, and from that casual touch an impulse not unlike an electric shock ran. . . . Latimer, I knew then if I could but get her to write for the paper. . . ."

Rebecca did write for the paper, and she did have talent, but apparently the demands of motherhood had won the day—until the sadness of loss sup-planted even that joy. Now Lawton was escorting a nubile young governess about the town. Where would that end? Latimer did not care to think. There was disaster enough to be dealt with at the paper.

"Remember," he said to his partner. "Remember the law and the profits."

"Yes," Lawton concurred. "The bottom line."

"The first principle."

"Each man pays his own way."

"Merry Christmas, my old friend."

"And a happier new year for us both."

The roller skating craze that swept Charleston in the late '70s had receded as all floods eventually must, but only in part, and especially then at Christmas, the rink was crowded, especially as it was Saturday. Hélène had this day to herself. With the assurance of a frequent patron, she had rented her skates and taken a seat in a second-row pew. Now, with a spirit of slight mischief, she raised her skirt well above the ankle, a flaunting act which a young man at rink's edge watched. She knew buckling on the skate showed her to a fine advantage. She caught his eye and smiled. Embarrassed, he looked away.

Not blades of gleaming steel upon the glistening ice of a Swiss millpond, but they were the next best thing, these rattling little wheels upon the board floor. She balanced herself on the bench end and prepared to push off into the current of humanity. Though already dark outside, numerous gaslights brightened as day that vast open shed where boys and girls, young ladies and young men came to circle—and where others of advanced age sat upon the bank and simply watched.

"Oh, yes, all are here." Suddenly the young man was skating beside her. "From both North and South, both high born and low—not the very highest or the very lowest but still a grand variety."

"Monsieur?" she questioned.

"In the paper today your employer, David Lawton, wrote that Charlestonians are not Americans, but who could see this spectacle and think such? Listen to the accents. Irish and German. And of course the Swiss." He nodded to her. "And the Coloreds. They do very well on skates." At this, he made an including gesture with both hands, and, indeed, numerous well-dressed Negroes did manage quite skillfully to circle about the thundering floor. "They have all started out even on this one account. None of them, black or white, had ever seen a sheet of ice thick enough to hold up a child. But here on this rink both races must start from scratch, Mademoiselle Burdayron, and you see the results."

"How do you know my name, Monsieur? How do you know by whom I am employed?"

She wished to avoid any impropriety. She wished simply to have fun, and regretted having teased this strange young man with her buckling of the skates.

"Common knowledge," he laughed. "On the lips of every lover of beauty in this city. And though you have not asked, my own is David Spencer!" He took her hand.

"Monsieur!" she laughed. "Monsieur Spencer! You do not talk to a young lady so."

"My apologies. But you do see my point." He motioned to the crowd. Around the rink were skaters who soared as birds might and those who cornered with business-like concern, and a fair number who bumped along, begging pardon and starting over. But all before her were laughing good-naturedly, or at least smiling their share. "You see, this is not just an example of black attainment. Here, too, is demonstrated the potential for peace between the races. A tiny example, true, but still we are witnessing the coexistence of all within the human race to move together in one direction and to laugh off slights and even crashes."

The rhythmic circling had carried Hélène back in memory to her girlhood, a frozen pond, and the communal pleasures of a Swiss village at Christmas. No matter how strange her companion, she would risk a smile and nod of concession. She knew they made a handsome couple, the two of them waltzing to the music. Now she felt his solid arm about her waist. The rhythmic sway of his body led them both, and then with a turn of that solid arm she was set free upon the floor alone—and there, for all to admire, was a handsome girl, moving with grace, her skirt switching from side to side and the weight of her body poised first on one gliding foot and then the other, until reaching a clear run, she spun about not once but twice. From all sides came appreciative claps.

At least here at the rink she was capable of expressing what was within. Beside her rolled this handsomely turned out young gentleman, this "Monsieur Spencer." He nodded to her with a good nature, and then as if the effort exhausted his concentration, he let out a yelp heard even above the thunderous rattling of the rink. His feet came out from under him, and this gentleman went hurtling into the wall. On her far side two girls sailed by in close union and giggled at the unfortunate's collapse.

Then Hélène was pushed further along the floor, and, unable to stop, she circled around a complete time and rumbled into the pews to find her escort bent over and clutching his arm. "Nothing," he whispered.

"You must see a doctor," she insisted.

"No, really, nothing." He bowed, grimaced, and added, "I enjoyed our conversation. 'Til we meet again."

"Adieu, Monsieur Spencer!" she called out and watched him stagger towards the exit. And quite suddenly, she realized that her breaths came now in quick and anxious pulls, not exhaustion but rather a strange excitement—was this it, romance in a foreign land?

David Spencer had broken his arm. And he had met the woman he was determined to marry. What worse could happen? You will see, Reader. You will see.

CHAPTER SIX

Sleeping in what seemed the dead of night, Thomerson was roused and guided to the window to hear the carolers. Where the music came from he could hardly say, but then he heard a silvery voice, a voice not loud but with a carrying quality that filled the very air. To the boy's ears, still in half a dream, the skies themselves were speaking, and some moments passed before he understood that what he heard was his father addressing the serenaders—telling them how happy he would be to have them return. Though the man said more, this was lost on the boy who listened not so much to the words as to the sounds of words uttered by his father. And only at the end did he realize, it was Hélène who stood beside him. One hand lay upon his shoulder, the other held together the lapel of her robe. Her hair was down, a feathering of gold across the shoulders, but not nearly so long as his mother's. "So very beautiful," his governess said. "Quite beautiful."

The two of them together, husband and wife alone, and she meant to match his enthusiasm joy for joy.

"Oh, yes," Rebecca teased, "your ship sailing upon the horizon." This she knew from the previous six Christmases was his true vision of himself, or had been his vision and would be again if he but held his course. "On the horizon you see it," she laughed.

"Yes," David laughed in return. "As ever, yon ship is treasure-laden, flags flying, music upon the deck. Fruits and candies, toys for a cargo, but when they are unloaded, I turn my back."

"That was not your ship, dear husband."

"You are right. My ship is out there still. Here it comes, freighted with my hopes, loaded with brightest dreams. Fame, Wealth, Home, Happiness, and Love are all onboard. See, on it comes, on through gloom and fog. Wait! A Rock! The sea birds flit through the fog and breakers roar, the sky grows black, and my ship sinks right there within my sight. Or perhaps not. Perhaps she makes the harbor and I see Hope shine from the stern. But still the waves are high and she must ride at anchor just beyond my reach."

"Wait! Wait! I do not believe that is your ship at all. No, those treasures come for others. There is your ship still upon the horizon!"

"Oh, Rebecca, you have heard my story." Now he was truly smiling.

"Yes. I must confess it."

"Then you grant me hope, at least. And at this time of year, I will exercise it. I solemnly swear to you that for the remainder of this 1888—ten days—all ten days of it, I will make my study only the union of human hearts. And I will let the season's mirth infect and enlighten my sometimes somber enthusiasm for humanity."

"Yes, David. Properly stated. The union of human hearts is the Christmas message. We have so many joys and consolations if we will only turn to them."

"Yes, my dear. As the poet says, 'Own our compensations as we own our griefs!'"

"Amen," his wife whispered as she had for each of the past six Christmases.

Yes, once a year, this "ship coming in" conversation was played out between them—he pretending discouragement, she providing laughing words of affirmation. Only his present discouragement was hardly pretended. And she understood this and voiced her support with even more conviction. Was that enough?

His Christmas editorial for the year began:

To the Christian, Easter's resurrection is the anchor of faith and the cornerstone of belief. And yet Christmas is more to the world than Good Friday or Easter. The promise is more than the fulfillment, the beginning more than the end. There is a reason for this in the very nature of man. In the whole course of human life there is naught that can compare with the solemn joy with which the newborn child is beheld in the weakness which is its strength. By the side of the babe whose eyes bear in their liquid depths some lingering token of the omniscience of the world beyond, there is peace and prayer, forgiveness and love.

That last Rebecca understood, understood only too well. But for her husband the promise had never been enough.

At last Christmas morning had arrived! Thomerson woke to the strains of "Adeste Fideles." At the foot of the stairs his father played the organ and sang, all done in the spirit of those days when he was an altar boy in Grosvenor Square's Catholic church. Yes, the very words *Grosvenor Square* and the organ's sound brought up a landscape as enchanted as any pertaining to St. Nicholas. Hearing that hymn Thomerson and Anna hurriedly dressed and, shepherded by Hélène, rushed down to join their parents in a triumphal march into the drawing room, a room sealed for many long days and now thrown open to reveal a Christmas tree ablaze with candles and bejeweled with ornaments and their stockings chock filled with magical contents.

"An exceptional day!" the boy wrote in his diary.

Christmas day. "The promise is more than the fulfillment." Certainly David had come to feel that way about his own life. Though the Bishop now chided him for being a poor Catholic, David's conviction that the next world was one of peace and rest went undiminished. The shadow of the cross was ever with the Babe of Bethlehem—a grim thought and yet joyous. He stared into the flames of the fire, the Yule log that marked the end of the Lawtons' Christmas celebration, and remembered, as he always did, the festivities of his boyhood.

On that single day his father somehow escaped his plague of pounds, shillings, and unmet expectations. Quite respectable the man appeared in tailcoat and cravat. He carved and marked the time of his song with swinging utensils. No matter how grim the financial circumstances, a rally was managed, a goose was cooked, carols sung. Presents appeared out of thin air. His mother smiled. The English understood Christmas in a way no other people could, can, or ever would.

Christmas in the New World? At once David summoned memories of bleak gray skies, a dim vista of blue-green pine woods and the long lines of entrenchment. That Christmas of '63 he spent camping on the rail line near Knoxville, a place where the men left bloody footprints in the snow. Yet in that dreary and pain-riddled countryside, they had managed a cheery Christmas. Eggnog was prepared from almost lethal applejack, and for entertainment he had joined a half-dozen other officers in the traditional tunes—and ended by singing, and dancing, as well, to "The Perfect Cure," an entirely inappropriate number borrowed from the London music halls. All of them had crowded into that happy if thread-worn tent, and within the year four of the seven were gone.

Then on the following Christmas, Christmas day to be exact, he had ridden with Fitz Lee straight into the camp of General Custer. Yellow hair! The Indian fighter had done hardly better against them. In grim silence and desperate cold, they approached through a sleet peppering the snow. By evening David's stiff hat brim was fringed heavy with icicles. The horses slipped and slid with every step. In the dark of night the five hundred men had crept upon Custer's sleeping two thousand, the enemy camped in the midst of a field, and the snake fence that surrounded them had been set ablaze. The flames still danced in places, and the smoke hung haze-like to the ground, and the smell of burning struck his nostrils almost as a blow. At daybreak they charged and in minutes routed the enemy from their warm tents. And General Custer, at rest in a nearby farm house, was sent fleeing in his underwear—which was far better than he had managed with the Sioux.

While chasing Custer, David, and three others had come upon thirty or forty horsemen, who because of their oilcloths were difficult to identify. "Well, Lawton, you are right, those fellows are Yankees, but there are not many of them," said General Rosser. "Let's charge them."

"Yes, sir," David laughed, and slapping his chest where the rosary hung beneath the fabric, he had joined his three comrades in that foolhardy attack. And to their amazement the Yankees spurred their horses and fled. He had killed two men in that encounter. On the faces of both he recalled the startled look that often accompanied death, and from the second, a man of some years, came the odd cry of "Why?" Odder still, there in that final year of the war, he was actually living his dream of the cavalry; his London stage notion of valiant combat had finally come to pass.

"Well, Lawton, you are right." How curiously vivid that memory was, and how apt a description for the years that had passed. Always charging forward despite the odds, always assuming that valor was the better part of discretion. His present enemies were no less belligerent. As he had recently explained to the governess, they now claimed he did not serve in the War at all. No, they did not question, as he thought they might, his handling of the munitions at Gettysburg, his supposed failure to inform Longstreet. Rather, they called him a runaway English bastard who had deserted from the Confederate Navy and spent the duration in hiding. Ridiculous! These enemies had been dealt with, and he would not let the thought of such miserable slanders ruin his holiday. He, who, staring into the flames, might bring forth any number of happy, if dangerous, adventures.

How different Thomerson's flame-induced visions must be. For his son no such memories of the past—nor hopes for the future. Not yet. And the boy could hardly be thinking of another book or toy. He had just received all that he requested. Perhaps he was meditating on that volume of Robinson Crusoe clutched to his chest, remembering, reinventing for himself a scene just read, perhaps the castaway coming upon the footprint of his man, Friday—and thus the promise of what will happen next. Yes, the mystery must be unraveled. Yet, it was *Morte d'Arthur* that hypnotized the boy. Tomorrow he would be back at Malory and his Sir Gareth the unsullied. Perhaps the boy was too bookish. Such could happen.

No need to worry over Anna. Anna would move through the world on her own terms. At that very moment, he saw an unreflected fire burning in her eyes. She was his child, Thomerson his mother's. And Rebecca seated there beside Hélène? The two seemed quite content to share the domestic duties and joys of this house, to smile now and exchange some words lost beneath the crackling song of the flame. Hélène and her would-be suitors? Another chore best shunted to the new year.

Oh, yes, the visions of maturity, these scenes he viewed while lost among those leaping flames. High hopes discouraged, desires defeated, plans unfulfilled, all these mingled with earnest resolves, eager plans for the future, castles that he built higher and higher. And what if they tumble? Were they not to be enjoyed at that moment? Perhaps. But on the morrow he stood at the basin and washed himself with the icy water, felt the blood rush with some satisfaction beneath the rough administration of the cloth, and yet considered his body—how quickly the muscle tone was lost. No longer an athlete. His stomach ulcerated and perhaps his liver diseased and what else he could not say, for Dr. Decatur would not say.

To be free of the body. There was the rub. He knew what they said of him in this town. How they still whispered about some arrangement with his shapely governess, Hélène. In truth, he still had such thoughts of her. A man does begin to slip. Despite his most earnest resolve, he was still taken with her beauty. He still watched her tending to the children with an open charm that Rebecca could not even pretend. He saw the pressure of the girl's bosoms against the light wrap she wore indoors and the silk-encased ankle revealed beneath the petticoat.

Hélène was a clever girl. No more than that. Yet that should have been enough, for in choosing a wife who was his intellectual equal, perhaps David had ignored the more important and potentially joyous portions of a marriage —the marriage bed, for instance. Yes, he still admired the Swiss girl and dreamed of some impossible future they might have together. But what could that future be, except one where his wife has died? Again he had had that despicable thought, and yet again he prayed to God to forgive him. Ridiculous, not his earnest prayers, but the fact that he was forced by his weakness to make them.

"Twixt Love and Law"—not a happy place to occupy. Only two days before, he had weakened and placed his fingers upon the girl's forearm. She had responded with a blushing smile. Perhaps she did understand the intensity of his feelings, but he realized, as well, that Rebecca would sense this and be made even more anxious. Yes, in the months since their arrival, he had managed through an act of considerable will to set aside such notions, to recognize his longings for the governess as the sinful betrayal they were. But in the months since he also set aside another restriction he had placed upon himself and began to frequent one of the city's better houses of prostitution. Of course, his political enemies soon caught wind of these visits and made a veiled reference to them in a speech, which David's own paper had unwittingly printed. And veiled though they were, the Bishop read this and understood immediately. David received a note from the man and in the ensuing encounter promised the Bishop he would desist. He had been good to his word. Of course, his growing frustration, his now almost total denial of all masculine pleasure, coupled with the difficulties of aging caused him (reluctantly) to accept hard facts. As with the newspaper, as with the man. Perhaps, just perhaps, David Lawton was running out of time.

CHAPTER SEVEN

January 2

Dearest Abbie,

Out with the old, in with the new.

Hélène has informed me that she is being courted by a young poet. A self-professed poet, I should say. That perhaps is forgivable, if barely. What David will not abide is that this young man is both penniless and a Republican. And David must be informed. I have told Hélène to prepare for the worse. She does not appear overly concerned, so I do not think this is an endless love we are about to assault.

Would that other matters might prove so pliable, especially those financial. Nonetheless, I should give thanks for this small triumph. I met the man in question while visiting the cemetery two weeks past and found his manner—his very essence—disturbing in the extreme. I have not told Helen of that encounter, nor will I tell David. As we both know such matters are not. . . .

Dear David,

Just a note of reminder. In good conscience, I cannot allow the bank to carry the paper's debt further. Also your own finances must be separated completely from those of our business. I know that you understand my position on these matters. You must find additional funding or we must close the doors permanently.

Yours,
Latimer

No, the competition provided by two rival papers had hardly lessened over the holidays. *The World*, in particular, had added modern and frivolous attractions —cartoons and serialized novels that drew in the younger readers. Judged by its year-end figures it was doing even better than David feared.

So he would go to New York. Yet, for the first time, no angel was waiting in the wings. The election of Republican Harrison over Cleveland called forth a national uncertainty, and, of course, nothing about the city of Charleston suggested that either David or his newspaper were a sound investment.

Compared to this weighty matter, the problems concerning his governess seemed minor indeed. When informed of the incident at the skating rink, he instructed his wife that Hélène was to have nothing more to do with this David Spencer. She agreed willingly, for she shared his misgivings.

Hélène did not have the heart to confront young Mr. Spencer with the news that she was forbidden to skate with him again. But to date that had been un-necessary. Through very little effort she had discovered that he had indeed broken his arm—and that he was a would-be man of letters currently employed in a pharmacy, and that he was a Republican. This last, of course, she had learned from her employers, and she had made her promise at that time.

Still, Hélène saw no harm in strolling past the pharmacy, which she had done, even halting to spy through the plate glass window. In all innocence she might enter this place in the capacity of a customer, but she would do noth-ing to encourage such an undesirable. After all he was only a clerk and rather wild in appearance and manner, and though she admired literature, she now knew that he had actually produced none.

Returning the following morning, she went in. He was there behind the counter, standing in the midst of blue bottles and brown boxes. He made no more speeches but did speak to her in an understandable if comical French. And though quite nervous, he showed delight in her presence, smiled and bowed when no bow was required. Once again she found herself attracted to him. She spoke of her errand. She mentioned a cough—a minor irritation of her throat that had annoyed her for several days. "I believe it is the cold. No more than that." What did he say? No sooner had Hélène voiced her concern than from the youth's mouth came the cursed word, "Tuberculosis."

Seeing her horror, he tried at once to retract his diagnosis. "I know noth-ing of such things!" he blurted. But apparently her look of alarm had not diminished in the least. "Here! Here," he added. "You must try this." He forced upon her a tonic, a popular tincture of coal tar. "No. No. A gift. A gift." He would not let her pay. As she left, he followed her onto the sidewalk, the sling-enclosed arm flapping like a broken wing. "Tea and honey!" he called out. "Tea and honey!"

At that she did turn and smile. "Oh, Monsieur, I am very fine," she said. "Do not worry." She even laughed and gave a little curtsey, which drew a glance from those passing by. She did wish to make him think the damage was undone and even that his modest attentions would still be welcome.

But at that very moment she was going in search of a doctor—a doctor who would not be known to her employers. It would not do for Hélène to visit the Lawtons' own physician, Dr. Decatur, for no matter what the diagnosis, this very action would distress her mistress. Simply hearing the word *tuberculosis* spoken would be the undoing of the fragile woman. If Hélène was suffering from consumption she would have to leave the Lawtons' house. If she were dangerously ill she would confess at once for she could not expose the children further. But if she were not ill then she preferred not to sound an alarm of any kind.

Having left the pharmacy, she found nearby another young governess and, suggesting that discretion was desired, asked for the name of a physician. Her friend thought she required an abortion and gave her the name of Dr. McCall. "Oh, no. Not that," Hélène laughed. She had been shocked but only mildly. "Just a cold. Just a cold." The recommendation was still Dr. McCall—her neighbor whom she had not yet met. She hesitated, but when two nights passed with the cough no better, Hélène went at midday around the block to the raised basement office of Dr. McCall. It was a common arrangement for a man to live on the floors above and practice his trade at the street level. The doctor had a wife and child living with him, and until recently a father-in-law had lived there as well. This man, a retired German storekeeper, had left after some harsh argument. All this Hélène had been told by her friend, and she took some comfort in the fact that the doctor was married, with family close by, for she understood that a certain intimacy would be required of her.

She rang the bell and heard footsteps within. The door opened wide. The doctor was a rather small man but quite handsome with black oiled hair, a trim mustache, and a manner which put her surprisingly at ease.

"Why, what a surprise," he said. "Bonjour, Mademoiselle."

So he knew who Hélène was, and she realized she had seen him at a distance on several occasions. "Bonjour," she replied and added in French a quick summation of her complaint and of her encounter with the clerk at the pharmacy.

He began to laugh and said, "I'm afraid I have used up my complete French vocabulary. Come into my office and let us try again in English."

He bowed with a half-mocking flourish, and she preceded him into the far room, a dingy place with damp masonry walls, walls from which a sad green paint was peeling. Little in that to instill confidence, but a reassuring diploma hung on the wall, and the doctor's desk was broad and cluttered with an assortment of important-looking paperwork and even an open medical book.

"Please, excuse the mess," he said. "I'm in the process of making medical history here and have simply forgotten all else." Then he laughed and asked exactly what her problem was. He did not sit or offer her a seat. In English she told him quickly that she coughed and feared she had tuberculosis, and perhaps she mentioned the clerk at the pharmacy and perhaps she did not. Dr. McCall told her that he must decline to treat her. He suggested that the Lawtons' family doctor, Dr. Decatur, would attend to her. His office, as she probably knew, was only five blocks down the street.

"But I cannot go and see Dr .Decatur," she explained. "I must know first if I have the disease. I will not be sounding the alarm if I am not ill. I spare my mistress the alarm."

"The alarm? Yes, I see." The doctor smiled. "All right, but I must say already on the basis of your color you are not gravely ill. Quite robust in fact." Then Dr. McCall slipped a spoon from an enameled drawer and saying, "Open please," did a quick examination of her throat. "A mild irritation, that is all." He set the spoon aside. "But to be certain I suppose I must listen to your lungs. Would you please step behind that screen and loosen your garments."

So Hélène did this and reappeared with the front of her dress completely open and the corset freed. In the meantime Dr. McCall had closed the shutters to guarantee their privacy and lit the gas lamp to counteract the ensuing darkness. Hélène presented herself to him with no shyness. He told her to sit and again examined her throat. He spied into her nostrils and ears with a small funnel-like device and took her temperature, which was normal. Her pulse was normal. He slipped his stethoscope beneath her clothing. She felt the touch of his fingers along the tops and sides of her ample breasts. These fingers moved, paused, and moved on. She could not see his face, which was just as well, for she was not certain what expression should be on her own.

Hélène took pride in the firmness of her body, and in addition to her daily walks, she followed an exercise of stretching. Also, she took care with her complexion, most especially avoiding the sun upon her face. Mrs. Lawton had warned her that women in the South often appeared worn and sallow, and the girl made use of both veil and parasol, and after each bath she applied a vigorous application of lotion not only to those portions of her skin that showed but also those that did not. Her skin was milk white and had the texture of unflawed silk, and this gift that God had given her she must reverently preserve. She noticed how neatly the black hairs were trimmed along the base of the doctor's neck and found in this evidence of grooming a curious reassurance. In any event, this doctor's hands were not the first to touch her so. In her village a boy, a quite handsome boy, had been given the freedom to explore so—but that was all. She would let him precede no further, which in that place was considered a remarkable restraint.

"Breathe deeply," the doctor said. Hélène pulled the air into her lungs and held it. "You may release," the doctor said. "It would not do to have you faint." He chuckled and after four more deep breaths told her to go behind the screen and restore her clothing. While she did this he asked if she had been hemorrhaging—coughing blood. The very question filled her with terror, and she shouted "Non!" Then he told her he was quite certain she had only a mild throat irritation and wrote her out a prescription, which any druggist might fill. She tried to pay him for the visit. He refused. She insisted, and so he accepted fifty cents, which did seem very cheap, and she left. Though she thought him a charming fellow, he was married, and she did not expect to see him again except perhaps in passing on the street.

But the very next day she stepped out into the garden, the garden of the Lawtons' house, and there stood Dr. McCall. His back was to her, and he was addressing Cecilia, the cook. Hélène said nothing, only stood watching, and when the doctor turned to leave he spied her.

"Bonjour," he called. She replied the same. Then to her surprise, and yes, her disappointment, he was gone.

She asked Cecilia why he came, and the Negro woman said that the doctor was treating her boy. The child was three years old and not of a sickly nature, but a severe cold had him bedridden. The doctor was a good man to spend his time on those who had little money. That was the opinion of Cecilia.

Alone in his meager lodgings, David Spencer cursed his lot. He had searched in vain for Hélène at the rink and even spied upon the Lawton house with no success. Then completely without warning, she walked into the shop. What does he say? Not even a complete sentence. Just the word. "Tuberculosis!" and this spoken in great haste—not to show off his knowledge of medicine, a knowledge learned only at his mother's side. No, he claimed no prowess of any kind. Rather he had quite involuntarily given voice to the violent emotion of love. In secret he loved this governess, and now she was ill and would die and they would never be together. All this was triggered by the word *cough*. And a quiet cough on her part, no more alarming than a sneeze.

But no damage was done, and he felt certain his attentions would still be welcomed. Attentions of what nature? A sonnet, surely a sonnet. Perhaps several. A book of sonnets

Of course, his principal concern was with the tormenting sexual desire that now filled his every waking moment. He had known several women in his twenty-four years and some months, but all were harlots, and his experience with them had not been memorable—or rather, they were memorable experiences but unpleasant. He was most certain that a sexual experience involving Hélène would be nothing less than bliss. He imagined them so, imagined her in every imaginable state of dress and undress, in every possible contortion. For this purpose he was aided by a pack of playing cards, the kind supposedly sent from Paris, France. And of course, such imaginings could only send the blood pulsing to his organ, a great galvanic surge that left him in a state of hopeless indecision. He had found over the years that the pleasures of masturbation were often offset for him by a crippling sense of guilt—sometimes accompanied by nausea. This would come on almost immediately and leave him in a black stupor that might linger on for several hours or even entire days. And yet, he must relieve himself or in some manner cool his rampant blood.

The solution, he found, was to soak himself in the great tin tub that his landlady expected everyone on the premises to share. The other boarders might complain from time to time, but none were all that interested in bathing, especially since the charge for warm water was close to criminal. Plaster-enclosed arm hanging free, David Spencer soaked in cold, and while in this state of containment imagined other occupations for Hélène—the two of them, the actions they might take together to bring justice to the common man—and the common woman, perhaps even a vote for women. Who could say? But first he must win the heart of this woman who was filling his every waking moment, and what better way to do that than with a sonnet—or rather a collection of sonnets? But he had not been happy with what he wrote.

"Shall I sonnet sing you about myself?" Browning's question. He could not bring himself to answer it.

CHAPTER EIGHT

NEW YORK, FEBRUARY 1889

On the first day of February David Lawton took the train north to New York. When he entered the sleeper berth he was suffering from a slight cold. A glance from the train showed the phosphate factories crowding Charleston's outskirts and a new a lumber mill beside the river. Great rafts of logs were still being floated to city's mills, and a fleet of lumber schooners waited in the harbor to haul away the product. Fine. No fault in that, except Yankee investors had reaped the profits, and such a resource would not renew itself for another century. Yes, fine, except that many miles of cotton fields bordering the tracks ahead were already thick with broom sedge and small pines. The state of South Carolina was drifting quickly back into the forested wilderness fit only for the habitation of red Indians. He jotted a note to this effect—an editorial in there somewhere—and gazed again out the window. Or he might write instead on the failure of the Pullman Company to design berths that actually accommodated a human being of normal size.

When David disembarked on the following day, the cold had expanded to a cough and a vague but encompassing listlessness. He checked into the new 5th Avenue Hotel, took a quick nap, and went out in search of financial support. He appealed first to an old friend, one who had run the Southern blockade with him twenty-five years before. To pass the time he had taught the young man French. Now, this friend took the editor to dine with a rising young politician, Theodore Roosevelt, and they passed a pleasant evening. Still, David's friend could provide only one possible source of funding, and after two days of frantic negotiations and rushing through the city, all the while blowing his running nose in the presence of the highest and mightiest, this single lead evaporated. Then to add insult to injury, he was forced to endure, at the hands of a stranger, a complete medical physical.

David hoped at least to insure himself for the thirty-two thousand dollars in personal debt he had accumulated. He could still survive this "war of the papers." After all, he was a seasoned veteran of that war. He even imagined that he might restore the paper to a healthy state and then sell his share. While he breathed even these snuffling breaths, he had reason to hope, but for the sake of his family he must secure some insurance.

The doctor who examined him was an elderly gentleman, one well into his seventies. David had been told he was a surgeon in the War and of the "old school," but the office, located in a finely chiseled brownstone, was modernly equipped and sparkling clean. Cloaked in starched white, a pretty, if aging, nurse moved silently in the corridor like a heavenly apparition. Ushered into the examination room, David was greeted pleasantly and asked some questions about his health, most on the level of "How are you today?" The answers to these were obvious: "I am suffering from a cold." "I have felt better." But perhaps there was some method to this excursion, for the old doctor did consult a folder as he spoke.

Next, David was told to strip away the garments above his waist. This done, the old doctor had him sit on a finely upholstered stool, and thus perched, David was once more sadly reminded of his defeated and aging composure. The interior of David's mouth was explored. The interior of his nose and ears were explored. Brief notes were made on a pad. The contents of the folder were browsed. The old doctor nodded to David. Then with a thermometer stuck into his mouth, the subject of the investigation was thumped and prodded about his chest and lower back. "Normal," was the reading of the mercury. The old doctor slipped the receivers of the stethoscope into his ears. Now the device seemed to grow out of his dense white sideburns. The old doctor was also well-mustached, and David took some comfort in this grandfatherly countenance.

"Breathe deep," the old doctor ordered. "Exhale. Fine. Breathe deep." The hard, shining circle moved from place to place across David's body. Once more the old doctor made a notation on his pad. "Now, I must ask you to stand and remove your trousers." David's stomach was carefully massaged, as was the track of his bowels. Questions were asked concerning pains and profusions—questions that required some discussion of bowel and kidney functions. Then David was examined for hernias. And then came the final order: "Bend over the table." Oh, yes, Dear Reader, David had experienced this intrusion more than once in recent years, and though the well being of his family required the ordeal, still he felt no little shame in having the finger inserted into his rectum.

"All right," the old doctor said, now washing his hands in the shiny steel sink, "You may dress." While David was pulling on his coat, the old man looked up from his voluminous paperwork and remarked, "You have suffered from hemorrhoids?"

"Yes," David said. "But my physician tends to them."

The old doctor nodded, making another note. "And you say you still find blood in your stool?"

"Yes," David said. "That is so."

"Please, have a seat."

Once more David perched as a truant schoolboy while the old doctor made some final notations on the many papers. Where had it gotten him? This man who had secured the nomination that made Cleveland the President of the United States, how sadly reduced was this noble knight of the Vatican. David struggled hard to find some saving grace of humor in his plight, to make some redeeming joke, but the old man suddenly swiveled about and began to speak for the first time in an earnest and extended manner.

"Captain Lawton, though it is not my part to do more than examine you on behalf of Prudential, I, having lived long and seen much, am not bashful and freely offer my advice whether asked or not. Your cold will pass. Your principal concern should be your ulcerated stomach. Exercise yourself. Diet is most important. Milk. I am sure you have been advised of the importance of milk. Of course, there are several preparations that offer some relief, but exercise and diet are the prime ingredients of any cure. And also, Captain Lawton, you must not allow yourself to be placed in a condition of stress. Ulcers, we are quite certain, are related directly to worry. Good day."

The old doctor was on his feet, and, grasped by the elbow, David was directed once more into the care of the nurse. With a pleasant smile, she led him to the exit and discharged him back into the bowels of an angry and calamitous world.

"Damn it to hell, Abbie!" David exclaimed. "They refused me. I telephoned the next day and was informed that in my present condition I could be insured for twenty-five hundred dollars only. And this amount was being extended to me as a courtesy. A courtesy! They mean that as a burial policy! And the old quack bastard demands that I go forth and live a stress-free life!"

The fact that her brother-in-law felt free to rant so in front of her, even to curse, suggested to Abbie that he was not his true self or, even more disturbing, this was his true self, and he now felt her to be the equivalent of some masculine buddy.

"They say he is a most capable man," she answered.

"Yes, I heard all that. He served as a surgeon with two of the New York infantries."

"He has treated Vanderbilts," she added.

"Yes, well, that is very damn fine for him, I am sure!"

This last was literally shouted, the red blood of anger flushing the editor's face to an almost royal purple. Abbie wondered if he might not expire from simply enduring the exam. "Unfortunate," she said.

"Never in my life . . ." David sputtered. "No, not since I was a child have I felt such a sense of powerlessness, such a complete lack of control over what tomorrow holds!"

Of course, Abbie was struck at the moment by the parallels that might be drawn between David's prospects and her own. If she, with no particular talents, could move here to New York and quickly make a survivable living as a clerk, David might come here and be quite comfortable as a cotton broker or anything else he chose. David had many options. Life need not end if the newspaper went under. Indeed, if David were to look upon the old doctor's remarks in the proper light, room for encouragement could be found there as well. But none of this could be said to him in his present state.

David blew his nose on his handkerchief and accepted a healthy shot of bourbon, and then another. "Let me apologize for my language, Abbie, Dear. I feel that of all in this world, perhaps you understand me best."

"Yes," she answered. "Perhaps I do." And so on his last afternoon in New York City, the two of them sat together, and as David's rage subsided they began to discuss her husband, André, and whether he might truly mend his ways and come north, and if so, should he be accepted.

David said no, André would not change, and no, even if he appeared to, he should not be accepted. The conversation moved on to other bits of personal news—and the last item was this: "Rebecca is most fortunate to have this young woman, Abbie. Hélène takes great care with the children, has a most happy disposition, and is, considering her circumstances, quite well educated. And yet I must tell you that over the fall she has begun to attract the attention of several young men. She is quite pretty in a fresh country way and has a most attractive figure."

"I have seen her, David. At the wharf when they came and later at the hotel."

He nodded. "She is only twenty-two, and naturally I do feel that she is under my protection, for being far from home, she has no father or brother to exercise that duty."

"Yes," Abbie said. "That is expected of you."

"Well, then," David said, a hint of anger returning, "those bastards may expect the bullwhip or the cane! One, in particular. There is a so-called poet that swooped down on her in the roller rink and continues to send her unwanted messages." Then came a laugh, but that, too, a short and angry declaration. "Abbie, the attention she is being paid is not of the sort I can allow."

"Yes, that is true," Abbie paused. "but, David, this young woman's wishes must also be considered. That, my daughter tells me, is the modern way."

"Yes," David said with a sudden, surprising and conciliatory calm. "In these matters I am clearly of the old school. No doubt you are correct."

Then for reasons which had no reason, Abbie embraced her brother-in-law. Despite his snuffling, she circled her arms around him as she had wished to do at the beach three years before. She held him to her and placed her face upon his chest. And though he brought a hand up to rest upon her shoulder, she realized with some embarrassment that she was not bringing him comfort. Not at all. "This does not comfort, David," she whispered. She did not think he heard her. She hugged him tighter for an instant and then stepped back.

He smiled at her, and with only a most ordinary show of emotions, made his parting. Abbie sent adamant messages of affection to the Southland, and David was gone. As was usually the case, Abbie had been pleased to see him . . . she hesitated to call him her "lover," and yet he was . . . no, he was not. . . . She was pleased to see her sister's husband come and equally pleased to see him go. Seated once more before her fire, she said a quick prayer for both David and Rebecca. It seemed likely that David had at last ridden that hobby horse of a paper into the ground. Dear God, let him have the good sense to dismount. Dear God, watch over David. Watch over Rebecca. Watch over us all.

Of the past, their summer together, that summer of the quake, of that she could sense nothing. Unless, when they discussed André, David had suggested for a moment or two that he had found her desirable—but hadn't they both grown old or older and wasn't that the fate of all mankind? But perhaps she had imagined that.

CHAPTER NINE

A full month had passed since Hélène's secret visit to the neighboring doctor, so she was quite amazed when he suddenly appeared. Captain Lawton was in the distant city of New York, and Madame was off visiting the fortune-teller, Mrs. Patrick. As Hélène was leaving the house to pick up the children from school, Dr. McCall approached her on the street and with an odd laugh announced, "You must leave this place and run away with me!"

To Dr. McCall she said, "Do not tease about such things as that. I am a young girl, and you are a married man."

"Yes, yes," he said. "That is so. That is so. I cannot deny it. But perhaps you will teach me to speak French. You know I have only that one word, 'Bonjour.' And a fellow needs more French than that if he is to make his way in the world."

"Oh, Doctor," she said and laughed. "I think you make your way in the world very well."

"Just a single lesson might serve my purpose."

"Yes, I am sure that is the purpose that you desire."

"And how is Mademoiselle's cough?"

"The cough is cured. Thank you, Monsieur."

And with a parting smile she set off down the sidewalk. That night in her diary she wrote "What a remarkable day this has been."

The next afternoon at the same time he met her again at the Lawtons' gate. "Run away with me to France," he said and thrust a bouquet of hothouse flowers into her hands.

"Doctor, I cannot do what you ask. I will not leave Mrs. Lawton for any-thing in the world. You must take away the flowers. I must go to the children." He took back the flowers, as she meant to lay them on the ground.

On the following day, he altered his request. "I will divorce my wife if you will go away with me. I will marry you. I am not happy with my wife. I will leave her."

"Doctor," she said. "You must not talk to me of these things."

"But I am so miserable in my marriage. I only married that woman so that her father would give me the money to start my practice. They are Germans. She is dull, and I do not love her and regret that commitment with all my heart."

"Doctor," Hélène answered at once. "I am only a young girl who has spent most of her life in the mountains far from here, but I can tell to you, Doctor, that you are not the only man in this city who is unhappy with his wife. You must content yourself, and you must not talk to me, for I have the children of my mistress to attend."

But on the next day, there he was, and not many days later, Hélène decided that he was sincere—or rather that it was indeed possible that the man would divorce his wife and marry her. It was possible that Hélène would then enjoy the possession of a fine town house with maid and butler and a coach with horse and driver. The current Mrs. McCall had all these. The governess began then to look cautiously forward to her encounters with the handsome and per-sistent doctor and accepted his gift of a gold watch and two poems, which he claimed to have written especially for her.

The young clerk had been promising her a gift. She had stepped into the pharmacy on two more occasions. She had spoken with him. He was charm-ing but wild, and she did not think he would make a proper husband. He would do nothing more than plan his wild projects, and she would be left with nothing.

Dr. McCall meant to take the governess from David Lawton. Take her from the editor's employ, not from his bed, for the doctor doubted such adventures were taking place in his neighbor's house. At least not yet. And he did intend to act at once. The time had come to claim Hélène as his own. He would, as the expression went, beard the lion in its den.

Even before the governess's arrival, Dr. McCall had hated editor Lawton, had hated him with a good and long-bred reason. Born upstate in Camden, a town where Celtic blood still pounded with exuberance, the doctor had been raised with little reverence for the English. In the Battle of Camden, his father's father had fought with distinction against them, understood they could be killed, and killed them. So had Thomas Ballard, his mother's father, and Dr. Thomas Ballard McCall was named for this English battling hero of the Revolution. More to the point, all honorable men of the upper country had come to view the Charleston editor as a meddler, especially when in print he relentlessly attacked Colonel Cash, a Camden duelist related to the McCalls by marriage. Lawton called the man a "killer and buffoon" and yet refused to meet him on a field of honor, claimed to be above such "barbaric" practices. It seemed that Lawton's self-regard knew no bounds—but then most occupants of the coast thought themselves superior to what they considered a crude backwoods population. Certainly, McCall had found this borne out in his medical practice.

Though he was the valedictorian of his class and had a thorough and modern understanding of his duties, in Charleston the better clientele happily remained in the care of talentless, even deadly, pontificators—men whose primary preparation for the profession might be the claim of a great-grandfather having owned a famous racehorse or a grandmother having danced with Lafayette. McCall's father-in-law (not speaking to him at the moment) felt much the same about the editor and the aristocracy. The retired grocer had been a prime mover among the Germans who had battled the Lawton "ring" for a decade.

In short, McCall had every reason to consider himself as good as any other man and better than most. But in addition he also had a genuine sympathy for those less fortunate. True, true, David Lawton might claim such sympathy, but what did it amount to? An insincere word or two in his newspaper. Well, Dr. McCall was offered a more immediate arena in which to practice his. He rose each morning and went off in his buggy to visit the diseased and dying, the Negro children with worms and rickets, and the arthritic and diabetic elderly. He traveled down Philadelphia Alley and Cow Alley and to the city's edge, to unknown regions, even to Danger Road. In both black and white quarters he patched up gunshot wounds and razor slashes. And he tended to the needs and complaints of women. In fact, he had once been on regular call at two houses of prostitution. And for all this, even the last, he was not richly rewarded —not by any single patient at least—but there were so many of the poor to be treated that cumulatively he managed to make a quite decent income. His patients, especially the Negroes, felt themselves blessed by his presence.

Also, Dr. McCall loved his little daughter, and at day's end he sat the child on his knee and in a pleasant way teased her about this and that.

On the dark side, the minus column—for the doctor dealt with himself with no little honesty—in his last year of studying in Tennessee he killed a fellow student. A mistake on his part, but both had been armed with pistols. The incident was much closer to a shooting fracas than a duel, and the cloud of that occasion did follow him on to Charleston. Also he was a committed womanizer. In order to marry he had been forced to abandon a mistress, a woman of the French Islands, of whom he was quite fond, and he did not abandon her completely for another three years. Then after the birth of his daughter came two other affairs, neither of which he took much care to conceal. His wife did not love him. He gave her little reason to.

Ah, but such was the stuff of any romance worth the name. Dr. McCall had read Flaubert's *Madame Bovary* twice through and still kept his pirated translation of the French novel close by. He saw there a ready reference for his current undertaking. A peasant raised above her station, Emma Bovary was a romantic, a lover of novels who allowed herself to be seduced by not one but two men. One of these was a bored despoiler of women, the other a young student of a poetic nature. Dr. McCall saw himself first as one, then the other. Seducer. Poet. Seducer. Poet. Back and forth. He did not hesitate to flip through the pages of this salacious manual and script a triumph for himself. Yet he loved Hélène and did wish to marry her—if it were possible.

Oh, such a woman. While examining her lungs, he had, for the first time in his professional life, felt an incredible urge to bury his face in the delightful crease between those breasts. Of course, to do so would have been his ruin. He had no business even seeing the girl and led her into the office only out of curiosity. He had said goodbye and put all thoughts of her out of his mind —where they stayed for perhaps a heartbeat. Yes, from that visit on he was haunted by the scent, texture, the milky whiteness of those breasts. They glowed as the pearly surface of a magnolia blossom and their firmness compared to nothing on this earth at all.

Through his practice he had seen more of female flesh than a hundred men might see in a lifetime. A thousand men, even. In his ministering to the prostitutes, especially, he had opportunities beyond his earlier imaginings—and those imaginings had been generous. But this titillation had quickly paled. The doctor found that he required at least some notion of conquest. The woman must be bested in some way, taken from a man or simply slipped from society's neat order. And the doctor must in the course of the seduction enjoy at least a modicum of romantic adventure.

Even with full-time wife and full-time mistress at hand, he had continued in these pursuits. But none—not wife, mistress, or pursuits—had ever involved him in love. At least he did not think so. And he felt he did love the governess. In every waking moment he thought of her. He would marry her if he could. Whatever it took, he would marry her. He imagined their future together, and he often imagined a different conclusion to the exam he had performed. He removing the garments, uppermost first. The voluptuous curves coming into sight. He stooping to kiss them, his lips feeling the firm round edge of each rising nipple. Then revealed would be the slender waist and the flaring hips and, surrounded by a pearl-white skin, the dusty brush of downy curls where he would next place his lips.

There was in the procession of a full-bodied woman a curious sensation. He had found it with his mistress. In truth, he had sometimes found it with his wife. On entering them he had discovered himself shrinking—not his member, which remained rod strong—but the sense of himself could be swallowed up by the expanding body of the welcoming female. The heaving breasts, the caressing motion of the other body. Even before ejaculation this rhythm could somehow lead to a displacing of his own person, that trouble-ridden creature that he knew all men to be. Surely, Hélène would bring this joy to every outing. Surely. Again and again, he imagined a different course for the examination of her breasts. The stethoscope is set to one side. "Perhaps, you should move these final garments," he says. "That is required if I am to make a proper diagnosis of tuberculosis." "Of course," she agrees.

Thus each day built upon the next until, on the morning of February first, the doctor had approached Hélène on the sidewalk there by the Lawtons' gate and, with a relaxed good humor that he did not feel at all, he had asked the Swiss governess to run away with him. Building upon this bold opening he had continued with some success.

David Lawton was still in New York. McCall did not fear the man, but thought this absence best for all concerned. He met Hélène at the gate and presented her with two poems, tokens of the high esteem in which he held her.

> Oft have I seen the city belle
> Display the charms that art has taught her:
> More lighter than the light gazelle,
> But never like fair Galila's daughter.
>
> Each line about her faultless form
> Is swelling soft and serpentine;
> Her head is clear, her heart is warm;
> She's nature's child—just sweet sixteen.
>
> Her soft, her brilliant, flashing eye
> Glows with a timid quivering beam.
> She feels, she knows not what, nor why,

Like one in strange mysterious dream.
More sweet than honey drawn from bees
Is the pure nectar of her lips.
Twould almost melt my aching heart
Could I but once advance and sip.

Each winning smile, such graceful stop,
Such everything has nature taught her.
I'd give—let's see—five years of life
Could I but wed fair Galila's daughter.

If I were a rose,
This would I do;
I would lie upon the white neck of her love
And let my life go out upon the fragrance
Of her breath.

If I were a star,
This would I do;
I would look deep down in her eyes—
In the eyes I love and learn there
How to shine.

If I were a truth, strong as the Eternal One,
This I would do;
I would live in her heart—in the heart
I know so well—and
Be at home.

If I were a sin,
This would I do;
I would fly far away, and, though her soft hand
In pity were stretched out, I would not stay,
But fly
And leave her pure.

The doctor had written neither, but they did express what he felt needed to be expressed.

Having just returned from the disappointing New York trip, David encountered yet another cause for worry—he met her on the street. Actually he had bumped into the plump, dark woman as she was leaving the bookstore with a large, wrapped parcel in her arms. He reached out and steadied her, this woman of perhaps his own age. He nodded, even thought to tip his hat, but realized in time that this was Mrs. Patrick, the fortune-teller that his wife was forever consulting. No. Such a woman might rate a nod, but she was not worthy of further courtesy. Only further complaint. And yet he had seen mischief in her eyes and something else, too—but what? That smiling visage seemed somehow familiar and, glancing back, he saw she remained in place and still watched him. She even dared to wave, a small glove-wrapped hand balanced above the large package, a small gesture, but done with no little impudence, and David, with a shake of his head, had gone on his way. Now with young Mr. Bailey coming up to his office, already mounting the stairs, coming to ask for employment, David Lawton remembered where he had seen the woman before. Mrs. Patrick. She was Mary Patrick.

RICHMOND, 1863. THE PAST.

The Magnolia Blossom Inn was only a block behind the Ballard Hotel, practically in the shadow of that venerable establishment. But not so grand, of course. Still, the women at the Magnolia were clean, certified, and for the use of officers only. That did not stop Asa Wright. On their arrival in Richmond he had obtained written passes for both himself and David. "Officer material," the permissions read, which caused the cruel-lipped madam to whoop with laughter.

Not much of that evening was clear to David. He and Asa were both drunk. No other word could be substituted. David rarely drank to excess, and it was not fear of the evening's doings that placed him in that condition. He had been with whores often enough in France. He drank to keep company with Asa, who needed reassurance, for as expected, the madam did tease him about his age and size. Of course, Asa charmed both her and the girl he picked, a thin, fair-skinned hussy, who went up the stairs laughing at his compliments. David had picked a more substantial companion, one with tumbling auburn hair and a sweet, intelligent expression, who called herself Mary. Actually, that was all he could recall of the encounter except the definite excitement of collapsing into bed and having his evil way with the actively willing Mary.

He searched for Mary now. Since being wounded last year, he had not been given such an opportunity, or at least not taken it. Was not feminine companionship of that variety a healthy necessity? He did not need to make excuses, not to his fellow soldiers. What caused him pause was his desire to see this particular whore—his Mary.

Richmond was filled with prostitutes. They numbered in the . . . who could say? By the time David stepped out on this adventure, one educated estimate claimed Richmond had more prostitutes than New Orleans—by another, more than New Orleans and Paris, France, combined. Gaudily dressed women did not wait until dark to ply their trade on the respectable sidewalks. Outrageous pimps lingered openly on street corners. In Richmond camp followers had found the ultimate camp. Still, as this was a military occupation of sorts, an order of sorts was maintained.

The majority of the women could be found inside the four walls of houses, houses which served either enlisted men or officers but never both . . . hardly ever. Naturally, the officers' women enjoyed better quarters, and the Ballard Hotel was among the best. Indeed, David strolled by its front door at that very minute. Every window shone, the sound of clinking piano chords slipped onto the street and also the sound of laughter. But since this was a Wednesday and the hour after two, the commotion was barely noticeable. Indeed, the poorly lit street before him, that leading to the Magnolia, was empty except for a drunk sprawled across the way.

Still he did not consider entering the Ballard Hotel. He went on in search of Mary—driven by a desperation of sorts. Those snatches of tune pursued him in vain. Ahead was the glow of a single lantern, reassuringly red, orange, at least. David leaped up the three required steps and pushed against the broad single door.

The interior was barn-like and uninviting. Thinking himself mistaken, he halted. Then off to the side but draped in the shadows, he recognized a grand piano, and propped with an elbow against it a redheaded woman with broad, flaring nostrils. "Well, look here," the woman said but did not bother to rise. "A late bloomer."

"Yes," David said. "After my bedtime, most certainly, but I imagine I'll be at war in a day or two and thought to find some companionship." He smiled and bowed and, fearing he arrived too late, took a quick look around the cavernous space.

"You're English," the redheaded woman said. "I can tell by that way you talk." And not waiting on his agreement, she rose and asked, "What kind of a companion do you require?"

"I was in here before," David said, still attempting good cheer—which sober was difficult indeed. "I went upstairs with a girl called Mary. An auburn-haired girl about so high." He raised a hand to his shoulder height.

"Auburn? We got one Mary. When was you here last?"

"Before the Seven Days Battle."

The woman nodded. "That would be her." With that she strode off into a dark corner of the barn-like chamber and snatched up what David had taken to be pillows. The women, at least some of them, were asleep upon a series of low divans. "Here she is," the woman announced. She held the sleepy girl hard by the arm, held her with needless cruelty, David thought. "Auburn hair, that would be our Mary," the woman said, and in that light David did recognize the girl and also saw that her hair was not auburn but only a darker red than the frazzled flame demonstrated by the harsh madam.

Six weeks before, his experience of the Magnolia Blossom had been altogether different. For one thing he was drunk. For another it was a Saturday night and the room was filled with boisterous women and their officer clients. The piano was being played. He had played a tune himself, though apparently this performance had not registered with his hostess, who, on that occasion, was a wealth of good feeling. Before, the two billiard tables were in active use. He distinctly recalled the click of billiard balls and the happy squawkings of a parrot. The parrot cage was here, sans parrot.

Yet on seeing the girl, David did take heart, for indeed she was a feminine creature. Though her face was coarse and hard, her bare shoulders were milky white, and pushed high by the bindings of her muslin wrap were firm and handsome breasts. And when the girl stumbled and was yanked forward by the madam, who still held her naked arm in an iron grip, David did reach out in a muted but gentlemanly fashion. Rescued from the clutches of the other, the girl smiled but said nothing. "Mary is a favorite with our religious gentlemen," the madam hissed, "those seeking a virgin." She gave a coughing laugh, fixed him hard with those scornful eyes and said, "Pay me now."

David did and then followed the girl up the stairs, down a narrow corridor, and into a dark room, a small and very plain room. He made out a broad, iron-framed bed, a washstand and chipped mirror, and a hand-size crucifix on the wall—a gentle and collapsed Christ was struck directly by the door-framed slash of light. In the single half-curtained window, the Richmond night shown as a much paler rectangle.

The girl lit the gas lamp, and suddenly the room glowed. Then she stared at him. She made no move at all. Once more David made a nervous survey of the room, nervous but he could not say why. "So your name is Mary?" he asked.

"Yes, sir," she answered in a strong brogue. "You may call me that."

"Or anything else I choose?" he said.

"In faith. That be so."

"And you are Irish and a good Catholic? Are you not?"

"I am. I will not deny it. Once a week I see the priest and tell him all the ways in which I sin."

"I envy you that," David said, though he knew she lied. As a precaution and perhaps in guilt, he had left his rosary at the boardinghouse. Well that he had. Before she could question him on his own faith, he took up her arm and turned it to the light so that the black and blue marks showed clearly. "She treats you needlessly rough," he said.

"She is not so bad as some," the girl replied.

"Still," he said, "there is no reason that I saw for you to be handled in that manner."

"She is not so bad as some," the girl repeated but did smile at him for a second time. "Suppose now we get down to it. In faith, you being a gentleman and an officer, I am particularly anxious to please." She reached out and touched him. And David had the most awkward notion to ask her then, "Do you remember me?" But he did not.

When they were done, they spoke for some minutes, and then, though it was not his intention, he slept through the night. Waking he felt a final brush of her lips and her fingers light against his chest. He opened his eyes and saw her leave the room—the door opened and closed with gentleness. He flung an arm out across the hard mattress and did not regret that he had come. Sunlight. Unfailing sunlight. He dreaded having to pass by the foul-tempered madam, being dunned for extra hours. But surely she would be asleep. He forced himself from the bed and used the chamber pot beneath the stand. No sign of disease as yet. As yet. He examined his face in the chipped mirror, not from any newborn vanity but to see if his night's efforts had not aged him to a small degree. A curse to be so beardless.

What he saw was the same young David Lawton, still unneeding of a shave, still a bit too innocent. And then he smiled at his own naiveté. At least he had this night together with his Mary. His last. He did not think it worth his while to return here. Indeed, in the future it would be best not to visit any of these Richmond establishments, for if the hostesses who entertained him, if the belles he danced with, were to discover the fact, they would say nothing but still find innumerable ways to make his life a waking misery. He left the room and went to war.

His present situation? His Charleston situation? Had the torment of exposure simply been postponed? Long postponed. Did this fortune-telling Mary Patrick mean to do him harm? If she planned to blackmail him, surely she would have done so by now. No, there was nothing on her face that morning to suggest a criminal intent. Something there, but not that. Compassion? Impossible. Amusement? Yes, most certainly.

A confident rap came at the office door. Lost in reveries, David had completely forgotten the business of the moment. An applicant was at hand.

"Ah, Mr. Bailey!" said David rising to his feet. "The son of my esteemed and venerated friend. Take a seat. Take a seat. Well, sir, I understand from your father, that you desire to try journalism as a profession. It is a rough road, Mr. Bailey. It is work in which there are likely to be more kicks than half-pence, but if you wish to try it, for your father's sake I will give you a chance."

"That is all I ask," a beaming Jim Bailey replied. "We must earn our half-pence before we spend them, but the kicks, I presume, we are permitted to repay at once, and in kind"

Of course, this was pure music to David's ears. "Ah, my dear sir," he replied, "young blood is hot blood, but a newspaper man should keep to his pen until forced to his fists, and to his fists until pushed to his pistol. Still, he must prepare for the worst, for we do still have a terrible Republican crew to deal with here, and many Democrats who are hardly better, and the *News and Independent* is determined to call a spade a spade."

Quite determined—but in matters of a personal nature, only great discretion would do. In those matters a spade was not a spade. To direct her life, his susceptible wife was consulting a card-reading gypsy. And this same woman was a whore he once frequented. Nothing there to laugh at. Rebecca would forgive him. He might confess to his early mistake. He saw himself saying, "The poor woman thought we might keep a shop together." He could shake his head with some weariness. Rebecca would forgive him, but she would be hurt nonetheless. He should talk to this Mrs. Patrick. Confront her? Offer her money? No, that would not do. But something must be done. Forbid his wife to see her. No, that would not do, either.

"We are determined," he repeated to young Mr. Bailey. But where was he to find a salary for Mr. Bailey?

She had seen him on the street that day, had passed him, David Lawton, for he was "hers." And she had seen in his eyes that morning the first glimmer of recognition. The two of them together.

RICHMOND, 1863. THE PAST.

She kept the lamp burning low. Only a faint gold tint lay across their proceedings. Her scent was of roses and her voice sweet. Her eyes were the dove's eyes and her cheeks and neck comely though unadorned. Her high breasts were as pomegranates, firm and brazened gold, and the expanse of her belly, the slope upon slope was as a gentle field of wheat. Her navel was as a deep well in which all thirst was quenched. The cleft of her rock a secret place, a bountiful garden of shadowed delight.

And the two of them bounded as young deer, and each saw to the pleasure of the other, and then in the hour before dawn they lay quiet and together.

David had one hand propped behind his head and the other flat upon his chest.

Mary looked not at him but at the gray ceiling. She had the sheet pulled across her breasts and her arms folded across them as well. "I remember you," she said.

"I thought you might," he responded, with just a note of boasting. No doubt he thought his prowess as a lover had made that impression. And perhaps his piano-playing and voice, as well, for he had sung a song or two on the previous visit. "I was with you before the Seven Days Battle," he said. "I was wounded then, and this was my first chance to return."

"You remarked then on my bruises," Mary said and raised an arm to the light. Ugly black and blue splotches glowed where the madam had held her—and held her and held her. "Few that come here remark on them bruises. And you be the only one saying I was cruelly treated. So I remember you. Your name is David. David Lawton is what you are called. I am . . . I am thinking that maybe David will come back and take me away from here. Of course, I know that is a dream, sir. I can recognize the real from what is the pretended—the dancing of fairies and the songs of foolish young girls. Still, it is pleasant to think of you, the English gentleman, and me, a common Irish servant, being together and having a place sometimes in the future, an inn or a shop or some such."

David Lawton had lain motionless, embarrassed, of course, by this declaration. "Yes," he said, finally. "We all imagine such things from time to time. I wonder at . . . this war may save us all a great deal of trouble."

At first Mary said nothing in reply then whispered, "Was your leg that was struck. I seen the scar."

"Yes," he said.

"To every man upon this earth," she recited. "Death comes soon or late."

"Where did you hear that?" David asked in surprise—even in alarm.

"A poem. Was printed in the newspaper—all that about the glorious battle. They claim you to be a most gallant Englishman."

"Yes," David said. "But others fought as bravely—perhaps more."

She had not argued against his denial—though no doubt he wished it. She spoke no more, and he fell asleep soon after.

Mary slept as well. She dreamed that she was in that very room, asleep alone upon that broad hard bed. A knock came upon the door, and she awoke and called out, "Who is it?" "Open up, my loved one," came a voice. "Open the door. I need to be with you." But I have gone to bed already," she called back. "Come tomorrow. Let me sleep." "No," came this voice of her lover.

"You must open now. I cannot wait. I have thought about you all this evening." He pounded on the door and rattled the knob. So she got up and pulled a robe about her and opened the door. No one was there. She looked both right and left in the narrow corridor, and then, still dressed in only the wrap and with her long auburn hair tumbled down, she passed through the cavernous hall below and out onto the night streets of Richmond. And at once she was grabbed by a provost guard, a man in ragged uniform with iron-hard face, and beside him were two detectives in dark suits and derby hats. "What are you doing out here?" the provost guard shouted. And from somewhere, Mary found the courage to reply. "I am looking for my lover!" "Your lover? Your lover," the man laughed. The other two laughed as well. "Richmond is filled with lovers. Every soldier is a lover. Armed with sword and buckle. Ready to storm the battlements, to mount and conquer." "Yes," she said. "But mine is different from all the rest." "How is that?" one detective shouted. "Describe this man, this soldier of yours!" shouted the other. "He is white and ruddy," she began. But then no other thoughts would come. Already, she had forgotten his face. "I am sick from love," she moaned. "I am sick from love." And then she woke and, seeing where she was, she kissed David Lawton on the cheek and left the room.

CHAPTER TEN

On that particular day his father seemed displeased. Over what, Thomerson could not say.

His father had returned from New York the week before, and soon his mother was to leave for Washington. She would visit his Uncle Asa, and his Aunt Abbie would be there, too. But for now the boy had both his parents at home and his sister, of course, and Hélène. For now they were all together, standing on the back piazza. His father had rung for dinner to be served, and they waited a moment before entering the house—he, his father, his mother, Anna, and the Swiss governess, Hélène. Then suddenly came the sound of scuttling, of claws scratching up the steps, and there rising towards them was a creature more ravenous wolf than dog. Still, Thomerson did recognize the animal, this playmate of his entire young life, his father's faithful old setter bitch Nellie. The boy stood paralyzed as, with slobbering jaws stretched wide and eyes afire, the dog sprang straight towards his face.

Thomerson ducked—for there is an instinct guiding even the most city-bound lad—and the monster passed over his head and fell sprawling on the piazza floor. But at once this Nellie, this nightmare vision of their domestic animal turned, crouched, and readied herself for a second attack. But his father stepped forward, caught her by the loose skin of the neck and held tight. The snapping jaws came down on empty air. Yes, certain tragedy had been averted, but the dog continued to twist in his father's grip while their puppy, Bruno, the Newfoundland, who at six months was already as large as a pony, came bounding up the stairs to join the fun. The sight of this new arrival only in-creased Nellie's thrashing tenfold, and now not only son and father might be bitten but also the puppy.

Oddly enough (even at that moment this struck Thomerson as a nightmarish incongruity), except for his father, no one seemed capable of acting. The boy was stunned. His mother stood frozen like a dead-white statue of alabaster. Anna looked on in puzzled consternation, as if all that occurred might be an act upon the stage. And Hélène seemed totally unconscious of the danger now facing the family and herself as well. In fact, she was laughing. But his father understood that with the bumbling Bruno added into the melee, his battle was a losing one, and so he shouted in a manner the boy recognized from his father's stories of the War. His father had used that angry bellow long before on the battlefields of Virginia: "Catch that dog—Catch that dog and drag him off! Catch and hold him!"

It was Anna who obeyed. She snatched the Newfoundland puppy around the belly just up from the hind legs and pulled for dear life. Thomerson joined her. Hélène made some motion in that direction though actually did nothing. But the battle had turned, and their father dragged Nellie away—Nellie snapping and digging her claws into boards of the porch floor and then scratching the marble of the steps and the brick paving of the walk below—until finally they entered the basement. He heard the door slam behind them. Then after a frighteningly long time their father reappeared.

"We must kill the dog," he said.

"Must we?" their mother questioned.

"She has hydrophobia," he replied.

"Are you sure?" their mother questioned further. "Did you try to give her water?"

"I did," their father replied. "You couldn't have hammered water down her throat!"

Now the puzzle of how water could be hammered down a throat fascinated the boy to such a degree that he actually put aside all thoughts of the danger just experienced and considered the problem involved in hammering a liquid. In his diary that night he recorded the event in brief and then set down the question in bold print. "HOW MIGHT ONE HAMMER A LIQUID?" It was a question that Hélène had simply shrugged away. But not the boy. The consideration of "Death on a Pale Horse" was nothing compared to this.

Indeed, Reader, he wonders at it still. A full eighteen years have passed, and I suspect this question returns to Thomerson in the watches of his sleepless nights. He stands at the window of his Paris apartment and looks out on a sleeping city—a city filled with foreigners, men and women who can never truly understand who he is—and considers a question that is unanswerable.

Rebecca Lawton has died. While Thomerson was on safari with Theodore Roosevelt, his mother passed. There was no evidence of illness. She died in her sleep. I attended the funeral, but, of course, he could not. Now he has returned to Paris and on several occasions came to visit my library stronghold. He shows some interest in this supposed biography of his father, but only of the nodding variety. He mutters a few words of encouragement. In the pretense of helping, he speaks briefly of his boyhood in Charleston and then at length, addresses questions like that of "hammering a liquid."

For spontaneous and complete expressiveness, he feels the phrase is perfect. "You couldn't have hammered water down her throat!" covered well that totally unique experience. After all, an expression that Thomerson could not forget throughout his entire life, however he might try to forget, may be unjustifiable from the viewpoint of a lexicographer, but still did I not see it had a validity, a lasting quality, which a purist could not possibly understand? And in all justice to the language, he had once heard of a nurse who broke the front teeth of a very ill but seriously recalcitrant child, literally trying to hammer medicine down its throat with a tablespoon, so perhaps the situation was not so unique as he imagined and the phrase applicable to a far wider variety of events.

But I should leave such distant matters to Mrs. Patrick. After all, that is to be Thomerson's future, his Paris future. Oh, how far he has traveled from that Charleston boyhood. The governess Hélène, his father, his sister Anna, even his mother, they seem but characters in a dream.

They seem that way to me as well.

"What is coming, Mrs. Patrick?" asked the young poet and perhaps novelist David Spencer. *Spencer* is but a name he uses—one borrowed from the rifle, not the English poet. *Patrick* is the one found on the baptismal records. Mrs. Patrick is his mother. As "Madame Chazzar" she tells fortunes and guides the lives of others.

"A steamboat," Mrs. Patrick answered. "The boiler explodes. See them there, bodies pulled from the water, most scalded beyond recognition. The men on the bluff roll them in flour. They do that to ease the pain, but it does no good, and the dying rise up and wander the water's edge, dusted so like ghosts. And oddly none of them screams. They talk among themselves and then lie upon the ground and die."

"Yes, Mama" he said. "But that was last week. On the Mississippi. All that was in the paper."

"Ah," she whispered. "Wait then. I see another such vessel. *The Lady of Baton Rouge*. Her bow points . . ."

"For me, Mama. Surely I am not sailing on the Mississippi."

"No, Mr. Spencer. I see you elsewhere. A quiet room. Books on all sides. And through the window I see wisteria running wild across the wall. A small woman of some age. She dresses all in black and sits as a doll might and speaks to you of a book that is to be written."

"Thank you," he said. "I must go." He dismissed himself from his mother's presence, nodded a farewell to the parrot and starlings or whatever else was now included in the woman's menagerie, and left the residence. He went in anger.

David Spencer understood at last that David Lawton had set the girl against him. She had told him so. David Lawton forbid her visiting the roller rink. He had obtained a promise that she not speak with him again, but she had disobeyed and come a final time into the pharmacy. She declared that she would do that no longer. She would make her purchases elsewhere, and he must forget that they were ever acquainted. He would find someone more suited to him. "I am not the only fish in the ocean. You will some day see that is the truth."

David Spencer was beside himself. The young pharmacy clerk and aspiring chronicler came to the iron gate and seized the grill, wrapped fingers around wrought iron, and considered that great oaken door set well back in the high entry. He stood before the Lawtons' grand house of grim, gray stucco, cement scored to appear as stone, and then passed on. He had heard of the doctor's advances to the governess. He had made inquires of his own and discerned that most probably it was his prognosis, his shout of "Tuberculosis!" that had sent the girl into the arms of her seducer. She had fallen into the clutches of a doctor with a reputation of the worst sort, all because he had uttered a single word. His efforts to write a perfect sonnet had come to nothing, and yet a single unthinking word brought ruin. The young man did think to act. To challenge the doctor to a duel seemed the bravest course. No. Not that. Best to wait. To bide his time. He could not blame Hélène for wishing to swap her life as governess for one of a comfortable matron. She would come to her senses. The doctor's attentions were but a test. Yes, he decided finally on a course that might just work this all to his advantage.

At seven o'clock on Wednesday evening, February 27, 1889, Rebecca accompanied David to his office. Then, instead of returning straight to the house, she impulsively told her coachman Isaac to drive to Madame Chazzar's. Madame Chazzar also went by the name of Mrs. Patrick, but when they were together, Rebecca called her by her given name, Marie, for she felt close to the woman and trusted her completely. It was raining, a gray winter rain, and the gaslights shone as small circles of sickly pale yellow. Rebecca was to leave for Washington the next afternoon and, despite the grim weather, felt a singular sense of well-being. Still, she was struck with the notion of having her fortune told and having it done at exactly that moment.

Now quite naturally, this caprice shamed Rebecca, for in addition to going against David's wishes, she had just been to this woman the previous week. Indeed Madame Chazzar was amazed to see her arrive—especially at that hour and in the rain.

"It is a shameful, foolish errand, that I come on," Rebecca said. "Lock the door!" It was locked, and with a gentle flourish Madame Chazzar ushered her visitor through the outer room, with its cages of canaries and finches, past the single parrot perched on the lampstand and two small dusty white dogs, and into the adjoining parlor, one decorated with rich draperies and rugs. At the center, of course, was the ornate round ebony table, at which both women quickly took their seats.

"Look into your cards, my witch," Rebecca whispered, "and tell me what is coming. Hesitate at nothing that you see!"

Though shaded as the dark Irish are, Madame Chazzar's wide and innocent features were hardly witch-like. Still she nodded solemnly at the compliment and spread out three of the cards—the Eight of Swords, the Three of Wands, and the Ace of Wands. Then after some surveying, Rebecca was told that she'd been visiting a dying woman. The fortune-teller's words rose and fell with a slightly foreign rhythm, with the rhythm of authority. But Rebecca was not fooled. Of course! Everyone in town knew she had been to see the mother of David's first wife, Mrs. Fourgeaud. "Skip that!" Rebecca demanded with raised voice. "Hurry on to what is awaiting me! I feel it near!"

"You will start upon a journey."

"Yes, tomorrow I go to Washington. Skip that! Tell me what is coming to me!"

Madame Chazzar closed her eyes and raised her head slightly. "Two women," she declared. "They be sitting in a house, a house in shambles. One has bitten deep into her own knuckle. That be blood runs down her arm! See, see, 'tis a house in shambles. Was soldiers. Soldiers have taken all away."

"Stop! That is my sister and myself. Young women. I told you that. What is coming now?"

The fortune-teller opened her eyes. She blinked and brought a hand to her brow. "Ah, yes. Coming next. Do you remember what I told you?"

"Yes! ten days or so ago," Rebecca acknowledged and rattled off a quick summary of how the next eighteen months of her life was to be filled with trouble but eventually the darkness would lighten and a certain peace would prevail.

"Comes near. Comes very near," Madame Chazzar resumed. "A change in your life where all that is, is no longer. A heavy story. Where you are wealthy, you will know want. Where you are shielded by love and tenderness, you will stand alone. Where you have all things—you will lack completely. It is very near. Comes near. Comes near. A great upheaval.'Tis dim. The rest is dim, but when all has passed, you will dwell no longer in this city." She tapped the Eight of Swords. "Oh! I see now. The challenge. Here is that awful accident. It is to a man! Do you remember me telling you that too? Well! It is coming. 'Tis near. Very near. It will fall like lightning from a clear and silent sky. There is no warning! No help! You are alone in the twilight. A piteous sight. Some men come to you. Men crowd around you. Not a woman is with you. You stand alone but for these strange men. Your fingers spread wide, but there is nothing to embrace."

"What is it?" Rebecca asked.

"Wait! Wait!" Again Madame Chazzar closed her eyes. "A key turns on my uncertainty. Such monstrous images swim towards my mind's eye. Violence. Bloodshed. This is awful! It is unexpected. The nearest and dearest in the world!" Madame Chazzar clutched at the rosary that hung before her ample breasts. She often did this, twisted the beads between her fingers when entering into a state of vision.

"Tell that to Captain Lawton, and he will laugh and say 'That's Asa!'" Rebecca shook her head in mock refusal.

"But the man who falls is not your brother!" The fortune-teller's eyes were again open. She stared at Rebecca as in accusation. "And you do not love your brother the best!" she said.

"Indeed I do not! I am only telling you that. What of Captain Lawton? What comes to him?"

Madame Chazzar hesitated. Then abandoning the rosary beads and raising fingertips to her forehead, she fixed Rebecca with that unblinking stare. "I cannot tell exactly. He has been through terrible persecutions." Madame Chazzar turned up another card. The moving card made a harsh whispering sound. But Rebecca barely glanced down. Her attention was on the woman. The stubby fingers touching upon the thick reddened lips, the blackened rings beneath those searching eyes. "The end is coming," the fortune-teller declared.

"Has come!" Rebecca exclaimed. "Heaven knows that all that—all the malice and wickedness that men can devise has been tried against him. He has survived it. It is over, I am sure."

Suddenly Madame Chazzar placed both palms down upon the spread cards and insisted: "Your husband is in terrible danger." Once more the woman looked into Rebecca's eyes. "You must warn your husband."

Rebecca shook her head no.

"There is someone who will take his life," Madame Chazzar insisted.

"Cantor at *The World* would murder him if he could stab him in the back, or ex-Mayor Courtenay would if he could hire a man to do it in the dark. But David is safe! They dare not!"

Again the woman insisted: "No. No. His life is threatened by a small, dark man—a professional man—he is a doctor! Listen to me. The assailant is a doctor."

"Surely you do not mean Dr. Decatur!" Decatur was their family doctor and treated both Rebecca and her husband.

"Oh, no! Captain Lawton does not know this man. He has never even heard his name." The woman had not bothered to turn another card. Tilting her head back she now announced, "Strangest of all, it is over a woman."

Rebecca reached across the table and clutched the card-reader by her plump wrist—which seemed somehow to be as hard as steel. "If Dr. Decatur expresses his opinion about some woman, there would be trouble. Captain Lawton cannot endure any aspersions against a woman's reputation. And Dr. Decatur knows some awful things!"

"Listen to me. This man is unknown to you. A very bad man, I tell you. All evil surrounds him. He is a low, obscure man. Captain Lawton goes in a room where he is. Something is said. I can see no more. It is as though a heavy cloud fills the room."

"But what do they say, Marie? What happens?"

"I see something." Now Madame Chazzar gazed towards the ceiling, and for just a moment her eyes rolled back. "Oh! the cloud lifts!" she shouted. "I see a priest enter. He kneels in the middle of the room."

"But Marie! Look closely! What does it mean?"

"See!" The woman pointed up above Rebecca's head and a cloud of smoke did seem to hang above the table. "Here is that awful shock for you! Horrible shock! What crowds. How many friends Captain Lawton has! They come surging around him like great waves. Thousands and thousands of friends! Fine upstanding men and women, too. And not only here! They come forward, even men of foreign lands!"

"But I do not understand, Marie! What becomes of the man who threatens his life?"

"I cannot tell." Madame Chazzar shook her head, then raised that dark finger to her temple. "Oh! Here is something clear at last!" She stared straight into Rebecca's eyes. She did not smile, nor frown either. She spoke in a calm flat voice. "In two weeks Captain Lawton will have his heart's desire, and great honors will be showered upon him."

"That's something pleasant to look forward to!" Rebecca cried.

"Oh, God's child," the other sighed, "the world's more full of weeping than you can understand."

At home that night, they sat at tea and Rebecca laughingly confessed the visit to David. His reaction was surprisingly gentle. He said, "Mrs. Patrick, I assume."

"Yes. She is the one I trust, the only one."

"You should not," he said with the same weariness. "I mean it is not wise to go out, especially in the rain."

"She had a message for you."

After a pause, he asked, "And what might that be?"

It was Rebecca's turn to mock. "In two weeks, you will have your heart's desire, and great honors will be shown you!"

"Let them hurry, then!"

"Have you a heart's desire, David?"

"If I had a heart's desire it would be for rest." His head drooped sadly forward, but only in mock contrition. "But eternal rest seems the only one available."

Rebecca hastened to add, "But we will not take it at such a price, will we dear?"

He laughed and tossed his head back. "No. Not at that price! Not at that price. God knows I cannot afford to die."

Then Rebecca told him all, except that which touched on his danger. That, she garbled. She wished him to believe, as she had persuaded herself, that the bloodshed applied to Asa and not to him. Besides, it could be true of neither! Why tell him Marie's entire prophecy? Rebecca said, "Asa's life is threatened. A violent death awaits him very soon."

David no longer laughed. "I have no confidence in so called fortune-telling! Nothing that this Mrs. Patrick tells you should influence you in any way, my dear. Go on to Washington. Enjoy your brother while he is of this world. That much of the future we all know. Asa won't be around for ever. None of us will."

The next morning, she repeated Mrs. Patrick's forecast to Dr. Decatur. He was doctor to both her and her husband and had attended the birth of all three of her children and the death of one. She must trust him. He knew her in a most intimate way, had touched her body as only a husband or a doctor might. She visited him that morning concerned with the pain in her back, a pain she'd endured for a score of years, and, of course, there was little he could do, except massage the spot and prescribe his blood tonic and bed rest.

She nodded as always and then spoke of the fortune-teller. Indeed, to Dr. Decatur she gave a more detailed account: she had not told her husband of the evil stranger who waited to assail him, but she did tell her doctor. And when she came to the description, "a small, dark man . . . a professional man . . . a doctor," she added, "Surely, Dr. Decatur, you would not be induced to say rude words to Captain Lawton?"

"I don't think I would," Dr. Decatur replied. "But if he does not want to hear the truth, he had better not question me about some people." That was Dr. Decatur's singular confirmation of Madame Chazzar's remarks. He did not offer more.

This physician of theirs was of a medium build, but some might say slightly smaller than average, and though he was fair-skinned and probably blond, his hair was oiled to a darker sheen. But it was silly for Rebecca to suspect him, for he had a club foot. Surely Madame Chazzar would have mentioned that. No. On most occasions Dr. Decatur had an easy manner and was hardly sinister in either person or reputation.

He did have an adulterous wife. But David considered him a friend, or at least valued him as the best possible physician in a city filled with medical charlatans.

CHAPTER ELEVEN

Captain Lawton had returned from New York, but he was at his office, and her mistress was off in Washington. So Hélène allowed her suitor to enter the house—or rather she did not stop him. At midmorning he simply knocked, and, expecting him, she answered and did not bar the entrance. Indeed, it was she who led the way into the library, and with the door closed, the two of them discussed a variety of matters.

Hélène sat in chaste seclusion on the edge of a chair. McCall sat close by on the sofa. From that vantage he peered into the scrapbook the governess held on her knees. The girl pointed out her broad-shouldered, ruddy-faced brothers and her sister who was a governess in England and her father, be-whiskered and proud. The doctor took an interest in each and inquired as to the prospects of each and complimented the sturdy countenance exhibited by the father. Then, as all were posed amidst that alien Swiss landscape of grand snow-peaked mountains and clean-swept village streets, the doctor teased her about the snow and how she must miss her "up and down" landscape.

"We have no Negroes," she said. "We have not the ocean. Here they have the salt smell. Very different, the heat and the rain that falls. And," she added laughing, "you have the bugs! I come here I sleep with a great veil on the bed. Here in Charleston you have the mosquito. You have the palmetto bug. Horrid black creatures. At the feet the bug. Mosquito on the head." She pointed from bottom to top, and he chuckled in appreciation.

Hélène turned the page a final time. "This is me," she said. The pose was formal, and presented to the world a pleasant, open face, eyes wide and staring straight into the camera—a wild animal, a gentle animal surprised. "Hélène, the mountain girl. This is me."

"*Très* beautiful," the doctor laughed. "Most naive."

"Yes. That may be the word. As you say."

Hélène's dress fell to both sides of the chair, and when the doctor reached over he stepped on the material. When Hélène shrunk away the sound of tearing came.

"Oh, pardon," said the doctor. "I only wanted this."

With nimble fingers he slipped the photograph of the girl from its bindings and sat back on the sofa.

"No. No. You must give me that." McCall only smiled and after a brief inspection slipped the likeness into his inside pocket. "I am not the woman that you think. I am bourgeoisie!" Hélène announced suddenly.

"Yes, yes. I understand that you are virtuous," the doctor replied with equal speed. "But I have told you that I want you for my wife. I respect you, Hélène, as a Madonna on a pedestal. I would do nothing to spoil that chasteness in your nature. But still I do admit I want you for your voice, your eyes, all that are so fresh, pleasing to the eye. And may I add to the touch. I must have Hélène the mountain girl to be my wife, my sister, the angel in my life."

"Oh, doctor, you talk such silliness." Hélène shifted on the chair as if to rise. McCall reached again and this time clasped her hand. But not with any force. No force was required. "You are the madman," the girl whispered.

"Mad for you," the doctor replied, in that gentle, soothing voice, that languid whisper.

"You do not divorce in this place," the girl said. "In my home many get divorced and marry again, and there is no shame, but here this is not done."

McCall leaped to his feet and began to pace before her, explaining that since the end of the Yankee occupation, divorces were no longer allowed in South Carolina. But he could travel to North Carolina and thus be freed. He repeated that he did not love his dull German wife and had only married her in order to get the money to establish his practice—money that had been returned to the German father long ago. If necessary, he and Hélène would live in Paris. He repeated that he was valedictorian of his medical class and not the "usual run-of-the-mill that practiced in the city of Charleston." Then he stood behind her, placing his hands on her shoulders, and whispered that his love for her knew no bounds. "I am crazed with longing," he declared, and, indeed, in his eyes was a hint of madness. He was a man lovesick and lost to reason. With an awkward bending he brought his lips to hers, which she did allow, but as he came away his cheek was scraped by the tip of her hat pin. He stood with hand on this wound.

"I must think about all these things you have told to me," she said. "Please, you must go now." After some urgings she managed to escort him out to the street gate—where he managed to steal a second kiss.

The kitchen with its pots and pans. There the heat of the great iron stove was coupled with the careless arrogance of the cook and of the butler, who stood around rocking on his heels. Even worse were the two others, who had little to do and less skill to accomplish this little. Her mistress spoiled them all. And yet, this place in the house did remind Hélène of home. Her peasant mother was always cooking or eating or loudly planning to do both, while her gentle father hid away in the attic room studying his books.

Oh, Hélène had no illusions about what might lay ahead. She did not view her virginity as a proof of moral superiority. Rather, she understood that if the doctor succeeded in seducing her, then no matter how sincere his feelings, he would not marry her. In short, her chasteness was a commodity that she must swap only for the married state. She had but one misgiving. The child who she often saw at play would miss her father. Yet, she reasoned, the unhappy doctor would certainly go on to find someone else. Better for Hélène to be the new wife.

Ah, yes. And sin was involved. They would all be judged in the hereafter, and her present actions would be construed as sin. Others sinned, but God forgave. Wasn't it for this that Jesus Christ had bared his blessed bleeding heart? She would pray. And she would make the doctor a good wife and have precious children of her own, and she would be forgiven. So it was settled. Except for love. She was most certain that the doctor loved her, though what a man might call love was always suspect. But she did not love him. Still, she was concerned over his unhappiness and thought him very handsome, and the sound of his voice brought her a curious comfort. As she lay upon her narrow bed in the privacy of her room, she did remember the touch of his gentle fingers along the tops of her breasts, the urgent pressure of his lips on hers.

She had not prepared for bed, had only removed her shoes and loosened her clothes. Now she stood and pulled free of all but the final layer, the muslin sheath. One thing was certain. She did not love that boy in the pharmacy. She did not love David Spencer. Two days before he had approached her on the street, and she turned away. Pretended rather clumsily not to see him.

She bathed her face in her small enameled basin and stood staring out her single window at a tile-shingled corner of the doctor's roof. Her single view. Then she stretched once more on the bed. She extended her arms and ran her fingers through her loosened hair and observed her own round alabaster arms and the rising of her own alabaster breasts. She placed her hands behind her head. Perhaps what she felt for the doctor was love of a kind. But she did not feel the ground move as it did in those romances she devoured. Still, it was common in her novels for a dark and villainous man not to be a villain at all, but rather the victim of slander. The girl, too, might be a victim of slander. But through courage and perseverance these two would unite and triumph. She did know with certainty that Dr. McCall was a brilliant man and industrious, and he was a handsome man, and she did not think she would find a life spent with him to be so difficult.

Love might come. She had read of that. In any case, she had been wrong to make love her first concern. David and Rebecca loved each other very much, and yet Hélène could see they were not happy. Not at all. She knew she still loved her mistress with the devotion of a child to parent, and she admired the Captain for what he had accomplished. But those affections would not hinder her, for in the months since Christmas she had felt Rebecca moving away from her again, treating her more and more like a governess and less and less like a daughter. She did not imagine that.

Her room once so spacious seemed but a cramped closet, and she resented the fact that her only entry was through the boy's room. And she had only one window. No matter how large. Only one. From that window she could glimpse the corner of the doctor's roof.

On the following day she met her suitor at the gate with a copy of *Twixt Love and Law,* a romance Captain Lawton had brought home from the newspaper office. Twice through Hélène had read this story of a beautiful young woman in love with a married man and how that man divorced his wife and married her. "It can never be the same between a man and a woman," she quoted to her suitor. "She—if she is young and innocent—has nothing to reveal, and he, being a man, owns a thousand concealments which can never be confided." She pressed the book into the doctor's hands, telling him that it held a message for the two of them.

David Lawton had received an anonymous letter—two letters, actually. The first, which read "Look to your home!," he threw into the trash. The second came in the morning post and warned: "Beware, Lawton. A married man preys on the governess. Look to your home!"

That same evening David Lawton called Hélène into the library and confronted her with his newly fortified suspicions. "You are like a daughter to my wife and me," he said. "We cannot stand by idly and see you ruined. I do not know the name of this man whom I am told you are seeing, but I know that he is married and that he is attempting to seduce you. My child, I will not allow you to venture further in that direction."

"Oh, Captain," she said, "there is no man. I am very happy to be in this house. I would not leave Mrs. Lawton for all the world."

David Lawton made a motion as if to cross the room to her. Both stood, he beside the desk and she beside the chair, the same chair where she sat to hear McCall's plea the week before. But David Lawton stopped, and she saw in his face not anger so much as sadness, a sadness unto tears.

"I do not believe you," he said. "It breaks my heart to say I do not believe you, but I do not. My dear, my wife and I understand that you might want to find a husband of your own and make your own way in life. We were young once ourselves, though you might find that very hard to believe, but we were young and do not begrudge you the happiness that marriage provides. If you are patient we will help you to procure a proper mate. There are ways these things may be accomplished. Especially in a city such as this, there are rules to be followed. I cannot allow you to see this man again."

"I have no man following me," Hélène said. "You must believe me. I tell you that I am very happy to be in your house."

Released from the interview, Hélène went at once to the kitchen and confronted the staff, telling them all— the cook, the maids, the butler—that what she did was her business alone and that if they told the Lawtons anything further she would denounce them all as liars and expose their petty larcenies. They, of course, exclaimed their innocence. They were innocent. The anonymous letters were David's only source.

Much was being revealed. On all sides. Only the week before, the doctor had sworn to Hélène on his mother's grave that her employer, Captain David Lawton, was a frequenter of whorehouses, a base hypocrite, a bully, and no friend to the poor. Hélène knew that such a man was in no position to be saying "I will not allow!" She was not his slave. Before leaving Switzerland she had been warned that in the American South she might be treated so.

The next day Hélène met the doctor once more at the gate, and though she was more abrupt than usual, she left in his hand a token of betrothal, a poem—"Hélène Burdayron: Mountain Girl." It began:

> On the roads here below.
> How does she know the path to follow?
> Without the guidance of God's angels
> She is lost.

Anna wished for a homemade telephone, one that would connect her to a neighboring playmate, and never able to deny his daughter, David had obliged. With the assistance of both children, he set about arranging the device—a lengthy piece of tight cord to carry the sound waves and a tin cup on each end to send and receive the messages of girlhood. This was on a Saturday, the morning after Rebecca's return from Washington, and she, too, was helping.

Standing beside him on the upper gallery, Rebecca carefully coiled the string, all the while calling out encouragement to their daughter, her playmate, and Thomerson, who all waited on the balcony of the other house. But the weather was cold, and Rebecca was not strong. She called Hélène onto the piazza and asked her to straighten the now tangled cord. Then she went inside and left David alone with the governess to whom he had barely spoken—or rather she had barely spoken to him—since their confrontation two nights before.

"When we are finished you may wish to call home," he teased the girl.

"Monsieur," she replied with a faint smile. That was all. But Rebecca had left the girl with a grand tangle of twine, which did demand her full attention. Still, David felt the need to fill up an awkward silence now stretching into its second day.

"In truth, matters mechanical are not my strongest suit," he laughed. "As a lieutenant in the artillery it was necessary to convert my navy coat into an army tunic—the most troublesome part the configuration of the Austrian knot on the arm. Oh, I was quite the gay blade. The gray tunic was trimmed out with scarlet cuffs and scarlet collar, knots of gold braid on each arm, two bars of gold lace on each side of the standing collar, and gray trousers set off with broad red stripes, and for a crown a scarlet and gold kepi, my 'woodpecker cap.' But working out the Austrian knot ornament was about the limit of my mechanical ability. And yet I was promoted and placed in charge of the armaments for half an army. Trajectories and ranges and a host of mystifying equations, somehow I would have to master those."

"Monsieur," she repeated.

"Hélène," he said.

"*Bon.* Quite handsome, I am sure. The uniform you have."

"Yes. Splendid. But I confessed to the old officer above me that I knew practically nothing of armaments. Do you know what he said?"

"No, Monsieur."

"He paused and then said, 'You know more than most, I suspect.'"

From the far house his children were calling out. He had meant to take this discussion somewhere. To say, "Don't you see? I was young and foolish and the old officer knew best. Or some such. But Hélène had turned away from him, half away, at least, and concentrated on her task.

"Let me help you," he said and through a motion, indicated she shift the coiled portion of the twine to his hands and thus be free to untangle the remainder. She did this but did so without meeting his gaze and continued her work in silence.

"Patience," he shouted across the abyss to the waiting children. "Do you think the Trans-Atlantic cable was laid in a single Saturday morning?"

"Yes, Father. Yes, Father," came the dutiful replies.

Only then did he glance into the next yard, to where a strange man stood holding a watering can. He was small and dark with clipped mustache, and on this neighbor's face was an odd expression, one of curiosity or perhaps annoyance. Was he unhappy about the shouting? Or simply wondering over the children's intended telephone? Perhaps neither.

This must be Dr. McCall. Though they had been neighbors for over a year, David had never met the man, only heard he was something of a libertine and treated prostitutes. And then it occurred to David that McCall might be the unidentified man making advances to Hélène. With astonishment he looked into the girl's face and saw there only concentration upon the last of the snarls, and when he glanced back across the wall, Dr. McCall, if indeed that was McCall, had vanished. So David dismissed the notion, for such could only be the fancies of his exhausted mental state—or rather his overworked imagination.

"Will you sing for us?" he asked the governess.

"I have the . . . voice . . . a chill," she replied.

"Yes. Well, by all means you should go inside." He thought she lied, but what was he to do? Too childish, all this business. It would be settled soon enough. The girl would come to her senses. He took the remainder of the coiled string from her and with only the children's help installed a quite successful telephone.

"What has God wrought?" Anna shouted into her tin cup end. The shout, of course, was a mimicking tribute to Morse's first message over the telegraph. And of course, you could hear this bellowing half a block away,· but still the neighbor's child was quite pleased and shouted back some piece of girlish nonsense about coming over some day for a visit. Back and forth they went for several minutes.

Throughout this exchange Thomerson simply stood beside him looking very grave, and it occurred to David that his timid, earnest son was still stuck on the question "What has God wrought?" And suddenly and for no identifiable reason, David remembered changing the boy's diaper. Long, long ago, he had raised up the tiny bottom and with a laugh wiped away all manner of noxious discharge.

Rebecca had gone off to New Orleans to visit her sister, and one afternoon, David came home early from work and relieved the nurse. He changed and bathed the boy and set about dressing him. And the boy held out his hands, fingers in miniature, but laughed aloud with a voice full-blown, and then made a most deliberate if inarticulate demonstration—joyfully bouncing himself on the mattress. Well he might, for had not David just dealt with all the nappy's mess and set him fresh before the world? Oh, such a child. From day to day David was certain he could see a change. The boy grew so quickly. The sleeves of his gown were tight at the wrist. His cheeks were rosy. He continued to laugh and coo for his father's benefit and waved his chubby fists. Wrapping Thomerson in his best swaddling, David had strolled his son in the perambulator, and from behind that simple vehicle looked on the world as only a king can. "Here is my future," he whispered so that only the baby might hear. "Here is my stake in all that is to come."

Yes, he had loved his son on that afternoon with an intensity he had not known before or since—with a complete devotion he had not felt for any human being, not even his wife. Now, here beside him was the son, a son soon to be man, and yet the boy seemed so tense, seemed frightened of so much. Had David failed on this account as well? Had his own father by doing his very worst managed to do better?

CHAPTER TWELVE

The meeting with her sister and brother had not gone well. The distance between them only widened. She, Rebecca, Asa—they loved each other, perhaps more than ever, for hadn't loss intensified their love? But Abbie thought them both still children. Asa, graying at the temples and slightly bent, still lived life as a daredevil boy—a retired daredevil boy. He raised dogs and drew on a small trust left behind by his first father-in-law to support his third wife and family. Rebecca? Oh, Rebecca came with the tale of visiting the fortune-teller—that Madame Chazzar she wrote of in her letters. The woman says David Lawton is to be killed. No other interpretation was possible. This was not some vague threat. Her brother-in-law was to be murdered. The woman was warning Rebecca, and Rebecca for reasons beyond reason refused to listen. Abbie had considered sending a telegram to David. She discussed this with Asa, who laughed it off—pointing out with some justice that he and David had walked the streets of Charleston daily under more dire threats than a fortune-teller's guesses.

"David will receive his heart's desire." That was Madame Chazzar's promise. David's desire? Much too close to Hamp's desire. And the doctor, Decatur, their family doctor telling Rebecca the same thing. Why couldn't the man simply name a name? Who was going to murder David and why? Didn't simple logic demand such answers? Her brother Asa laughed at her. He only showed interest in the attack of "the mad dog" and in the growth of the new puppy. As ever, his were the concerns of a boy, and Rebecca, too, seemed beyond the reach of adult logic. Indeed, Rebecca's principal concern was that Abbie not return to her own husband. David had sent the same message.

Marriage? What an unrelenting joke! Abbie had managed to take control of her own life. She had saved herself, and she had saved her daughter. She could do no more than that.

Fate.

Was her brother-in-law in love with the governess? Not on a conscious level, perhaps, for Abbie knew he considered the custodian of his two children to be "under his protection," to be in a sense his "daughter." And, of course, he did not wish to cause his wife pain. Still, David would have for Hélène a lingering affection, something akin to what he had felt for Abbie two summers before. But she knew it was Rebecca, her sister and his wife, that David Lawton loved deeply.

Oh, in the South all was deeply felt, and, of course, with love came a commitment to romance and to anger—and to death. Politics? Business? Even marriage? In the South weren't all tainted by this binding passion, this ill-fated direction of their energies? David's desire? What choice did David have? Sadly and truly, her brother-in-law crossed God's wide plain on a narrow track, one bounded close by this odd, odd chivalry. Wasn't this the realization of the Great Earthquake days, this understanding that had led her to take daughter north and start anew? All of Charleston lay before David Lawton, yet each afternoon he took the blue line trolley.

That last thought caused Abbie to laugh out loud. She did hardly better, for weren't her own memories and regrets still binding her just as tightly? She had sent emphatic word to her husband that there would be no reconciliation. He had sent back word that there would be no divorce. He had not changed. She had learned from several sources that André was still a drunkard, one making a pathetic living as a gambler's "accomplice," whatever that might be. Daughter Catherine was right. Not about wishing his death, but about Abbie's right to chose someone else. Here in New York she might be granted a divorce. She could certainly take a lover. The city was filled with displaced women, many from the South—the majority from there—and with propriety, they made all manner of concessions. But Abbie could not bring herself to do that.

Though the city of New York held many pleasures, she had settled on a meager handful. Five blocks from her apartment the theaters began, and an opera house was almost as close. Every week she attended either one or the other. She had come late to the enjoyment of opera, but she found great satisfaction in the grand passions announced therein. Considering her family and listening, as well, she sat now in the midst of strangers with the tears openly pouring down her cheeks.

What mistakes she had made . . . or had she?

For their honeymoon she and André had gone down to the Gulf Shore. For two weeks they stayed in a clapboard cabin set well away from others. "A place of honeymoons," André called it. There was none of that cloying pretense she had grown up around. To enjoy a honeymoon a couple apparently needed several miles of privacy. By the end of the first week, she had come to agree.

They made love in the morning. They walked on the beach, kicking at shells, and swam in the surf—which was never more than a hand-high curl of white. They ate their modest lunch and made love again. Then they napped and, waking, swung together in the hammock until late afternoon. There, encased in that cocoon of webbing, he would run his hands across her in an indolent fashion, caressing, and then halt—which was almost cruel.

It was on those afternoons that she truly began to appreciate her husband's ability to relax. This was not laziness, though André possessed that, too. No, what she witnessed was simply an uncoiling. And in the hammock she allowed herself to study the composition of his hands, the joints fitting one to another in such a taken-for-granted but fortunate arrangement. Of course, the same could be said for his entire body, which was a lanky arrangement of dark, sinuous muscle. And from fingers to toes, all seemed to coordinate around that single most important organ.

In those first few days she could not bring herself to look upon him naked. But in the surf she could at least study his limbs with impunity. Appearing to play she would touch his elbow, touch his neck, all those portions not covered by his costume, and this not out of wantonness so much as pure wonder. Perhaps, in the hammock he did the same, touched her in wonder as well.

With twilight coming she would rouse herself, leave his absent-minded embrace, and take a bath in the deep tin tub set in the middle of the living room floor. Then she would hear her new husband stirring on the porch. He would rustle whatever paper was at hand (news a week old at best and never a book—she realized that week that she had never seen her husband with a book) and come to find her. And with suds up to her neck, she would beckon him with an upraised hand. Already he would be pulling off his shirt. His interest in her was quite evident. She would be pulled up from the bath, and he would rinse her down with buckets of sun-warmed water and set to touching and kissing her until she thought she might swoon. And then he would take her to the bed, except for the time when he simply placed her on the floor beside the tub.

On the seventh afternoon, they had walked far down the beach, to what passed as a community. At a small restaurant they had eaten shrimp in a sauce of some Creole concoction. André played the Frenchman through all this and, whether believed or not, was certainly accepted by the rotund and red-faced proprietor. They split a bottle of wine, and compliments of their host, they split a second. This left her unsteady on her feet, almost stumbling. Laughing together and singing, at times separately, they now braved the night and headed back towards their cabin. Only a sliver of moon showed, but the luminescence of blanketing stars and an ocean's silver surface made the way distinct enough.

"Here," her husband laughed. "Here should suit us."

"André! No!" Even drunk she thought him crazy to consider such. She could hear a guitar being played in the restaurant and even the faint voices of the clientele. And worse, she realized he was not pulling her towards the dunes, but toward the gentle surf.

"Here!" he continued.

"No!" she continued. But after shedding her shoes and outermost skirt and watching him, with much haste, leave behind every stitch and sole of his own clothing, she allowed herself to be led waist-deep into the ocean, allowed the smell of brine and the soft, sweet sting of salt to sweep over her. When he released her for a moment, she fell back and began to pull away with an assured stroke. Before coming here, she had been able to do no more than paddle, but her husband had given her instructions, held her parallel to the sea, and assured her she would not sink into oblivion. She must simply relax and slide through the water, which, despite the strain of the undergarments, she did now, slipping away from him with a laugh, going deeper—heading it would seem to Mexico. But he followed, a centaur, half-man half-ocean, plowing toward her and snatching a foot to bring her laughing and sputtering against him.

With kisses applied to her face and neck, she allowed herself to be undressed from the waist up and then from the waist down, so that her husband lay cloaked in layers of dripping fabric, and she, bare to the skin, kissed him in return and pushed herself against all that dripping paraphernalia.

"Do we really need all this?" he asked and made a threatening motion to set her underclothing off with the flood.

"No," she said. "I suppose we don't."

He released it all.

"Adam and Eve," he laughed. "And the snake, of course."

She felt him entering her. But not such a pleasurable feeling as she expected, for the water proved a poor lubricant. She whispered that they should go ashore, which they did, each pulling the other with equal enthusiasm. He laid her down upon the abandoned skirt and entered her with hard thrust, and within moments she felt a familiar pleasure spread throughout her body—an impulse that she could only consider to be of a heavenly nature. And at that moment Abbie Dubose began a moan which ended in a howl of utter joy.

"My heaven," she sighed. She lay upon her back spying on a night ocean of stars.

"Exactly," André laughed.

On many like occasions Abbie's husband had redeemed himself.

CHAPTER THIRTEEN

CHARLESTON, MARCH 12, 1889

Dr. McCall thought of Hélène. He now thought of her only. . . . While in her company (only minutes), he dreaded the parting that must quickly come. Apart, he counted the long hours until they would be together. The sound of her voice passed through his body as a mild shock. To touch her hand brought even grander stimulation. Of course, McCall recognized the symptoms as those identified with love, but he was certain this expanding passion was far beyond the ordinary. No mortal man was meant to feel so. No mortal constitution could stand such strain.

Though he lacked the financial resources to make such a move and still spoke only a few fragments of the French language, the doctor was now determined that he and Hélène would live together in Paris. The young student Leon had proposed the same to Emma Bovary, but then French was that fictional character's native language. In any event, Dr. McCall imagined himself and Hélène off somewhere together. Yet he knew that if he could seduce the girl he would not marry her. Yet if given the chance, he would marry her, for his every waking thought was of her.

His fantasies of Hélène now stretched on into wild days of lovemaking— yes, into a complete loss of himself in that most perfect of female bodies. Also, he had begun to suspect that the editor had already enjoyed "a slice from that loaf," and though he did not truly believe this, the notion persisted and drove him further into raging envy. How could such a posturing fool have those pleasures thrown before him? Undeserving. The editor was a hypocrite and a bully, and such a man could and would be bested.

Mrs. Lawton had returned from her trip to Washington, and Hélène now insisted that a meeting in or near the Lawtons' house was out of the question.

Indeed, the doctor heard in her tone a distinct coolness—a drawing back from the precipice, so to speak. But she did agree to meet him in the upper reaches of the city at the Reverend Porter's church—this being the doctor's substitute for Flaubert's Paris cathedral.

With the children delivered to their school, Hélène took the trolley of the second blue line, and he boarded at the next stop. Fortunately, they did not acknowledge each other, for the doctor realized a police detective watched him from two seats away. At Bee Street, Hélène pulled the cord and stepped from the right of the car, and he stepped from the left. Both walked on, but on opposite sides of the street and he further ahead. At the Porter church, the Church of Holy Communion, which the good Reverend Porter had built with so much help from Yankee contributors, she caught up with him.

"You must not speak to me anymore," she said at once. He said nothing but took her by the arm and walked on into a Negro neighborhood of small rambling cabins, and among these were houses of assignation where a white man might take his paramour for an hour. Flaubert's rude Rodolphe would have accomplished this weeks before. He would have simply taken the girl by the wrists and led her into the nearest boudoir, which the doctor intended to do.

McCall whispered, "A man I know is coming in that buggy." And taking the governess rather roughly by the hand, he went through the gate. "May we go inside?" the doctor asked the aged black woman who sat on the dilapidated porch in her bright yellow rocker.

The old woman said, "No, they in there now." He knew the old woman lied, that she saw trouble standing in her yard.

"I do not go into that house," Hélène said.

"A policeman is on this block," McCall said. "He will see us if we do not enter the house."

Such a great mistake she had made. The doctor gestured over his shoulder, but she saw no one on the street. Still, Hélène did, at last, understand that he meant to get her into a bedroom of this cabin, and that was to be the extent of their marriage and their running away together.

Only the day before, Mrs. Lawton had told her that divorce was not possible in South Carolina, and Hélène had disagreed. Oh, she should have confided in her employer when the doctor first approached her, should have at least hinted at the nature of the attentions being paid her, should have trusted herself to the judgment of Rebecca Lawton.

"I am going now," she said to the doctor. She jerked free, and he followed.

Again they took the second blue line, but on the return trip they sat together. Dr. McCall pointed out the detective, who now stood at the rear of the car, and whispered, "That is a policeman. If I were not a gentleman I would go and push him off. He is following us."

"You do not tell me a policeman is following us!" Hélène whispered harshly. "Everyone will know what we do. You take away my reputation."

"I do not care what these people in this town think. Why should I care?"

"The Lawtons treat me very well. I do not . . . I cannot . . . You have tricked me!"

"If David Lawton comes for me he will find me ready!" the doctor whispered with a renewed fierceness. He said nothing more until they approached their respective homes. "I must see you tonight," he insisted.

"No," she answered.

"We are in this together," he hissed. "Do not forget that we are in this together." Then he declared he would come to the front door if she did not agree to meet him in the cook's house. To be rid of him, she agreed to do that. A block early he stepped from the car.

At her own stop David Spencer was waiting. He approached and bowed. "I wish to speak with your employer," he said. "I feel the time has come to state my case."

"You have no case. You must go away. You must not come here!"

"Tomorrow. May I call tomorrow?"

"No!" Hélène whispered harshly. "No! No! No!"

"I will be heard," David Spencer declared and turning on his heel marched away. "I have the right!"

"No! You do not have this right!"

"Love!" the suitor shouted across his shoulder. "Love gives me the right!"

CHAPTER FOURTEEN

David Lawton stood before his dressing mirror and with hesitant finger made a final adjustment to the collar's rim. On the previous afternoon, he had received a third unsigned warning. "FOOL." Only that one word was printed at the page's center, but he recognized the sender's hand and understood the reference.

Had he waited too long? Had David, indeed, played the fool's role? Over the years, he had received hundreds of such notes—and not all unsigned—but few had grated as this one did. He had acted. Even before the note's arrival, he had made inquires, inquires which would gain results. Still, the brazen warning chafed, angered him to a surprising degree, and to that fiery emotion he could now add the confusion of last night's dream. Awful.

He'd been wrestling for his life with a stranger on the edge of a cliff, yet he had no real feelings against the man. Finally, he gained the upper hand. But suddenly the man held a pistol. David grabbed for that but was too late. He heard the shot and went over the cliff. And of course, he did this all in that helpless state of dreams where every effort is doomed to fail. But as he fell he managed to grab the heel of his opponent and drag him over, so that together they went whirling through the air and crashed to the bottom of the cliff, annihilated. Christ, it was all so vivid, and oddest of all, in falling he realized the stranger had his face—and on that face was a most apologetic smile.

Naturally, he had no intention of mentioning either note or dream to Rebecca. Absolutely none. Yet when he went into her bedroom, he found himself pacing to and fro.

"David?" she said, and he faced her. Rebecca rested on one elbow, palm to her cheek, still-glorious auburn hair spread about her. "David?" she questioned once more.

"Do you believe my life is in danger?" he asked.

"No more than usual. I am always anxious about you."

"But do you believe anyone would murder me? I have no enemies." He paused and laughed. "At least, I know of no one who wants to kill me—just now."

How could Rebecca reply? She who lived her entire life in constant concern for his safety? She would speak the truth. "David," she said, "I had a dream last night which may pertain to your question. I dreamed that you and I went walking hand in hand through the parlors. We were barefoot, and a woman shrouded in black crepe went before us scattering burning coals upon the floor. Our feet were bleeding and torn as we stamped out the fire!"

"What does that mean?" David asked. He approached the bed.

"It means that a woman will make trouble for us—trouble that you and I must bear alone."

David took Rebecca in his arms and kissed her, saying, "No woman will ever make trouble for me and you. I can promise you that. Did any woman ever come between us?"

"Never!"

"And none shall. What did she look like, this woman of your dream?"

"She wore an obscuring veil, but I believe it was . . . no, I cannot say who."

"She shoveled burning coals on our floor?" David threw up his hands and returned to pacing. "A singular dream," he mused. "I suppose it could contain a warning."

"Please, David, speak no more of dreams." How odd that she would say that. David was the scoffer, the one impatient with the supernatural and dismissive of dreams. But Rebecca could go no further.

The previous evening Hélène had confided that the young man from the pharmacy, David Spencer, the self-professed poet, had met her at the trolley stop. She tried to send him away. He insisted on coming to the house, perhaps this afternoon. With tears in her eyes, Hélène had begged Rebecca not to tell her husband. If the boy came she wished Madame to send him away— "shoo him away." Would that Hélène could be dealt with as easily! No doubt that she was the woman of the dream—the veiled figure. Yet Rebecca knew that her husband would never betray her in such a way.

She waved aside the question of the dream, urged him down to breakfast and followed soon after. Their tête-à-tête meal was almost happy. A letter arrived from Virginia requesting aid for the widow and orphans of an old wartime friend. He told her he meant to give. Then a neighbor's child came bearing a pair of partridges tied in a fancy basket. They teased with her, and then he asked Rebecca to see the child to the gate. When she returned he clapped his hands and asked, "Do you want an oil portrait of your husband, Mrs. Lawton? Speak. This is your last chance. Unless you make me sit to that artist before half past three o'clock today, you will never have that portrait."

"I shall make you sit, then. But you know my heart is divided between a portrait and a marble bust."

"Oh, eventually you will have the bust, but the portrait artist is here now! If you can be at the office at three o'clock and make me leave, you will have that first sitting. Then we will come home to an early dinner, and after that we can call on whom you please at our leisure. I want you to have this portrait. Don't let me put it off."

Rebecca ran upstairs for her hat and cloak. Hélène entered the bedroom, a strange look on her face. It was almost ten, and Rebecca told the girl she would no longer be allowed to loiter on the street in the mornings. The children were due at school before nine, and twenty minutes should suffice for the slowest return.

"Madame, do you think that I'm late?"

"Madame thinks that you've been late for some time and that it won't happen again."

"But I was only a minute! Surely Madame can't find fault in that!"

"Indeed, I can. The poet? He was not on the street, I hope."

"Certainly not, Madame. Certainly not."

David called out that it was later than he thought, and Rebecca took her veil and flew from the room.

"Do I need to come down?" Hélène asked.

"No!" Rebecca called back.

In the entry below, David asked if she had just been speaking to Hélène and wondered why the girl was not seeing her to the carriage as usual. Rebecca said she had excused Hélène. He said, "I have not seen her since Saturday morning. We installed the 'telephone' for Anna. She helped quite willingly, but since then she seems to be hiding from me. Is anything the matter?"

Rebecca laughed. "No, she plays with the children and is very attentive to me."

"Nothing is wrong?"

"I have just told her she stays too long on the way from school. She seems sorry. Perhaps she thinks I told you or that you heard me."

David answered with a single unintelligible word, and they hurried out to the carriage. (What was that word? In the years after, she would remember with precision all she had said and all David had replied, except for that single word, and, of course, she would wonder if the missing utterance meant more than all the rest together. But on that morning she did not question him. All their dark concerns were set aside.)

Traveling to the office, they discussed her numerous morning errands. Most especially she was to order a gravestone for Mrs. Fourgeaud, the mother of David's first wife.

"Please God," David said, "when my time comes, I pray my friends may not have the inconvenience of standing in such a rain as I stood for her."

Once halted in front of the office, Rebecca remained seated and handed out to him twelve books—all of which he managed to balance in his arms. But she dropped the final one, the thirteenth.

"The first symptom of approaching age I have yet detected in you, Mrs. Lawton. Let me see no more of it, I beg."

"You shall not, I promise."

Then while saying his goodbyes to her, his "more last words," every book slipped from his hands to the pavement.

"Captain Lawton, this is the first symptom of old age I have detected in you," she mocked. He laughed so loud, several passing by joined in.

Stepping inside the building for just a moment, she was greeted by the young reporter Mr. Bailey and told the freshest of news. *The World,* as usual, was scandal-ridden, and the day before the *Sun* had been seized by the sheriff. "Bailey," said her husband with a laugh, "why do you fellows keep all that is disagreeable for me and tell Mrs. Lawton all that is pleasant? I never hear anything endurable, save through her."

"Captain, you would not listen to us as Mrs. Lawton does."

"Perhaps that is so," David agreed. "Now, Rebecca, I must go and you must go."

"Remember the appointment with the artist," she said. "Three o'clock sharp."

"Yes," he said in parting. "Yes, of course." He gave a tender smile and added his familiar *"Au revoir!"*

Arriving home at twelve, Rebecca was met by a man who had come to plant a huge palmetto and twelve other trees. Running upstairs to throw off her cloak, she found Hélène sewing quietly in Thomerson's room. Since the girl always sang, Rebecca cried, "Something is wrong. Something happened to the nightingale today?"

"So Madame knows of my worries?"

"The young man of the pharmacy. Spencer? I will deal with him as I promised."

"No. More than that."

"What, for example?"

"While you were gone I suffer so with the kitchen help!"

"Kitchen quarrels? No one complained to me about you. Sing as usual, please."

Rebecca ran outside to the palmetto and remained in the garden supervising until almost two. Then she telephoned her husband to tell him the tree he had his heart set on was planted. A clerk relayed the message and returned to say Captain Lawton was very busy, but would she please call back soon? But her wish to place every tree as her David wanted kept her late, and she did not call again. At three Hélène told her the telephone was ringing. Three hours of standing had exhausted her. She was not dressed to go for her husband, and perhaps he was waiting for her. But his first words were "I am glad you are there. Don't come for me today, please. I have to go up in the trolley."

Rebecca started to ask "Why?" but he always had some good reason, and untidy as she was, she could not rush straight there. Instead she said "I know I am late. I have planted thirteen new trees for you. Your palmetto is gorgeous! Fifteen feet high, with the leaves tied up and bigger around than you, my husband."

"Well done!" he declared. "Well done, my wife. I am delighted. And I will be home very soon to thank you. I leave in a few minutes."

"But wait, David!" And for no reason she could think of she added, "A man was shot up the road. My old vegetable woman told me. . . ."

"Mr. Bailey!" she heard him call into the newsroom, "Quick, go see about this shooting up the road." Then to her went on: "What is this state coming to with all this bloodshed? No man can be sure of his life from one hour to the next." He asked her particulars, which she knew little of, and ended, "I am coming soon to thank you for the palmetto. *Au revoir!*" She heard his laugh again as he turned from the phone. Hélène stood in the doorway. She appeared uncertain, perhaps frightened.

David Lawton was forty-nine years old and still carried himself with the proud bearing and contented courtesy of an English gentleman. His voice was rich and sweet. He was, as the Augusta paper eulogized, "the embodiment of a charming companion for a beautiful spring day." They remembered him so. The witnesses. His light brown mustache was full but trimmed short of the lower lip, and the gaze of his blue eyes was steady. He wore a pale gray suit, calfskin gloves, and carried a silver-headed majorica cane. As he stood before the office of his newspaper, the *News and Independent,* he spoke "pleasantly" on topics of business and general interest. And though this mild, overcast day in mid-March lacked spring's customary explosion of azalea blooms and fragrant tea olive, the promise of spring was there.

"To the end he was an optimist," said one. But few knew of the disappointments of his New York trip, and none knew of the heartbreaking interview with Hélène, the unsettling notes received, or the nightmare of the previous evening. Whatever problems he faced, whether financial, political, or personal, he did not let them show. Certainly, the editor did not speak of them to those standing on the street corner. He remarked, instead, on the prospects of baseball's new Southern league.

Since their midday meal was served promptly at four, he nodded a farewell and boarded the trolley. He took the blue line—the second blue line, not the one running out to the cemetery. Captain Lawton took the second line. To the nation he was "Captain" Lawton, and it was certainly as Captain Lawton that he entered into that afternoon's mission. Once more he felt the exhilaration engendered by a cavalry's charge. He was a bannered knight going into battle.

At the editor's request, the chief of police had placed a detective in the Lawtons' neighborhood. This was done the day before, and now David knew that the married man in question was indeed Dr. McCall. This disreputable doctor, this villain, and his governess had walked together on Bee Street and entered the yard of a Negro's house. David Lawton exploded at the news.

The police chief then warned David that his opponent was surely armed and probably expecting him. Dr. McCall, he was told, had killed at least one man in Tennessee. The law, he was told, could and would deal with the situation. Yet David knew his duty to his family and especially to the young Swiss girl living beneath his roof, and he understood that the blinding anger he felt was just and ordained by society. He planned to use his cane. Already he imagined himself swinging it upon the narrow shoulders of the black-hearted doctor. At the least provocation he would do so.

Of course, he had not told his wife of the interview with their governess and her denial of involvement with a married man. And he certainly had not shared with her the most recent knowledge that this man was their neighbor Dr. McCall. In every sense David went alone.

The trolley swung north on Rutledge Avenue and preceded at a walking pace past the gentle ripples of the newly impounded salt marsh—the ten-acre square with promenade where the governess Hélène sometimes brought the children, "the pond" where their Newfoundland puppy would splash and frighten off the ducks. Nothing in Lawton's composure suggested he was now embarked on a mission of personal import. As one passenger recalled, "He spoke for several minutes to a young man on the subject of the sonnet." Both men seemed quite well informed and enjoyed a pleasant exchange of views. Captain Lawton had even quoted something at length. Perhaps Shakespeare. The young man smiled and bowed. He had an intense look about him. Perhaps he was a poet himself. "Captain Lawton's discussion of the sonnet form was quite interesting," testified another witness to this exchange. "The young man was rather ill-kempt. He wore a black frock coat, quite soiled. Captain Lawton's suit was of a light material. As usual he was finely dressed."

When the blue line trolley reached the corner of Bull Street, the editor pulled the cord, said his goodbyes, and stepped down. But instead of walking the few paces to his own door, he crossed the street to the house of his neighbor Dr. McCall. The doctor's office was on the ground floor and opened level to the sidewalk. Lawton knocked and entered.

Watching from the second-story window of the Lawton home, Hélène saw him enter the doctor's office—as did Anna. From beyond the door Rebecca heard Anna call out, "That was father! See! See! He left the streetcar and entered that house!"

"No! No! That was not Captain Lawton," came Hélène's loud denial. Rebecca went in to see the meaning of Hélène's words. "She is mistaken," Hélène said. "Mistaken," she repeated and felt the creeping inevitability of nightmare entering into her life.

Rebecca descended to the parlor. And the governess went immediately to her mistress's now empty bedroom, threw herself on the Brussels carpet, and wept.

At the ringing of the gong, Dr. McCall rose from his desk, crossed the room, and opened the door.

"Are you Dr. McCall?" the man asked.

"Yes, I am Dr. McCall."

"I am Captain Lawton."

"Please, come in, Captain."

David Lawton walked in immediately, pushed past the doctor, in fact. McCall closed the door behind him.

"Dr. McCall," David Lawton said at once in a voice rich with accusation. "I have just been informed of your ungentlemanly conduct towards one of my servants."

"What you say is untrue," the doctor replied. He had crossed the room and stood beside his desk. In the low, small room the irate editor loomed above him. The sleeves of the intruder's overcoat spread wide as the wings of a great avenging bird, and in one hand he raised a silver-headed cane.

"I give you to understand she is under my protection," the editor declared, "and if you speak to her again I shall publish you in the papers!"

"And if you do that, you scribbler bastard, I will hold you personally responsible."

"God damn you! Listen to me, you son of a bitch! I forbid you to speak to her."

"I will speak to her as long as I please, until you show me you have the authority to prevent it. Now, get out of my office!"

With this last the doctor pointed towards the door, and as he did so the editor struck him across the hat crown with the cane, at the same time pushing him backwards with his other hand. The doctor fell across his lounge and was struck a second time with the cane. Then, as David Lawton raised his arm for a third blow, the doctor pulled a pistol from his back pocket and fired. Struck beneath the arm, Lawton staggered away a single step.

"You have killed me," he whispered.

"As you meant to take my life, so have I taken yours!" Dr. McCall shouted in reply.

The editor contemplated his assailant. A momentary look of disbelief was replaced with one of complete sadness. His face blanched. He turned, and rather than moving towards the door, took a reeling step towards the rear of the office. Then clutching his side and with legs twisting out beneath him, he collapsed against the far wall. He made a sound which may or may not have had a meaning and lay still.

Staggered by his deed, the doctor watched as one locked frozen in a nightmare. "You will not cane me," he finally whispered. He half-expected a response—an apology, some admission of wrong. None came, and to remedy the situation the doctor next offered aid. He knelt, and pulling Lawton free of the wall, straightened the body flat on the floor. But already the breathing had ceased, and the eyes opened upon the living in sightless accusation. The doctor rose to his feet, brought hands to his head, and realizing that he still held the pistol, placed it calmly on the desktop. And then he raised both hands again to the sides of his head. If he were to shoot himself, he must do it now. If he were to kill the governess Hélène, he must cross the street and do it now.

Dr. McCall considered all that he'd done in the name of love. He had lost her. He had lost her when they stood in the Negro's yard. And Lawton, who had loomed so large, that phantom obstacle to his happiness, how quickly and needlessly reduced that barrier had been—reduced and mountainous at the same time. At that moment it did occur to the doctor to pray as he'd been instructed to when still a child. He considered that he might ask God to return David Lawton to life, yet that notion struck him as even more preposterous than the course of his present disgrace. And then he thought to salvage in some way his original intent. He took up his battered hat and meant to cross the street and ask the girl to flee with him, to confess to her and beg her to go with him. But then came a knock on the door behind him, a timid rap at the inner door of his office.

At once the doctor cracked it open. Beyond stood his butler asking an unspoken question and attempting to peer into the room.

"Go!" the doctor shouted and followed the Negro upstairs, where, in the presence of that one, the cook, and his own wife, he announced, "I have shot the son of a bitch. He is dead. You are to tell no one. If you do, you will pay. Believe me you will pay." The butler brought his hands together as in prayer. The cook, who was new to them, rose from her straight-backed chair and stared at him with open mouth. His wife already stood with hands to her face. What of it? Indeed, he could see nothing that could be gained by denying the deed to these three, but already he imagined that he might deny the crime to the world. He walked onto his veranda and looked out at the street—left, right, and finally straight down. Peering into his open window was the ancient hag who sold roasted peanuts. "Get away from there!" he shouted. Muttering beneath her breath, the woman scuttled a step or two and halted. The doctor reentered the house, instructed the cook to drive away the groundnut vendor, and, ignoring his wife and the butler, descended the stairs.

Lawton was just as he had been left—no miracle, no rising up for a sinner such as the doctor. And all notions of God's approval and even God's existence left him, for what good were superstitions in the face of this reality? He slammed shut the window where the groundnut lady had peered in, and set to work. Taking up the man's cane and hat, he carried them into the yard and pitched both into the privy. Indeed, he meant to pitch the body in as well but realized he would quickly be found out. To carve David Lawton into manageable pieces also crossed his mind. Once reduced the victim could be carried away in packages. Overhead he now heard rushing feet. Apparently all had set upon their own courses of action, and he must work quickly. He returned to the interior stairwell and opened the closet beneath the stair. The floor was of boards, but they might be easily pulled up, and beneath was dirt that might be dug and the editor could be disposed of—at least for a time.

Dr. McCall returned to the body, bent, clutched it by the lapels, and allowing his legs to do the work, pulled. The body moved. The head lolled to one side. He stopped to close the eyes, and as he did, a knock came on the outside door. He answered, dealt with the detective in a remarkably calm manner, and resumed his removal of the body. Tugging, rolling finally, staggering beneath this awful embrace. "What a fool I have been," Dr. McCall whispered to himself. "What a fool I have been." And perhaps he whispered to the corpse as well, a passing of unction as an unholy priest might do into a dead man's ear. "What a fool. What a fool."

Once the body was clear of the office, the doctor went to the stable and found a spade, and using this, he pried up the floor of the closet. The joists were closer together than expected, but he managed to scoop out a small hole beneath these. At the end he used only his hands, burrowing in the dark closet as an animal might. A rat. He could see himself as such and repeated his lesson of "What a fool I have been."

Then satisfied with the entirely too shallow grave, he attempted to push the body into the closet. The door was too small. He wrenched away the framing and at last managed to pitch the man in face forward, causing an awkward doubling over, which denied all humanity to his victim, all peace and grace to the dead. "What a fool I have been. This will not do."

There was not room enough, and even to close the door upon the body, he would first have to rehang it on the frame and rebuild the frame to do that. But what if he stopped now? Reversed all that had been done? If he were to pull the body out, return it to his office, and to the original place that it fell? Might he then not claim self-defense? No white man in this state had ever hung. But no other white man had committed such a crime as this. And yet, with a first inkling of rational thought (if that is the word), the doctor saw that with luck such could be accomplished. He braced himself on the threshold of the door, caught Lawton by an arm, and pulled sideways. The man did not move. In death he was more an obstacle than ever, a dead weight upon the future. "A dead weight," the doctor whispered to himself. He ran his fingers along the interior of the little enclosure and realized that the exposed ends of nails were pressing into the body, or rather into the clothing. But he had realized that only by touch, for with the coming of evening the interior was growing dark. Candles. He decided he must have candles. He returned to his office and for a moment sat panting on the lounge.

To think he had once been jealous of David Lawton. His rival! This torturer of his life! What a joke that was. "What a fool I have been." And then he was struck as by a flash of light—as if he had suddenly waked from the blackness of sleep into a brightly lit day, though in fact, only the gas chandelier burned there. No. No, he had simply slipped from the grip of rage and panic. And now he was aware for the first time of the rapid beating of his own heart. He clutched at his chest, thought for a moment to take his pulse, and realized he had simply awakened to the truth of his present situation. He must follow through on the plan to return David Lawton to this room. He rose and left the office by way of the street door—once out, being careful to turn the key completely in the lock and rattling the knob for assurance. Here now was true light, an afternoon shadow laid upon a wide city street. He adjusted his hat square on his head, brushed at his coat and trouser leg, and then noticing the attention of a traveler (did he know that man?) on the far walk, nodded in that direction and set off towards the corner grocery.

"Good day, Mr. Molloy," he said on entering.

"Good day, Doctor," the grocer responded. "What can we help you with this afternoon?" (The grocer thought best not to comment upon the fact that the crown of his customer's hat was crushed in, that his clothing was streaked with whitewash, his face flushed, and his eyes wild. The policeman Gordon had been in the store minutes before remarking that something was amiss at the doctor's office.)

"I must have some candles," the doctor said. "How many may I purchase for a nickel?"

"Two," said the grocer.

"Two it shall be then," said the doctor. "And while I am here I believe I will buy some apples. How many apples may I purchase for a nickel?"

"Five. The apples are a penny a piece."

As the grocer retrieved the candles from the shelf, the doctor moved to the far end of the counter and began with care to retrieve five of the better-looking apples. He placed these in a line between the two of them. "Will you wrap these, please?" He handed over the two nickels. The grocer quickly secured the apples in a brown string-wrapped parcel. The doctor accepted this and put the two candles in the inner pocket of his coat. He nodded to the grocer and stepped onto the street, where he stood once more blinking in the light.

It occurred to him now that he wanted to eat an apple. Perhaps it would even benefit his case if he were to be seen eating an apple. Unfortunately, he could not return into the grocery and no one else was on the street. Still, he unwrapped his parcel—and of course, all five apples spilled on the pavement. With a considered calm he retrieved them, slipped four into his then bulging pockets, and took a healthy bite out of the last. The juice flowed down his wrist. With a brush of his forearm he wiped his lips. He began to walk towards his office, but coming opposite of the Lawtons' house, it occurred to him that he must somehow communicate with the governess. If he were to extract himself from this current predicament, and he saw that such could be accomplished, then perhaps not all was lost. After all, he had killed Lawton for the sake of the girl. It was in defense of his right to court the girl that the editor had reached his end, and so to give the efforts of both men their due, it would certainly be expected of him that he now divorce his wife and marry the Swiss girl. He finished his apple, tossed the core into the gutter, and walked directly to the Lawtons' gate. He rang the bell and waited. From inside came the sound of hurried footsteps. The girl rushing towards him? The door opened, and he saw before him only the distraught mistress of the house—Rebecca Lawton. The doctor looked both to his left and right as if some escape was there. Then he bowed to the shocked and unspeaking woman and exited once more to the street. Then hearing the door shut, he circled the house, walked boldly into the kitchen, and asked the cook the whereabouts of Hélène. He asked twice, shouting the second time, and was answered, "At the dancing school." The girl was beyond his reach.

The bottom had been reached. He walked with a deliberate pace back to his office and set about at once to correct his situation. With the candles lit and placed within the closet, he was able to see the nails that held the body and bend them away. Next he rolled the corpse—the corpse now stiffening—into the hallway, and taking it by the ankles, bent back, sliding and sliding, until once more the editor lay where he had first fallen. Using a damp rag he wiped the whitewash stains from those fine clothes, and with the same rag wiped the dried blood from where it had collected around the nostrils and mouth of his victim. He returned to the privy. The hat had fallen too far, but he extracted the cane, and he placed this beneath the body in what seemed a natural position. Yes, he had already taken care to present the entire body as a fleshy statue, the fallen Gaul, a dying warrior.

Only one chore remained. With surprising deliberation, he slowly fed his medical records into the flames of the office brazier. In the treatment of some prostitutes and some quite ordinary women his practice did violate the letter of the law, and there was not time to separate the illegal from the rest. The pirated edition of *Madame Bovary* he offered up last. Its cheap brownish paper curled quickly into an ashy nothing. When discovered, Emma Bovary had eaten rat poison and died a horrible death. That Flaubert's contrivance was a tragedy only now occurred to the doctor. He used the pistol barrel to poke at the ash with force. He did not intend to eat rat poison, nor did he imagine that Hélène would come to that end either. "Son of a bitch," he said of the novelist. "Fucking French scribbler."

141

He began to weep, for he thought suddenly of the woman from the French Islands, the mistress he had abandoned for the sake of his marriage. She was a good woman, a nurse and skilled midwife, and he had cared for her. Perhaps that was love. Still on his knees before the brazier, he wiped his face on his sleeve. But he loved his daughter. He could not love both mistress and daughter. He loved his father. His father was also a doctor. He had disgraced his father. And he had failed his wife.

There were two children lost. Born in the winter of '80, his son Charles had lived eight days. The second, Mabel, a daughter, came in May of '82 and lived four days. McCall's wife had failed him there. She had borne children who could not live. He had failed his wife. As a doctor he had failed her, had allowed both children to weaken and die before his very eyes—in his hands. As a man he had failed her, had engendered in her body children who would not live. Perhaps . . . oh, it was possible that his midwife mistress could have saved at least the first, the boy, but unthinkable that she could be called in. And it was possible that God was punishing him because he kept a mistress. So the doctor abandoned the mistress and was rewarded with a living daughter, his little Molly. Then to get the better of a God who would make such bargains with a mortal man, the doctor had gone with other women. Now David Lawton was dead, and the doctor took his pistol by the barrel and smashed the butt into the floor—as if to drive a nail—and tossed it aside.

With his thoughts ordered thus, Dr. McCall went upstairs to the kitchen. The house was empty. He would be informed on soon. Unreasonable to expect those three he had threatened to hold their tongues for even this long. He paused to appreciate the beauty of his garden and considered how much of this domestic security he took completely for granted. Exiting by his office door, he walked up the block to where policeman Gordon was peering at him from behind a tree. Reaching the man, he said, "I have killed David Lawton. I am giving myself up."

Then without the benefit of cuffs or shackles and using the doctor's own buggy, Officer Gordon drove the man to the station house. On the way the doctor made only one comment. "He caned me," the doctor said with no little indignation. "No man allows himself to be caned."

On the street, a young black coachman, G. W. Yeats, had been waiting for his fare. Yeats took pride in his apparel and in his rig as well. He wore a starched shirt with cravat, a dress coat, and brushed top hat. His carriage was polished to a sheen, and he was waiting with patience. He, too, had watched Lawton enter the doctor's office. He knew to watch. Everyone in this quarter knew that the doctor had been courting the governess. Anyone with eyes had seen. Anyone with ears had listened.

The coach driver heard the crack of a revolver, followed by some muffled groans, and a man's voice cried out from the doctor's office: "You meant to take my life, but I have taken yours." Three to four minutes later, a slight man dressed in black with a neatly trimmed mustache appeared on the piazza above. A woman with a child in hand paced back and forth behind him. Of course, this was Dr. McCall. The woman was his wife, the child his daughter. The doctor looked over the rail and saw a vendor of peanuts, an ancient crone in layered skirts, peering into the ground-story window of his office. McCall disappeared from the piazza, and in moments his cook, a portly black woman in white apron, appeared at the house's wrought iron gate to shout away the spying vendor—who, picking up her skirts in one hand and clutching her wares in the other, passed by Yeats muttering something about a murder taking place. The McCall's butler appeared on the street next. He was an elderly black man. In an obvious state of confusion, he ran a short distance, stopped, and then returned to the house.

By now coachman Yeats's fares had arrived, and without mentioning the gunshot or accompanying incident, he placed them in the carriage and started down the street. But at the next corner he saw policeman Gordon's head peering around the corner. The coach driver slowed enough to point to the doctor's house and shout: "Some murdering has been done there!"

If there was a coach driver in the city who did not know that the doctor was courting the governess, G. W. Yeats had not met the man—or heard of him either.

Gordon had been the one shadowing Dr. McCall the day before, so he was half expecting trouble of some sort. At once he trotted to the doctor's door and knocked. McCall answered. He was well dressed and appeared unperturbed. He responded to the patrolman's inquiry by stating there was no problem at that address. After the door closed, Gordon heard what sounded like a sack of potatoes being dragged across the floor. He went off to find his superior and report, a lengthy process that was only recently completed when McCall turned himself in three hours later. And only then was David Lawton found, stretched out on the cold tile floor of McCall's office. His light gray suit was stained with blood and dirt, and—and as was quickly noted—the editor's gray felt hat was missing.

"Considering what he'd been through, Lawton weren't in all that bad a shape." That was how Gordon summed it up for his drinking companions—and everyone else he met.

The third witness—the fourth if we count the old peanut vendor (and, of course, we should)—the fourth was I. Yes, it was I, David Spencer, who shared the Captain's trolley and even spoke with him. For the first time I had found the courage to express myself to this man who might be my father. We discussed the writing of sonnets. I lacked the courage to say more, to step from the car with him, to introduce myself and say, "You who are my father, how dare you deny me the company of the beautiful Hélène? You who abandoned my poor mother, how can you select our rights and wrongs, make decisions on how I, your never before acknowledged son, must now live his life." Instead of voicing this, I nodded a silent parting. I rode a block further, returned on foot, and secreted myself in a shadowy corner. Yes, when the good doctor stepped from his office on his way to purchase candles, he saw me there. Saw me decked out in frock coat and white spats, the perennial spy. Young Oedipus. The meddler. The omnipotent chronicler. Novelist. Murderer, even.

But is this fiction? I have warned you it is not. In Charleston, South Carolina, on that day a newspaper editor was killed in exactly the manner described here. And his wife learned of his death in the manner which I am about to describe. Fact or fiction? It cannot matter. I must write on, redeem myself, and I am in need of witnesses.

At four o'clock, Rebecca grew extremely anxious, and from that striking of the clock on, she was convinced her husband had been murdered. Ten minutes, at the latest, could bring David home, and he never failed to warn her by telephone, note, or messenger, of any delay. He understood her anxiety. For the entire course of their marriage she had feared daily for his life. Their acquaintance had begun in just such a threatened tragedy—her brother Asa shot in the back. She never doubted that would be her husband's end, and despite his faith in humanity, he shared her belief.

At five, she had dinner for the children served. She would not eat. She told them it would make him sad to eat alone. The children were due at dancing school, so at ten minutes past five they ran from the dining room, each catching up a piece of cake and wondering why "dear father" did not come. They were followed by Hélène. From the window Rebecca saw all three pause before McCall's office. (By which time the villain had pulled their father's body from its hiding place and back into the office. Yes, and as a widow and they as orphans, Rebecca could weep and cry out how the children had stood below wagering which of the approaching trolleys would bring their father. The murderer must have heard their laughter—heard it even as he concluded his ghoul's work and planned his plea of self-defense!)

Left to herself in that great house, Rebecca could no longer dissemble. She could neither read nor reason because she could only imagine her husband murdered—doubled up in a dark corner. She shamed herself to think that. No reason to. At exactly six she went on the front porch to hear his step sooner. She knew it was six, because the gardener, who never worked after the first stroke of six, was putting away his rake and spade. She begged him to take along the dead vines she had pulled down as she waited. He wrapped his gnarled black hand around the proffered bouquet, and with a white-toothed smile and humble nod, he left her. She continued to stand and listen for the step she was never to hear and to gaze at a beautiful sunset sky she would never forget. Suddenly at the gate, looking intently at her through the light iron latticework, was a slender, very dark, dirty, and disheveled man. He had the face of a devil in anguish. The eyes were wide and red-rimmed, and the blanched white skin was stretched taut. In complete dismay she gazed at this incarnation of a lost soul, repeating to herself, "It is a devil. He is a devil." Why, just his piteous, godforsaken look was a defilement. Then a more earthly notion crossed her mind, and she feared that by standing so absorbed on the front porch, she had attracted the attention of a drunken tramp. She quickly entered the house. (She did not realize this was the murderer, who having buried her husband, had come to carry off Hélène.)

She had hardly entered the parlor when the neighbor's daughter, the same who brought the partridges at breakfast, returned for a visit. Reluctant to draw questions which would be difficult to answer, Rebecca hid her anxiety, even attempted to be gay. The girl, in the first years of maturing and slenderly pretty, asked why Rebecca had not gone out driving with her husband. "This is your hour!" the girl teased. "I confess I did not expect to find you."

"I will go soon to the office," Rebecca answered. For a moment she was about to add, "I believe he is murdered!" and so create a painful impression of her sanity. Instead she saw the guest out and fled upstairs to her husband's room, where she sat by his bed, looking at the sunset, and in vain attempted to read *The Century* clutched in her hands. If only she had an excuse to call the office, one that would not reveal her fears! The clock that he kept so exact struck half-past six. She flew to the telephone and reaching the newspaper office asked, "Were the wood and coal ordered for me today?" The clerk would inquire. "Oh! no matter," she said with forced casualness. "Is Captain Lawton there?"

"No, ma'am! He has not yet returned."

She closed the telephone mechanically. "Returned!" Then he had gone out—and so the haunting question of all those years remained—murdered?

Again she stood by his bed, staring at the fleeing rays of the sun, dreading to move or speak for fear of the formless horror on the threshold. From four o'clock on, she had seen him only as murdered, doubled up, and thrust in a corner. She could not rid herself of that sight. Again the telephone rang. Praying that he called, she dashed to answer. But it was the office manager. Strangely enough, her own needless question was asked of her: "Did you get the wood and coal?"

"No—but—"

"Is Captain Lawton there?" the manager asked.

"No! No! I believe he has been waylaid and murdered."

Then, not waiting for a response, she cut off the telephone. Yet she was angry with herself for not compelling that man to listen to her pain. (She did not know the manager was even then repeating her cry to the chief of police.) Again she turned to her husband's window. The dimming sky held no meaning for her. She said to herself: "If my husband now lies stark dead, lies doubled up in a some corner, I will remember that I went for hours doing nothing when through quick action I might have saved him."

She turned to the clock: twenty minutes to seven. She dashed out to the telephone, determined that someone should hear her concerns. The assistant editor, Mr. Armstrong, answered. She said, "Mr. Armstrong, Captain Lawton has not returned to dinner. This has never before happened without a note or a message. I am very anxious."

"What are you afraid of? He is in perfect health and strength," he laughed.

"He is in perfect health, thank God, but you do not know what I have suffered since four o'clock! I believe he has been waylaid and murdered." As she uttered that word *murdered,* a wail not of this world came across the telephone wire. It was a soul in anguish. Was it her own? Some call from beyond? "Is this my sin?" she almost asked aloud. And yet in the next moment she heard Mr. Armstrong's voice: "Did you remember the Granite committee at seven?"

"No, or I would not have spoken. But please go to the committee room. Tell him I am sorry to be unreasonable, but I will have no rest until he sends me word that all is well."

"Trust me, Mrs. Lawton. I will not leave his side until he stands under your eyes! You shall see for yourself that he is unharmed."

"Thanks! Quickly, then." she said and hung up.

Having just returned from dancing, the children had paused on the stair to listen, and now they came running to her. Anna threw her arms around her mother. The servants had also been listening. To give them some purpose Rebecca told Cecilia to change the dinner to a hot supper and not to forget a cobbler dessert he'd requested—that in itself was most unusual. To Isaac she gave orders to reset the table, substituting the plain blue china for the Minton dinner service. Jane, as usual, wanted to borrow on her wages. She was given five dollars to change. Peggy began a very bitter and impertinent tirade. Rebecca informed the girl that she was very tired of her ingratitude and inefficiency, that she had borne her patiently for God's sake, and would feel greatly relieved when she found another place.

Rebecca had turned to finish a letter to Abbie, when her neighbor opposite, Mrs. Griffen, was announced. Mrs. Griffen talked for fifteen minutes, neither sitting nor pausing, and then Rebecca ran back to her letter. Hardly the second page was finished when the young reporter, Mr. Bailey, was announced. Running down the steps, she met him under the crimson hall light. Open faced and yet apologetic, he seemed no more than a boy—another of her husband's adopted sons.

"You bring me a message from Captain Lawton?" she cried eagerly.

"No—"

"No message? Where is he?"

"Is he not here?" The young man's lips were twisted into an uneasy smile.

"No. If you bring me no message, Mr. Bailey, what has happened?"

"Nothing. I thought I would like to call is all."

"Oh, I beg your pardon, Mr. Bailey. Pray come in! The fact is I am very anxious about my husband, so anxious that I am not civil. Where is he?"

"At the office!" he declared and threw both hands up as if the answer were most obvious.

"And sent me no message? Is anything the matter, Mr. Bailey?" for Rebecca suddenly perceived that Mr. Bailey was either insane or deeply agitated.

"Oh! nothing is the matter! He is well. Very well!" And he burst into tears and fell kneeling at her feet. She knew that at least one of Mr. Bailey's villainous relatives deserved death. And David often swore he would be forced to kill ex-Mayor Courtney. Two famous slanderers. Had her husband killed one of them? Strange to say, this notion only gave her strength.

"Has he killed anyone? I do not care!" she cried. She meant that nothing could separate him from her love. Not the sin she had once committed nor any sin he might now accomplish.

"He has killed no one. He is quite, quite well," Mr. Bailey moaned loudly. "In the office, you know."

Then she understood that Mr. Bailey was a madman. She must humor him and temporize until she heard David's step. He must be at the gate. But her own haunting fears were beyond endurance. "Mr. Bailey," she whispered, "I am in a very critical state. I feel I shall die before many minutes. Will you put me out of pain and tell me what has happened to you?"

Tears rained on his hands as he knelt before the chair where she had collapsed—where she thought to die. He only sobbed "Nothing. Nothing has happened to me."

She heard hurried steps! Surely David's was in this crowd! He would save her from this madman. The door burst open. Two men stood frozen upon the room's edge, then came forward. Her husband's lawyer, Mr. Griffen, was first and just behind him, the young man from the graveyard, David Spencer. She flinched at the sight of the latter, for his eyes were wide, his lips twisted in some confused horror.

"Mr. Griffen! What has happened?" she asked.

"I know nothing. I came to ask."

"Mr. Bailey knows something! Make him tell me, or I shall die!"

Mr. Bailey could only cry on in anguish. Mr. Griffen led him from the room. She faced David Spencer. "Hélène does not desire your company," she said. He nodded but could not face her. When the other two reentered, she advanced calmly.

"Is my husband dead?"

"Yes," came the answer.

CHAPTER FIFTEEN

David Lawton, who had survived three years of Civil War battles and a dozen more years of warlike Reconstruction, a man who had seemed invincible, was dead. For his wife, Rebecca, and the governess, Hélène, and his twelve-year-old daughter, Anna—for these came a world of unbounded grief. And for his ten-year-old son, Thomerson—for Thomerson it seemed the world had turned upside down. When told that Dr. McCall, the murderer of his father, would hang, the boy replied, "Then I feel sorry for the doctor." And yet he did not cry. Did not shed even a single tear.

"Dead! Dead! Dead!" began the first editorial of the now unguided *News and Independent,* and from across the nation other papers joined in outrage and condolence. The citizens of the city, the state, and the nation had lost a great friend. And the cowardly libertine who cut down the courageous and progressive editor deserved only the hangman's noose. Certainly the immediately available evidence suggested this. The unarmed editor had been shot in the back by Dr. McCall, who then attempted to conceal the body. The obvious conclusion: Foul Murder!

Not surprisingly McCall was denied bail. Still, he was quickly reconciled to his father-in-law and visited by his aging father, and through the efforts of these men was provided with the excellent defense team of Major Mackintosh and Asher Cantor. And under the influence of Cantor, he had halted all newspaper interviews—fortunately, for these were all of an inflammatory and often contradictory nature. Now, the doctor would only claim he looked forward to his day in court. "Taught from childhood to lisp the accents of truth," he announced, "I can never eradicate them from my bosom. Let me assure you

I am neither a cowardly assassin nor self-confessed 'rake and libertine.' I have nothing to fear before a impartial jury."

The doctor dressed each morning in a well-cut dark suit. His linen was always fresh. A barber was brought in to attend with particular care to his hair and mustache. His meals were sent over from one of the better restaurants. And once certain the danger of suicide was past, the police chief allowed the cell to be curtained. The prisoner walked upon a Turkish rug. A writing desk and numerous books were provided. The vase on the desk was filled each day with fresh flowers. His wife provided those.

The funeral: In the front pew of the Catholic chapel—a building of some size if not splendor—were Asa Wright, Rebecca, her children Thomerson and Anna, the governess Hélène, Abbie and her daughter Catherine. Behind them every single pew was filled to capacity, and every aisle save the central one also was filled with mourners. Indeed, the mourners overflowed onto the great wide church steps and far out along Queen Street in both directions. Standing in a drenching rain, those last mentioned were of all classes, creeds, and conditions. Not since the death of Senator Calhoun had the city seen such a heartfelt outpouring of grief, such admiration and respect as this.

Slowly the pallbearers made their way towards the front of the church. A choir sequestered high above filled the cavernous space with a heavenly volume the likes of which none could remember. With a somber shuffling, all in attendance found their seats. Bishop Northrop rose to speak, a great black-robed presence, a face of broad expressive features. On the family he placed a sad but silent acknowledgment and then cast his gaze on the multitudes. And after a full minute without utterance, he began. As ever, his voice was rich and full but touched by the broken chord of great emotion held within.

"My dear brethren and Christian friends: In the presence of the illustrious dead and in the awful shadow of the tragedy that has been enacted amongst us, in the presence of death itself, what is there that I can say? I feel the truth of a remark made to me by one of the gentlemen in the sanctuary, 'Better to say nothing or you will have to say very much, if you attempt to speak of Captain Lawton.' Better I think to . . ."

Asa Wright only half-listened to this catalog of his friend's virtues. On receiving the telegram he had wept, wept with an open and unashamed anguish, allowing a broken heart to vent in sobs and then to be salved by the concerns of his wife and the caresses of his little daughter. The time for his tears had passed, and surely none in this great church-gathered throng knew better the worth of David Lawton. Oh, what adventures the two of them had! What risks they had taken, what victories they had won!

As for this killing at the doctor's hand, Asa Wright was not greatly surprised. Such a death was the inevitable end to such a life, to such an all-out assault on the status quo. Sad for his sister, certainly, and he wondered if that little woman sitting so stern-faced and stiff beside him had the fortitude to continue on in this place. Charleston was a difficult community in which to dwell. Had always been so. Despite this overwhelming show of laudable affection, David had many enemies here. Many. Oh, yes, Charleston still might turn her back on Rebecca and the children. And Asa also knew of the financial reverses suffered by the paper, for David's recent need of funds had led to sharp words between them—the only spoken in their lifetimes. But that was all forgiven. The two had parted friends.

Still, David had left behind a multitude of unfinished businesses, and stormy days were surely on the horizon. Already his sister hissed accusations against the paper's other owner, Colonel Latimer. And Asa Wright simply could not fathom keeping on the governess, the well-endowed Hélène. Yet Abbie insisted it was the proper course. Not only was the young woman friendless in a foreign land, but to dismiss her would be to acknowledge that Hélène and David had been in some way involved. This last both Abbie and Asa agreed was highly unlikely. Though Asa did see a clear temptation there. Yes, even to a slightly bent and deeply mournful Asa Wright, the girl held no little charm.

As to the murderer, McCall, Asa wished the man dead, and in his younger days he would have made certain of this occurrence. But times had changed, and his disposition to anger and mayhem had changed with them. Justice? That would be up to the court to decide, and Asa was wise enough to Southern ways to know McCall would go free. For punishment in this life, they must depend on the murdering doctor's own guilty conscience, and for the next— oh, hell was a possibility. Asa was not a regular churchgoer, but he had seen hell for himself on more than one occasion and could at least recall from Milton that the mind could make "a heaven of hell or a hell of heaven." Nightmares came. Asa remembered nothing of them. He would wake screaming, sit up straight in bed, and at once the loving arms of his wife would encircle him.

How fortunate he had been in these last years! Already twice widowed, he was informed by the doctors that his third wife and their newborn child were in danger as well. His only hope might be to carry them off from the city, so he bought a farm in the pleasant Maryland countryside, a place to breed horses. Not only did mother and daughter live, they thrived. Of course, no one wanted pedigreed horses. That market was glutted beyond hope, but he raised a breed of terriers, happy little dogs he had brought back from Australia. And from these meager profits and his few investments, they managed an austere but comfortable existence. He might even be able to lend some assistance to his sister, to repay those past generosities of his stalwart friend David. Perhaps, he. . . . What course was the Bishop now launched upon? Once more Asa Wright gave the robed figure his full attention.

" . . . Yes, David Lawton was a strong man," the Bishop expounded with arms raised, "not only in physical strength, not only in intellectual strength, but he was strong enough to lift himself above the weakness of our sad inheritance.

"Some months ago at a meeting of an exciting campaign, I read in that paper of which David was the creator and the brains and soul, words uttered by a political opponent in the forum and on the street which stung me to the heart. I took the liberty as his pastor of writing David a note and begged him, for God's sake and for the sake of his personal honor, never to permit anyone, however hostile, to be able to hint at such a thing again. I have the note in reply thanking me for mine and written in words of deep humility, coming from such a man, telling me that he had promised himself with God's grace that he never would, and he has not, and that I know.

"A month ago he came here and said that as he was a member of the vestry, and certain things being in the case, he wished to know whether his name should be . . ."

What? What was the Bishop speaking of? Whores? The previous summer David had begun to visit the Charleston whorehouses. Yes, Asa had heard this, for word had drifted north, but such a lapse was considered by Asa's associates to be merely a sign of normal urges. Indeed, the news had only surprised Asa Wright because he knew in the past how scrupulous David was in finding his comfort in other cities. But now here in this eulogy, in this public forum, those occasions must be revisited? The conscience of the Catholic? All that strange bother over the most natural of habits—sins of the flesh. Poor David.

Asa glanced with care at his sister. No sign she understood what had been said. Perhaps she did not listen. But young Thomerson's face was creased by a frown. That one was always listening, puzzling over the meaning of every word, troubling himself with the very sound of language. But no, a tear was on the boy's cheek and no true flush of confusion or anger. They said he had not wept, but now he did, and Asa saw how Rebecca and all in this pew wept at least to some degree and that many more within the church did the same. From behind him came the sound of muffled grief, while before him the Bishop continued in a voice still broken with great concern, and Asa felt the contagious trickle of a tear forming in the corner of one eye.

"We cannot understand the mysteries of God's providence, nor need we inquire why a man so grandly endowed and with gifts so nobly used, with years of hope and promise before him, should have met a death so sudden, so awful. But if we believe the words of the man who slew him, and there is no reason why we should not, God gave David Lawton a few brief minutes; and we know that in those few moments, with the darkness of death closing in on him, he turned his thoughts not to his busy office or to his hopes in this life, but to heaven, with forgiveness in his heart for him who stood by his side with blood-stained hand. Yes, we must forgive as Jesus Christ forgave. There is no blasphemy in the comparison. Let us hope that he whom we mourn has attained his reward in that life everlasting, whose glories never fade."

With eulogy completed, the coffin was escorted out, and a procession of twenty-five carriages traveled through the rainswept streets to the far distant graveyard. Businesses were closed, and black bunting hung on balconies and lamps. Along the way many stood bareheaded in the wintry elements. And finally at the burial grounds, a most beautiful if now inhospitable spot, there beside his infant son Stephen, the great man was solemnly interred.

The winds howled out their grief. The drooping trees dripped nature's tears on that final body of mourners. As the coffin descended Rebecca stooped to retrieve a bedraggled wreath of lilies, a tribute from her husband's comrades in arms. She hugged the muddy offering to the black satin of her mourning. I was there, Reader. Hidden in the damp gray shadows, I, David Spencer—David Spencer, the young clerk, he of the pharmacy—saw this. I stood beside Mrs. Patrick, my mother, and cursed myself.

I saw Asa Wright put his strong arms about Rebecca's shoulders. Abbie drew Thomerson and Anna to her, and Abbie's daughter Catherine was left to look shyly upon the governess, Hélène, who pressed both hands to her face and shook with uncontrollable sobs. Then all in that bleak assembly were escorted back to the carriages and returned to the Lawton house.

That night in the dry, warm comfort of their homes, many in the city of Charleston recalled in disappointment the Bishop's words. They had expected a hell-fire condemnation of McCall, not a plea that the fiend be forgiven. Oh, yes, very fine for the murdering doctor to sit safe and happy in his jail cell while David Lawton began to molder in the muddy lands of that graveyard! Worse yet, how could the Bishop have chosen such a time to dwell on the deceased's visiting of whores? Yes, all men are frail—no news in that sad fact. But the courageous man's funeral was not the time to speak on the enjoyment of certain women in certain houses, which all knew existed and were accepted and expected to remain unnoticed. Forgive the murderer? Acknowledge the failings of the slain? Clearly the bishop was getting old.

But, of course, there was much else to discuss around these hearths and kitchen tables and in these bedrooms (not to mention the taverns and gaming parlors—for few in these were silent). Would the doctor hang? What was the true relationship of the editor to his governess? Of the doctor to the governess? How could Rebecca Lawton keep such a woman in her employ? What would become of the family? What would become of the newspaper? And who would win the weekend's baseball game? What settlement of expenses could be expected at the city hospital? And what price might be paid for an Easter bonnet? Oh, Lord, yes, and what could be said for the Negro women, the cooks, nurses, and laundresses, who now wanted as much as a dollar a week to attend a family? What would they have for supper that night and breakfast in the morning? What would happen next? Where would it all end?

It was left only to David Spencer, the would-be man of letters, to look for deep, deep meaning. He had begun this tragedy with the blurted word *tuberculosis,* and finally and most importantly, he had sent the anonymous notes to David Lawton—three notes in all, each meant to goad the man to action. He, David Spencer, had set one supposed foe against another. Two men stood between him and the object of his desires. Why not pit them one against the other? He had not expected murder, though. What had he expected? Now he could not say. In his way, he had killed the man, the man who might be his father. At least, he had helped, hadn't he? What would his mother say to that? He could not bring himself to ask her.

There was no active part left for him to play. He had accomplished all the worst that could be done. The time had come to step aside, to earn forgiveness. Is that possible?

Whores? What could the old monsignor know of such? Mrs. Patrick laughed aloud. There was no one there to hear. She sought out the company of none. Her David Lawton. It was as difficult to summon up the past as to glimpse the future. So many to choose from.

RICHMOND, 1865. THE PAST.

On that third and final visit, David Lawton presented himself as a maturing gentleman. Yes, better than a year and a half had passed since he had come in search of female companionship. No, not the silliness found in Richmond drawing rooms—that he could find easily enough, for he was still young and handsome and still a hero. Of course, the pleasures of society were now much subdued, the songs muted, the dancing of a decreased tempo. No, she saw at once that he traveled in the direction of the Ballard Hotel, approached that venerable establishment with no sense of shame. From the doorway across the street she watched him.

Who could deny that at least in Richmond the Rebellion was unraveling? Even there, before the Ballard Hotel, one smelled the stink of sewage and saw the weary travelers on the street. Soldiers dressed in rags, these veterans of so many battles, and equally worn were the whores, who still stepped openly forward and in surprising numbers to offer their services. Her David waved away one, then two, three—he waved them all away. From within the Ballard came boisterous laughter and the musical pounding of a piano, but he ignored this implied invitation and continued down the boarded walk toward the Magnolia Blossom Inn—strode with perhaps some theatrical notion of haste and purpose.

He wore his saber, in part no doubt from vanity—but also for defense. His left hand grasp the hilt, causing the scabbarded blade to trail behind in tail-like fashion. And, of course, a pistol was strapped to his side. Richmond was no longer safe to walk in, at least not these neighborhoods. Not even in the broad light of day. Though descending, the sun still shone bright—brighter than usual, as the stacks of the iron works emitted only thin streams of noxious smoke.

David Lawton's path now appeared quite open, for the portion of the street below the Magnolia Blossom Inn was empty. Why? At the door of his intended destination stood a great black bird of a man, a railing stork who perched on one leg (for he had only one) and propped himself on a tree limb of a crutch in order to hold a Bible high with both hands. Mary was separated from these two only by the width of that sad street.

"Son of Dust!" the preacher screamed at David. "Son of Dust!"

"Good afternoon," David answered back with a smile.

"The Lord says I am against you!" the man raged on and spread his arms to halt the soldier's progress. "City of Murder. City of Lewdness. Young girls, harlots, creatures of filth. The walls will be broken down. Whores! Whores of . . ."

David dodged left, then right, then left again, and slipped beyond the raging sentinel, whose open mouth showed only blackened stubs of teeth and whose eyes burned round the edges with the reddened fires of hell. A retired soldier. Who else would declare in such a fashion?

"Yes, I'm very sure," David said with a nod.

"You are English?" the preacher questioned in a suddenly rational tone.

"Why, yes," answered David, halted now by his curiosity.

But the preacher only wailed anew: "Son of Dust! No foreigner shall enter the sanctuary! Son of Dust!" the man screamed and fumbled through the pages of his Bible searching out a proof.

But her David had his hand on the china doorknob, which he now turned. The door still resisted. He leaned his shoulder in and pushed, had no choice, for the vehicle of his salvation was approaching, crutch-end thumping loud, black-cloaked arms waving once more. David slipped through the door and slammed it behind him.

She waited a single minute, hardly more. Stepping with ease past the waving prophet, she brought her face close, whispered, "Out of my way, you old fool," and followed David Lawton inside. The vast room was empty. Dusty and in abandoned disarray, it had been empty for some time. Only a single pool table remained, and that lay on its side. From the remnants of the chandelier hung the mangled remnants of the parrot cage. The bar had been dismantled, its boards propped against the wall. A single cushion remained, filthy cotton spilling out and trampled underfoot. All this was seen dimly, for the windows across the rear had been boarded over. A year and some since David had visited her here, had braved that cruel woman for her sake, and Mary did smile then, for that had been a night of surprising happiness, or so it had seemed in the long months since.

Above her in the dusty somewhere of the second story, she heard David call out, "The Son of Dust!" and laugh. Her finger traced a line down the filthy column beside her. "Retreat!" he shouted. "Retreat, hell!" and again laughed. With his saber clanking against each step, he was climbing to the third story. Behind her Mary heard the quiet scuttle of rats—no, something larger. A cat of prodigious size broke from hiding and streaked into the shadowy recesses of the hall. She took the stairs. But she went with feminine quiet and, reaching the third floor, counted the doors of memory. David had done the same and remembered well, for he chose correctly. The abandoned room was not so very different. The crucifix was gone, but it had left behind a faint impression on the sun-bleached wall. The mattress remained on the bed. No linens. Raw ticking only. And gone were the washstand and basin.

David stood with his back to her. He was looking out the window, looking down at the prophet. Then he stepped back and, with back still to her, took a clumsy, saber-rattling seat upon the bed. "A shop," he said aloud. "She and I together."

She smiled, not a smile of a malicious nature, simply a smile. He stretched himself full length upon the bed, and when he did he saw her watching him from the doorway.

"David Lawton," she said. "Ah, my weary eyes, it is he."

"Mary?" he questioned, and she knew she did not look the same. Her hair was no longer red. Her hair had never been auburn and was now jet black.

"And is love worth the pain of losing?" she laughed.

"I have no usable money," he said. "Only paper."

"That will do."

"Here?" he questioned.

Already she was closing the door behind her. A thick wire was wrapped around the interior knob, and the free end of this she stretched and wound about a nail driven in the frame.

"On occasion I have used this room. There are other rooms, but most men find them all to be the same." Already she had seated herself on the bed beside him. She spread out the folds of the nicely cut dress of dark satin, a dress long since discarded by its first owner and probably several more since. Beneath her breasts the seams were splitting, and the white muslin sheath and even two thin crescents of flesh showed through. The girl knew there was nothing in this attire to allure, nor was her face an inducement to action. The skin was far coarser now, and when she applied her makeup it was done in a hasty manner.

Yet she knew that beneath that paint was not the face of the conventional fallen woman but of what was perhaps an angel. The Virgin Mother? She smiled on him, now, gave that beatific smile borrowed from some religious painting viewed in her childhood. She could not place the painting but knew with certainty the lips turned up just so and the eyes seemed bedewed with a curious maternal concern. She did not affect this smile. It had come to her with the birth of her child.

"Perhaps some other time," David announced with a suddenness that surprised her. And he rose upon his elbows—but still remained abed.

"To every man upon this earth," she whispered, "death comes soon or late." With a practiced hand she was already unbuttoning his fly. "You were wounded. 'Twas your leg. I recall the scar. Oh, a handsome young man. Handsome enough to set a poor girl dreaming." Already she had pulled his member free of the trousers, and despite himself (for it seemed he did wish to halt this performance), that part of him was swelling in response. "There he is. A fine soldier, red capped and standing at attention." With those lips of innocence she kissed the head, touched it with her tongue's tip. But red? The golden light of late afternoon had found its way upon the bed. Gold, a luminous if dusty gold, was imposed upon the scene. And then, with an act of what might be construed as violence, Mary was suddenly upon the bed, straddling David, ragged black satin spreading on both sides. She lowered herself. She wore no undergarment. She felt David's hardness enter, and then followed a bouncing performance in which his saber became impaled on ragged satin and holster and pistol were flung to the floor, and he spent and spent again, and all the while she only smiled and smiled as if in some effort of maternal solicitation.

Finally, an end came. She lay beside him. Head beside his, both of them gazing at the broad water stain on the ceiling above.

"Has been foreseen. Abe Lincoln will travel here in a balloon." She said this to him in the manner of a confidence. Not whispered so much as imparted as a fact to be wondered at together.

"What?" David asked. "When will this occur?"

"Has been foreseen. 'Tis near. When the city falls Abe Lincoln will sail across the river. His balloon is yellow as the sun is yellow. I have seen that balloon. Others have as well."

"The balloon is for observation, not travel. And I can also tell you that Lincoln will not enter the city of Richmond. Even if the city falls, he would not dare enter."

"Abe Lincoln does not fear the likes of us." In saying this she laughed. "But we should not quarrel. 'Tis man is the master and woman but his helpmate."

"So I've been informed."

She hardly listened to him. She rose on one elbow and seized his flopping member with her free hand.

"David Lawton, I have a request to make of you."

"I have no spendable money," he repeated. "But you are welcome to the Confederate paper."

She released him and gestured towards the door. "No. I only ask that you come along with me?"

"Where?"

"Has been foreseen. You are to hold the baby."

"What?" David asked. "Who?"

"A son . . . ," she began, then saw his look of terror. He reasoned that she meant their son—that on his last visit he had unknowingly engendered a life in her and now she had this monstrous claim upon him. "No!" she laughed. "I make no demand on you. I found a husband and was a whore no longer. But didn't he come home and leave and come again. I had married a sailor. And off I was to collect my notions, pots and tins scavenged about, for nothing would do but that I have my shop. War or no, I must have my shop. But this man and me did have some times, some fine times together.

"Still, I did not love him. But when he was wearied, when he was asleep, I held him in my arms. And then I loved the child in him. And now I love the child. Oh, every woman knows what no man can, that love is a narrow thing best kept on a high shelf, and for that sin I must do my penitence. Ah David, and such a penitence it is."

Then to demonstrate she yanked again upon his still-limp member, yanked with enough force to bring him also to his elbows. She only laughed at this. "I have his child. I love his child. Will you come along with me and look upon God's child?"

"Yes," David said as he pried her hand from his body part. "Yes. Fine. Allow me to rise."

She knew he was lying but nodded and eased aside.

He sat up, attended to his buttons and spoke again. "Well, I cannot think that your husband would care for that. Not in consideration of what has just occurred."

"God rest his soul, my husband is risen up to heaven. Here, didn't he drown at these very wharfs?" She motioned towards the window, rectangle of golden light, and out there somewhere was a river. "They tell me he was sober. Perhaps that's so. He could not swim, and the night was dark."

"Yes, well," David repeated. "Some other time."

"A Negro woman keeps the child. 'Tis close by. But a short stroll on a delightful evening. Or would you be ashamed, David Lawton? Would my company shame you?" Here came a tone, not so much of pleading as a loss of patience. "When last you came, you wished to preserve me, rescue me from the madam, for you saw the bruises on my arms. David Lawton, what I ask of you now is so much less." She rolled from the bed and stood smoothing the ragged skirts. She knew she had won. He, too, left the bed, straightened his saber, retrieved his pistol, and followed her out onto the street.

Of course, the one-legged preacher had gone nowhere. He gloated in silence at the spectacle of her leading David away and launched into a denouncement that involved Judah and the Moabites and a great number of fallen woman.

"He means no harm," whispered Mary. She had hitched up her skirts with one hand and held his arm with the other. "A fine sight we make," she whispered next.

"Son of Dust," David muttered. "'Idiot' comes closer to the truth."

But he kept her arm, and they strolled off in the direction of the canal, which some thought to be a particularly dangerous section of the city. "'Tis close by," she repeated. On and on they went. Fewer soldiers were in evidence, replaced by more and more ragged civilians. And Negroes, too, men leaning in doorways and women at the window sills. Mary spoke to one and then another. None threatened her. Neither black nor white. She simply made her way, until turning a corner they came upon a tall Negro man armed with a rifle. From beyond a nearby door came the vigorous shouts of a betting mob and the frantic ranting of competing gamecocks. David could not help but stare and whispered to her, "A law prohibits Negroes from carrying arms."

"What is you looking at?" the black man snarled. A front tooth was capped in gold. Mary yanked David off to the opposite curb. Ahead buzzards flocked about a carcass of some unknown species. Not human, at least. She doubted he would pass farther if the remains were human. The birds did not fly but only shuffled aside to let them by. The sun was low in the sky. David tightened his grip on the saber's butt. The scabbarded weapon wagged behind him like a great tail. Now, they saw few others. The buildings appeared vacant—windows broken, doors missing from the hinges, bricks broken, and boards coming away. He looked over his shoulder, craned his neck.

"What is it you search for?" she asked.

"The Ballard? I thought I might see it."

"The street is narrow. We see no landmark here. There be no church steeple peeping up." Ahead of them was heard the faint tinkle of a bell. And then a curious bleating and a great flock of sheep crowded them at the next turn. Here, too, were other Negroes, large men with scowling faces, these, too, armed with rifles, some the very best of armaments.

"That is a new carbine," David whispered.

"Come along," Mary said. She saw the renewed alarm on his face. She held him by the arm, nodded at the men, and led him on through the midst of the sheep. The two of them, man and woman, waded across that great river of dirty white.

"How long have these men gone about armed?" David asked her when they had emerged on the far side. "These . . . these shepherds?"

"There be wolves," Mary said.

"Surely not in America," David said. "Not in the city of Richmond."

"Perhaps they be dogs," Mary said. "In the dark of night they come upon the sheep."

"I see," said David. "And how much further must we travel?"

"A step further and another, and in truth we have arrived."

Ahead was a shadowed alley but no sign of man or any place for one to hide. "I do not mean you harm, David Lawton. If I meant you ill, I hardly would have brought us all this distance."

"Perhaps you would. This tale of a child? Of a drowned husband? How do I know?"

She held him by the arm and led him on, and suddenly they were before a doorway. She reached into the recesses of her dress and produced for his inspection a small brass key. This she inserted into the lock and turned. They entered a great vaulted warehouse, and from beyond the open light of a court-yard came the sound of cattle.

"Yes, of course," David said. "I know this place. The market and then the river. We have not traveled so very far."

But Mary hardly listened. She still held his hand, pulled him along a final corridor. Ahead of them hung blankets of different color and texture, a great house of cloth created in the abandoned stalls of this adjoining stable. Though the sun was sinking, good light still entered from a series of windows set high above.

From behind the barriers they heard a low murmur—the voices of women and of children. Then from close by came the cry of a baby. "Catherine," Mary called out. "I have brought someone." She had paused before a drap-ery of army-issued wool.

"Who?" was the answer.

"A son of the dust."

A throaty laugh was the reply.

Mary led him in. A Negro woman sat holding a swaddled infant. Her coal-black face was strangely unlined and circled above with a white turban of ker-chief. The woman was blind. Her eyes were open but glazed with an opaque pale blue finish. She nodded a greeting and held the baby out to its mother.

"Here he is," Mary said. "Here is my son. Now tell me, David Lawton, is he not a handsome, bouncing baby boy?" She held up the reddish bundle of weeping flesh. The diaper was wet and rank to the heavens. The streets they had just abandoned smelt better than this, but she did not care. The child was her delight.

"Very fine," David said with a much-forced enthusiasm. "You should be quite proud." Mary wiped the face with a quickly retrieved rag and coaxed a smile from the tiny lips. The alert brown eyes peered deep into her own. A pink hand of miniature fingers reached out as if to wave in David's direction and then found its true destination—the bodice of the satin dress. "How old is the boy?" David asked.

"A year and some. A year and some this coming Sunday." She offered the child up to him, and when David raised a hand in protest, she scolded, "Take him, David, 'tis only for a moment." So he did, and the boy did not cry. "Let his bottom rest upon your arm. That coat had been exposed to worse," she laughed, and he nodded in agreement.

Mary struck a sulfur match and lit three candles that were placed on a high board. The dropping sun was now supplemented. David joggled the baby, who frowned and could not decide if tears were necessary. Reaching behind her back, Mary undid the dress's snaps and stood bared to the waist—her breasts swollen with milk.

She retrieved her child and stripped the soiled diaper. This she passed on to the Negro woman. The private parts were rubber red, David's own equipment reduced to miniature, hidden now when she positioned the child to suck with greedy contentment on a pink and broadened nipple. The child tapped at the full breast with his free hand.

"There is my boy," the mother crooned. "There is my little David."

"You call the child David?" The soldier spoke in alarm.

Mary smiled at him. Her beatific smile. "I called him after you. With such a hero's name might he not grow up to be a fine gentleman, a fine man of both strength and nobleness?"

"Yes, well," David stammered on. "I am not sure your husband could agree."

"Oh, God forgive me. I lied to my husband. I claimed to have a brave uncle called by that lovely name. No, no, I could not say your name. My husband had made your acquaintance and spoke on many occasions of his hatred for you. He was boatswain mate upon a ship, and from that ship you had fled. He spoke only ill of you, David Lawton. Made you out to be both a coward and a fiend, and I let him go on as he wished, for he was good to me in other ways. Then he fell into the river and drowned himself. The baby not three weeks old. David, I have forgiven him. I knew him to be a drunkard. A careless man, he had become that in those last months. He had no ship to sail. No purpose in life other than wife and child, and for so many men that is not enough. Will that be you, David Lawton? A man who must have more? A greedy man who must stretch himself out upon the world? Have his say about this matter and that? Strut upon the stage and forget those simple souls who wait at home?"

"I must go," David said in way of answer.

"I have surprised you?" Mary laughed. "Do not be alarmed."

"I have nothing to give you," David added. "Let me leave you these." He pulled a jumble of worthless notes from his pocket and pushed them into the crease where her flesh met dress at the waist. Some of the notes fell free and fluttered down upon the stable floor.

"Oh, and thank you, your Honor," Mary mocked lightly, and then she smiled on him once more. "But in truth, David, I do not need your money, for I am most certain this cruel war is ending."

"Yes," David answered her, "I know. Abe Lincoln will come in the balloon."

"Yes," she said. "Has been foreseen."

"Goodbye, Mary," he said.

"Who this Mary?" The blind Negro woman spoke, and David gave a start. Perhaps he had forgotten she was there. "Who this Mary?" she repeated.

"He calls me that," Mary explained. "I have used that name at times."

The blind Negro delivered her deep-throated chuckle, nodded, and said no more.

"I can find my way," David said and, bowing, he left them.

Mary watched him go without comment. Saw him step free into the corridor. He let the blanket drop but then paused. Again the blanket rose, and he placed a gift in her hand—tucked it quickly beneath the baby's leg. And before Mary understood the nature of his gift, he was once more in the corridor. He had left his rosary with her. He had opened his tunic collar and lifted it from his own neck. "You will be prayed for!" she cried—but already she heard him exiting through the front of the stable.

A week passed, and from the stable she heard the shouts and cheers of the Negroes and soon after the orderly tramp of invading Federal infantry. A band played "The Star-Spangled Banner." But soon joined to those sounds was the booming crackle of a great advancing fire—set by one side or the other, who could say? She went into the streets and watched the Federal soldiers fight the blazes, but to no avail. Soon after, only smoldering ruins marked the boundary of this and that lost thoroughfare, and among these ruins stood in odd abandonment the stately blackened columns of bank and courthouse. The railroad stations went to ash. The post office burned to ground. But who had ever written to her?

Soon after, Abraham Lincoln arrived in Richmond. Taking the hand of his young son, Tad, the victorious President walked the streets of the conquered capital. Once again the emancipated Negroes and the town's lower element shouted with joy. Mary was among these. Most certainly, her lot in love and life could only improve. Holding her son in her arms, she cheered wildly, as did so many others.

In the years since, Mrs. Patrick had made her way in life. With the divining skills learned from the ancient blind Negro, she had cobbled together a living as a fortune-teller. There was not much skill involved, for were not the futures of each and every searcher written on their faces. Mrs. Patrick had only to nod and peer with seeming interest into the crystal ball, listen and watch, and repeat back all that was known to come. Had she not seen David Lawton's future? And done nothing more than warn his wife for what was to be done when fate was working its unchanging way. If not dead today, then dead tomorrow. She had seen that on his face many, many years before.

"How can man die better?" Mrs. Patrick whispered to herself. On David Lawton's two acts of kindness she had built a life. With the first, his attention to her bruises, she had summoned the courage to leave behind the cruel madam and find a husband. And with the second, the gift of the rosary, she had found the courage to endure all that had come since. And she knew that second kindness had cost David dearly. Within three days he had been shot through the shoulder. As Richmond burned, even as she had heard the alarms and smelled the smoke, the surgeons in that city had tried and tried again to extract the ball from her lover's shoulder. They had failed and left it there. She had read David's memoir of the War years. She knew the ball was in him yet. It had accompanied David Lawton into the grave.

Of course, she had been among those who went from church to cemetery, been among those who stood in the wind-whipped rain, stood close enough to see the widow and the rest lost in their own grief and unaware of hers. She would be seeing Rebecca Lawton soon enough. Soon enough, and for what purpose? Mrs. Patrick, otherwise known as Madame Marie Chazzar, pressed her forehead against the rain-streaked pane and wept.

Mourning? Abbie felt great sorrow, felt it on Rebecca's behalf and on her own as well. She too had loved David. She had loved him as the "brother-in-law," provider for them all, and as a brave man, deserving of her tears. And for that short summer they shared, she had loved him simply as a man. Yet, despite all that devotion, Abbie barely managed a presentable grieving. Long before she had cried herself dry.

Both Abbie and Rebecca had trusted God would send their brothers home from battle, had assumed that was His will. When word came of Miles's capture near St. Louis, they convinced themselves it was for the best. In the enemy hospital he was better cared for than in the Southern ranks. He would be paroled. Yet one evening, after complaining of a sore throat, Miles took a swallow from a glass of water, then seeming to drown on that alone, he struggled for breath, pitched his hands into the air and died. Shelby, too, was in a hospital, a Confederate one in far-off Virginia, one he died in only four days later. He, too, died in bed—where he was being treated for a disease he did not have and not the one that killed him.

Absurd. All of it. Still, on that occasion Rebecca had done the soldier's part. At the death of Miles and Shelby, Abbie had wept and wept for weeks on end—months on end. Her baby sister had been the strong one, the nurse administering to Abbie and to their mother. What grief Rebecca felt had been contained inside . . . and what more was there? With Rebecca she could not say for certain. Abbie did not think she would ever know completely Rebecca's inner struggles.

Three nights before Hamp's death, the two sisters had come upon him in their mother's room. Their brother stood before the wall-length mirror, admiring himself in that infernal black coat of his. He had buttoned it up to the neck and stood sideways to the mirror. At once they recognized this pose of dueling, and Rebecca ran straight at her brother and threw her hands at his face. She meant to claw him and would have if their brother had not raised an arm and if Abbie had not pulled the girl off. The three of them, such a tableau, and all Abbie could think to do was whisper, "Stop, Sister. Stop."

"She mourns for no reason," Hamp laughed. "I shall defend my honor. And I shall gain my heart's desire. We will live most happily ever after."

He had not. They had not. At the death of Hamp, Rebecca had come undone. Running through the house, she pulled wildly at her bodice, screamed and screamed. She had gone unaccompanied in the street and wailed at any who would listen.

They brought Hamp's body back in the deep of night and buried him without notice just at dawn. She and Rebecca had only learned this on the following evening. Their father showed them the Paris coat, now scrubbed of bloodstains and pressed. This was to hang in Hamp's chifforobe. Apparently this garment and this alone was to be the memorial to their brother.

Of course, Rebecca had slipped from the house that night and walked to the graveyard, climbed the iron fencing, somehow leapt across the fatal spikes. With only the light of a moon's sliver, she had found her brother's fresh grave and lain upon it. That was where their brother Asa found her. He came before daylight, raised her to her feet, and to calm her drove the buggy the long way home. They had seen the rising sun burn the mist from the river. Rebecca said nothing to her brother, said nothing to anyone for several more days, only clutched herself and moaned.

And now another death, and this one, too, hinged upon a cane. Mr. Sparks struck by Hamp with a gutta-percha. Dr. McCall struck by a majorica. The first was a sword cane, but sword aside, the majorica was still lighter. South Carolina's Congressman Brooks had used a gutta-percha to cane Massachusetts's Senator Sumner—that distant event but another fine cause for war, fine cause for a nation to split in two, fine cause for Miles and Shelby to lay aside their lives.

The weight of a cane—apparently that mattered. Could David's walking stick be considered a weapon? Such a question! Enough that David had mimicked Hamp in that way, and of course, Catherine had made the connection.

They spoke at length on the subject, but Abbie had not mentioned canes to Asa and certainly not to Rebecca. The repetition of events would have occurred to both—the majorica taking David from them, the gutta-percha sending Rebecca out onto the street, wrenching at her bodice, screaming into the night. Yet with the death of her husband, Rebecca was quite composed. Steely even. Determined to see justice done. Determined to protect her children. Determined to carry on in this strange place.

At the funeral, and both before and after the funeral, it was Abbie's daughter Catherine who wept the most.

CHAPTER SIXTEEN

From the *New York Sun:*

It was a raw, chilly morning in June, and a blustering wind drove a penetrating rain in every direction. But once more the masses did not stop for that. They hoisted umbrellas, donned oil coats and overshoes, and plodded in the direction of the courthouse from every section of the city. As early as eight o'clock a stream of pedestrians poured to the corner of Broad and Meeting streets, and the bedraggled people either sheltered themselves as best they could under the porch of St. Michael's Church, in the courtroom lobby, and around the city hall, or stood on the sidewalks growling at the weather and the slow flight of time, and discussed the merits of the case as each one understood it.

And there were many others who perhaps only wished to satisfy their morbid curiosity and see a prominent and intelligent man who had shed the blood of a more prominent citizen. Hundreds lined the route which the prisoner McCall must travel, and at the corner of Queen and King Streets the police directed the crowd to move on, for they blocked the roadway. McCall was expected to be taken to the court; it was necessary for the police to make the crowd move on—they had overflowed the sidewalks and filled the roadway.

At a quarter to ten o'clock Judge Tyler entered the building. He was followed at short intervals by nearly all the bar of this city, besides a number of visiting lawyers, half a score of newspaper men, and a host of other privileged characters. When these were seated, the big doors were opened a little wider and the room began to fill rapidly. One noticeable feature of the audience was its respectability. Nine-tenths of the people who gained admission were white men of the class known as "solid citizens"; the remainder were colored. Although several had been expected, not a woman was in the room.

At about the same hour a closed carriage was driven up to the jail door on Magazine Street. Into this Dr. McCall, with a deputy, stepped and was driven at once to the courtroom. He alighted at the main door and went directly upstairs. As he passed, all eyes turned and all necks craned to catch a glimpse.

The doctor was clean shaven, except for a small black mustache, which drooped slightly at the corners and gave an even firmer resolve to a firm mouth. His olive complexion was clearer after long confinement away from the sun and wind, but otherwise he was not much changed from when first incarcerated.

Stepping into the prisoner's dock, he flicked the dust from the chair with a white silk handkerchief and sat down. He was attired in a well-fitting frock suit of black and wore a black tie, dark gloves, and highly polished boots. One quick glance around the room was all he made; then he shook hands with the friends within reach and nodded to others further removed. Meanwhile a continuous hubbub was going on at the door, which finally grew to be so annoying that the sheriff had to interfere.

Presently St. Michael's clock chimed and struck the hour of ten. As the last stroke died away, Judge Tyler stepped from his robing room to the bench. The attorneys in the case stood ready, the ruddy countenance of Major Mackintosh and the snowy head of Mr. Asher D. Cantor, forming a striking contrast with the dark bearded and younger faces of Solicitor Taylor, Jonathan Griffen, and Jeffery Johnson. The crier announced the opening of court, and after a comparative degree of quiet had been effected, Judge Tyler declared "The State against Thomas B. McCall, for murder," as the order of the day and inquired if the gentlemen were ready to proceed. Then followed a small degree of other court business and a listing of the thirty-six witnesses to be called. And finally the selection of the jury began. It had been predicted that this alone might require two to three days, but in less than an hour the panel was completed. Of the twenty-nine names drawn from the hat, six had been objected to by the state and eleven by the defense. Three men had expressed opinions on the case; one of them could change his opinion if the testimony warranted it, and was sworn. The other two were afraid their minds were biased, and were objected to. Seven of those chosen were colored and five white.

Asher Cantor of the defense considered the case won. In the three months since the murder, he had had private detectives investigate every possible juror on the court's summer roster, and he did not think a single man now seated by the court would look on the evidence and find his client, Dr. McCall, guilty. He was confident, and appearing confident was more than half the battle.

Cantor was a tall man and thin, but wiry hard, and when the need arose, he managed to stride the courtroom with the pace of an athlete. Yes, and he still possessed the energy of thought and purpose that when channeled into a healthy debate gave him, if not the strength of ten, at least the assurance of ten. He was Jewish and had the bent and protuberant nose of the Semite. His skin was of a slight olive hue, and the eyes dark and sparkling as two diamonds uncovered in the mines of Arabi. Cantor was not young. He was over sixty, his hair fully white but still thick and curled close to his scalp. And his voice still held its clear and robust power, that ability to berate with shaking finger or croon a lullaby of calm. No juror could resist him. No witness could withstand him. His wife thought him the most handsome man in Charleston and the best criminal lawyer in the South. Cantor let her make that claim on his behalf, but if he was truly vain, it was concerning one matter alone: like the lately passed David Lawton, Asher Cantor dressed very well. For the selection of the jury he wore his alpaca coat with the broad collar and a polka-dot tie.

The jury? Since the War's end one white man might kill another without fear of punishment. White jurors refused to convict other whites. The customs of the place did not allow that. And the very presence of the black jurors probably meant at least a hung jury. The great majority of McCall's practice was among those people, and the services of this very capable and even concerned medical man were not taken for granted by the poor. Further, Lawton's paper had frequently referred to the Negroes as various animals of the jungle, and the editor's own recent remarks on the chastity of Negro women had been preached and spread throughout the dark-skinned community. Of course, Lawton's Catholic faith had been played on as well. In the bottom drawer of his desk Cantor kept an anonymous card delivered by mail the week before. No doubt left over from some political contest, it declared in bold type: "DAVID LAWTON IS A CATHOLIC!" and below was a carefully etched picture of a bound, half-naked servant girl being whipped by a hulking, hooded monk. All that was going on in the cellar of some monastery. The lawyer could not resist chuckling to himself. What was depicted for the Jews? The Christ-killers? Worse no doubt, but what could worse be? Oh, faith was an easy card to play. In his opening remarks Cantor had, as always, evoked the name of Christ and quoted, "Let he who has not sinned cast the first stone."

David Lawton? Well, the editor had many enemies, and not just among the Negroes. Asher Cantor was one. His brother, editor of *The World*, was another. Lawton ran Charleston—or tried to, anyway—and in the course of fifteen years he had probably insulted every white citizen in the city at least once. Perhaps everyone in the entire state of South Carolina. Tyler, the presiding judge, was no friend of Lawton, for when the man was president of Camden's anti-dueling society, Lawton had, in print, branded him "timid." Timid? A veteran of four bloody years? Such was the tyranny of the press. Indeed, seen in that light, David Lawton had simply acted in intemperance once too often. And what was a caning? Only a lesser form of that same dueling the editor had railed against. Clearly, a cane could be a weapon—a weapon of insult, but a weapon nonetheless.

Was Lawton's relationship to the governess improper? Possibly. Did it matter now? No.

Rebecca Lawton's pain? To keep references to his client's many other sins (his rumored sins) out of the record, Cantor had threatened to call the already publicity-battered Rebecca to the stand. No regrets there, for an aggressive defense was his client's due. Chivalry he would leave to Sir Walter Scott—to Lawyer Griffen and his crew. No regrets about Mrs. Lawton. No regrets and hardly much curiosity either.

No. What struck Cantor as truly interesting was the conduct of his client. Of course, McCall was an erratic Scotsman, a race no better than the Irish. Both Celts. Both as bad as the Negroes. To be honest, weren't they? No surprises there. No. What interested Cantor was the role of rake adopted by the doctor since the crime's commission. The crime? Yes, it was a crime, a crime of passion, clearly the deed of a love-crazed suitor. Yet the doctor could not admit to that, nor would Cantor have wanted him to. No, better to have his man strutting and smirking, for this implied that the governess was willingly submitting to a seduction. But in reality the girl had had no intention of un-crossing her legs until a wedding ring was on her finger. So much of life was theater. . . . So much pretending, and to what purpose?

Asher Cantor was confident of victory.

What did Rebecca truly know of the trial? Only what she read in the papers. But, of course, that was all of it—for many papers gave extensive summaries, and her husband's paper printed every word. She had intended to be present at least on the day of Hélène's testimony. Had insisted on this, in fact, but two days before they had met in the parlor to review the coming examination. There, before the prosecutor and her own lawyer, Mr. Griffen, Hélène confessed that she had allowed herself to be kissed twice by the doctor. After hearing that, Rebecca could not continue. She felt she must protect the girl, but she would not subject herself to public scrutiny—not under those conditions, not when Hélène confessed to an involvement with the married man. Did she truly know this girl? Only on hearing that confession did that question occur to her. No. She had wondered earlier, had always wondered. What was the true intent of this young woman, whom some of the papers insisted on referring to as "the French maid"?

Following that revealing interview, Mr. Griffen had remained behind to warn Rebecca. She should not expect a victory. Since the War's end no white man had been convicted of killing another in this state. That would not change. And she should realize that the Negroes would not vote to hang a doctor who tended them with such regularity, and there would be Negroes on the jury. Cantor would see to that. She should not underestimate the Jew Cantor or his partner, old Mackintosh. Both were foxes. They would win this case. Mr. Griffen would do his very best to aid in the prosecution, but the defense would win. He had no doubt. Best she know that in advance.

"Thank you, Mr. Griffen, for your candor. Quite refreshing," she had said.

Q. Do you read many novels?

A. Yes.

Q. French or English?

A. French and English.

Q. Did you ever read this book entitled *Twixt Love and Law*?

A. I never read it. I sent it to Dr. McCall.

Q. You know what was in the book?

A. Yes. I know.

Q. Did you know that the parties in this novel were occupying the same position as you and the doctor?

A. I don't know that. He was not obligated to do what was in that book.

Q. Didn't you know that it was an unmarried woman falling in love with a married man?

A. Yes, but it was the woman that loved the man, and that was not the case with me. I lent him the book and told him that it was Captain Lawton's book.

Q. By lending him the book did you mean to show him that his conduct was wrong?

A. I could not show that by lending him a book.

Q. Why did you lend it then?

A. I cannot say. Why does he lend me books?

Q. Because he was in love with you.

A. Oh, yes, I expect so.

Q. And if the point of this book I hold was to show that the unmarried woman could love the married man, wasn't the doctor obliged . . .

A. I do not know what he was obliged, poor man. . . . I do not know.

Q. He kissed you, did he not?

A. Yes.

Q. How many times?

A. I do not know.

Q. Didn't you count them?

A. Two times, and two times too much.

Q. Only twice.

A. Yes, only twice. You want some more?

Q. And where were his hands at this time? Did he rest one on your shoulder?

A. Yes.

Q. Did you throw it off?

A. No.

Q. You let a man's hand rest on your shoulder without reproving him?

A. Yes.

Q. He can put his hand on your shoulder whenever he pleases?

A. Not when he pleases.

Q. When it pleases you?

A. Yes.

Q. Miss Burdayron, can you explain how this poem "Mountain Girl" came into the doctor's possession?

A. Of course. I give it to him.

The public spectacle that followed did nothing to ease Rebecca's grief or to mitigate the horrible reality of events. Certainly the trial contained many moments of fine drama, some even of bright comedy and, of course, great evidence of pathos. Within that high-ceilinged but still dreary hall, many views were expressed, views both confident and timid, and opinions voiced of how and why the killing of the editor had taken place. And five days later the issue was settled.

Did it matter? Rebecca had begun to wonder. She took the various newspapers into her hands and throttled them, vented on the newsprint the rage she felt not just towards McCall but to every living man involved.

The *New York Times* saw all this courtroom "dueling" between defense and prosecution as particularly absurd and concluded: "The people of Charleston enjoyed all the dramatic scenes, the beauty and naiveté of the Swiss maid, the bursts of eloquence of the counsel, the coolness of Dr. McCall, and had no time at all for the consideration of the awful crime of murder."

The *Times* was right. Any trial is but a crude approximation of God's own judgment and, often enough, not even that. But then Rebecca considered the same could be said for all of reality. What was justice? A farce? Surely not? Not completely. Despite what Griffen had said, some miracle would occur. Surely, her husband's fate would be revenged.

No. It would not. *The Herald* gave this conclusion:

Only two hours after retiring the jury returned. "We find the defendant not guilty," the foreman said. A faint smile played upon McCall's lips, but he remained motionless. Then upon the instant a yell arose—one mindful of that Rebel Yell heard long before. An exultant yell. Not one of joy so much. The Negroes yelled in unison with Dr. McCall's many white friends. Judge Tyler administered a stern rebuke and dismissed the jury. Mr. Cantor congratulated his client, who was then surrounded by his well-wishers. Dr. McCall walked from the courthouse a free man. A coach was waiting. The doctor was driven home, Negroes and others running behind, and many more remaining about the courthouse to cheer. The exaltation of the Negroes was thought to arise from an antipathy to Captain Lawton and to the fact that he was a leader of the Democratic Party.

Immediately, the chief prosecutor blamed his defeat on a series of editorials written several months before. Upstate a white man had committed an outrageous assault upon a Negro girl, and this man was afterwards lynched by a colored mob—a crime for which two of their number were later convicted. And David Lawton in urging clemency for these two and arguing their right to revenge, made an unfortunate allusion to the chastity of Negro women as compared with that of white, and these portions of his editorial had been used by his enemies to cause mischief.

Vindicated. Dr. McCall had hardly doubted the outcome of his trial. But who could say what fickle jurors might seize upon. At last he was a free man. His father said otherwise. Already, the old man was urging him to abandon his practice here in Charleston and come upstate. Why? Had not the cheering crowds in the streets proved his right to this place? And now here in the office, the scene of his misfortune, a happy group of family, patients, and close friends had appeared. He still wore the clothing of the trial and sat behind his desk. He still maintained his impeccable grace under what for most men would be unbearable pressure.

The reporter from the Georgia paper had a question. "Doctor, have you anything to say about the case? What did you think was the strong point in the prosecution?"

"Mr. Cantor told me to keep silent on the subject."

"Do you intend to remain in Charleston?"

"Yes, oh yes. I've the largest practice of any young physician in Charleston, with possibly one exception. In fact, a lucrative practice—one that pays me a good competence—and I know my patients will excuse my little indiscretion." The doctor lowered his voice, but only to utter in the whisper of the stage, "I have a weakness for women." The reporter smiled, as did several others close by.

Then his Molly came chatting and playing her way towards him. His little daughter—she was the one he truly loved. The only one. He bent over her and kissed her upon the cheek and was satisfied to see that the reporter took note of this affection.

"She is a bright girl," said the doctor. "She is but six, and already she is beginning to read and print her letters."

"It is a family trait. I believe you are a smart man, yourself," the reporter said.

"Yes, and being a smart man, I will answer no more questions." He held his hand up palm out to show his resolve.

"Just one more, and it is a pretty sharp question to ask you. What are the chances of getting your picture? Maybe one with your daughter in your lap?"

"Daughter or not, the answer is 'None at all.' I have had enough notoriety. However, if you could say anything to correct the injustice that has been done me, I would be glad if you would. I don't know how to describe my feelings when I had shot Captain Lawton. It is a feeling unlike anything a man ever felt. But I am speaking on what my counsel told me not to and must not talk on the subject." Dr. McCall paused to sweep his hand across the interior of the office. Here in this room he had killed Lawton. The bookcase, desk, table, all referred to in the great trial, all were present, but there was nothing to indicate a death struggle had taken place in that office—nothing there to tell the truth of what had happened, what it had felt like to be set upon with a cane in his own place, to be struck as one would strike an insolent servant or child. And over what? A governess. A part of him now thought Lawton's end too kind by half. "When I read some of the reports in the papers," he said, "I felt like getting a shotgun and going hunting for the reporters, but that is all past now."

The reporter smiled in retreat. The doctor gave him a nod.

The doctor does not know, cannot guess the future Madame Chazzar has for him. As his father warned, he will lose most of his white patients. But he gains new black ones. Still, he drinks more—stays drunk for weeks at a time. His wife and daughter begin to spend the summers at a mountain retreat in North Carolina, and one autumn they do not return. McCall sinks from sight and from the concern of almost all. And in the hot summer of 1905 he dies. He lies dead in his house three days before the body is discovered. The *News and Independent* will give only two paragraphs to this morbid event, but on the editorial page it is remarked that on the streets of Charleston one white man might still shoot down another and expect no punishment. But all that is for the future.

For his final summation, Asher Cantor had approached the jury in his usual manner of confiding fellowship. He stood before them and nodded. His diamond ring flashed before the eyes of those impaneled. His nimble fingers traced along the looping watch chain that fronted his flowered vest and produced a grand and golden watch. He would speak for three hours—but their time, he meant this panel to know, had value to him.

"Gentlemen of the jury: No troubled traveler at sea, with the waves surging around him, ever longed more for the sight of land nor beheld it with greater joy, nor measured with more anxiety, mile by mile, the distance overcome, than did this prisoner at the bar. . . ."

And so on and so on. But the points of the defense were actually quite straightforward. If the doctor felt that the editor was threatening him with death or even grievous bodily harm, he had every right to pull his pistol and fire—especially as all this was occurring within the bounds of the doctor's own office. A man's home was his castle. As to the evidence that might suggest otherwise, they were fortunate to have the testimony of the coachman waiting across the street, a respectable colored man who had heard the shot and then the shout "You meant to take my life, and I have taken yours." That the bullet had entered beneath the editor's arm but slightly to the rear could easily be explained by the configuration of the struggle, but the ineptitude of the examining physician certainly ruled out any evidence provided by the autopsy. And the Swiss governess, or as some called her "the French maid"? Clearly she had encouraged the doctor's advances. True, those advances were improper, but the editor's threat to publish the news of them in his paper was hardly a fatherly tribute to his governess. And what the doctor had done to conceal the body in a moment of panic was not a true sign of guilt but the actions of a man who felt certain he would be denied a fair hearing. A man's home was his castle, and from a swinging cane and pounding fists McCall had every right to protect himself. A cane, even a light majorica cane, could inflict grievous bodily harm.

It did not help, of course, when Judge Tyler instructed the jury that an office was neither a home nor a castle and that David Lawton had every right to enter McCall's office and object to the attentions being paid the governess. Still the judge made it equally plain that once the editor entered, he had no legal right to strike the occupant. Apparently past slanders against the judge had been forgiven. The playing field was tilted neither one way nor the other. Before the law all were equal. That was expected. In summation Cantor had stressed to that jury, containing seven coloreds, the importance of their (his and their) shared Anglo-Saxon heritage. That, too, was acceptable. Logic was not a requirement of such oratory.

As for the predictions that no white man would ever hang and that the Negroes would protect their doctor, the proud counselor did wish McCall's fate to rise above those crude prejudices, and it had. Yes, he saw in the speed the verdict came a proof of his considerable abilities. On this jury, this hand-picked jury of Cantor's, there were at least four intelligent and reasonable businessmen. Two were white, and two were black. At least these four men could be counted on to vote their consciences. And immediately on retiring, that jury had voted—and they voted unanimously to free the prisoner. Fifteen minutes to do that. The remainder of the two hours was spent waiting for the judge's return.

And all things considered, Cantor had been treated well by the press, he and his partner, too. The cross-examination of the governess was widely reported. Yes, yes, from a legal standpoint her testimony—all of it—was totally irrelevant, but at least Cantor's companion in the law had been entertained by her explanation of the flirtation. *Flirtation*—that was Mackintosh's word. The entire world was entertained as well.

All that hesitating, that searching for the proper English words—not an act, but still the girl had managed to erect a great wall of prevarication. Had she spoken the complete truth even once? Her name perhaps. Yes, and at one other point: when speaking of the kissing, his courtly old friend had asked, "Only twice?" And she replied, "Yes, only twice. You want some more?" Oh, even Judge Tyler had laughed at that, the sour old bastard raising a hand to cover his mouth. "You want some more?" She was a charmer, all right, but certainly as guilty as McCall—as responsible for Lawton's death.

Odd. All that commotion over two kisses.

The Flirtation.

Just two kisses. Life in the city of Charleston was indeed cheap.

CHAPTER SEVENTEEN

The death of André Dubose occurred in August of 1891. Though it came as a shock to his wife, Abbie, and daughter, Catherine, apparently those frequenting the lower reaches of New Orleans had long expected the event. Only they had expected his heart to stop when a knife or bullet entered it and not simply to stop one fine bright morning when he was staggering down the block to get his coffee and roll. The sun was out and the birds singing, and over he went—dead. At least that is what Abbie was told.

There would be no reconciliation. There would be nothing but a final emptying of that particular portion of her own heart. And of her daughter's heart, of course. Catherine wailed, wept and wept for no discernable reason other than the drunken scoundrel who had fathered her no longer breathed the air that might be used by some approaching saint.

Abbie said, "Yes, he was your father. You must remember that and forgive his weaknesses as you would wish your own to be forgiven." And none of this sounded like the platitudes they were, but rather the sincere advice she wished somehow to give herself. Indeed, André had had his strengths. For one, he did not read.

CHAPTER EIGHTEEN

In November of 1891 the rival *World* suspended publication, that putrid sheet snuffed like a candle after wretchedly burning for three years and eight months. Such lies they had printed. Yes, founded in the vilest hate and encouraged by every wretch that Rebecca's husband was impelled to frown on, the rag was finished. Even the bottomless purse of its millionaire backers, men who stated they could "pay any sum necessary to revenge themselves on Captain Lawton," even such funds proved inadequate. Without warning *The World* closed up shop. Did that mean her *News and Independent* dividends would be coming in January—that her great epoch of sorrow and want was ending?

Of course, the answer was "No!" Now Rebecca saw a pattern in what Mrs. Patrick forecasted. All that was exclusively evil came to pass. Of the good promised Rebecca had seen nothing and never would, for the demons involved amused themselves by foretelling a good that had no foundation.

No, wait, of course! On January 1 the dividend was declared.

But Rebecca was the only stockholder to receive nothing! Legally her husband's vile partner, Colonel Latimer, was forced to pay her dividend, but immediately he confiscated her share for the payment advanced to her in the fourteen months since her husband's death.

Oh, how horrible Life, Death, Time, and Eternity must appear to such as Latimer! And yet Rebecca calmly sat through the stormy meeting with hands folded, as her lawyer, the bold Haskell (not the timid Griffen) openly accused her enemy of theft. Every man present raged or cowered—each according to his talents. Colonel Latimer, of course, contended in a rage. Of course, she lost that day, but before adjourning, she stood and made an appeal for bread—at the end, turning contemptuously on her enemy to declare, "Considering that the paper is my husband's creation, such an allowance would not be overly liberal." (Even then she took care to place her gaze above the ignoble villain.) A death-like silence followed. No man spoke. Colonel Latimer gripped the table edge with claw-like hands. Finally her lawyer moved that she receive the small amount asked for.

"No!" bellowed Latimer. "Here are my 257 votes against her, and their proxies, and these." He heaped over 300 against her.

"I demand a record of this vote," she calmly declared. The next day her personal lawyer, Mr. Griffen, spoke to the Colonel, and she was granted half of her request. And in the next confrontation she bested the Colonel, for she managed to avoid an additional hundred thousand dollars in debt. But this gained her no more in living expenses.

Of course, worse was to come—and quickly.

At last, Rebecca came to understand the entire significance of Hélène's story —the governess's strange account of the telephone. Certainly, the girl told the tale often enough, each time voicing her suspicion that McCall had decided to murder her husband on that day— an assumption too unreasonable to discuss.

Anna had wished for a homemade telephone, a simple device, no more than two tin cups connected by a tightened cord, so on a Saturday morning David set to work arranging this, and Rebecca lent a hand. But having just returned from Washington, she was tired and the weather cold, and she called Hélène out onto the balcony to take her place.

With Hélène's prompting (well after the trial), Rebecca remembered that a neighbor, a man she did not know, stood in his garden holding a watering pot and watching them. At the time she saw nothing in the sight—only a neighbor staring intently as if to understand their purpose. David did not see the man. At least, he did not seem to. No, David was quite happy as he signaled to the children and said funny things to both wife and governess. Rebecca had, in fact, left him bowing and laughing at Hélène, teasing the girl in some harmless way that made her laugh as well—offering to make a call on the can phone to Geneva or any other place of her choosing. Still, Hélène had seemed subdued, and now Rebecca understood why.

As Hélène explained it, on that day McCall was already in a frenzy, and fearful that he would do something desperate, she longed to drop the cord and hide. But Rebecca and David had suspected nothing. They had never seen McCall. Oh, they knew they had a neighbor, and for months after Rebecca's return from Europe, they had meant to inquire. In December she had finally heard the name mentioned, for the doctor had attended their cook's child.

And in January news reached her that the man's father-in-law had abandoned the household because of some scandal—an act of infidelity committed by the doctor. She did not repeat this gossip to her husband.

Of course, she knew now that David had been receiving anonymous notes concerning an unidentified married man preying upon his servant. But David had not mentioned these to her. Such notes were not exceptional. The week before he had shown her several unrelated to this matter, and all made threats against him. No doubt he meant to shield her from further worry. Indeed, it was only after the diary incident that she learned her husband had confronted the governess, urged her to confide in him and been rebuffed. Yes, it was only after Hélène's departure that her staff found the courage to confess that sordid tale.

April, the twelfth day of that all-too-handsome month, but the morning held no springtime joys for Hélène. Hélène lived now in a world without seasons or even bright sunshine and certainly not one where flowers bloomed. No. Each day was connected to the last only by weary gloom and the repetition of a governess's duties. And Sunday was no different from any other day. Except this Sunday she entered the day with the previous night's dream held before her as an offering. Rebecca Lawton was still abed but sitting upright and clothed in a silk dressing gown.

"Madame interprets dreams like my mother!" Hélène began and, with a friendly nod from her audience, rushed on. "Last night I dream that Madame, the children, and I are on a carriage going up a beautiful mountain. Madame was so good to me! But in all quickness, Madame reach out and take me by the wrist. She let me fall by the road, and she and the children go away faster and faster. I see you disappear over the peak. Madame is calm and happy. She beamed. And I cursed her miserably. Madame, would you believe that?" Hélène stood now in supplication—but an expectant supplication.

"Certainly, Hélène! No doubt the day will come when you will abuse me with pleasure." Hélène murmured in protest, but Rebecca continued. "Here on this earth people do change! You know my feelings regarding these confessions, my faith in the absolute power of dreams."

"But . . . but Madame, when I see I gain nothing by rolling on the ground and screaming, I decided to follow Madame and beg forgiveness. I am starving. While climbing up the mountain, I see a bush covered with grapes. As I move towards it, the bush change into an oak tree. I see Colonel Latimer. He want to keep me from the grapes. He say that they belong to him. I snatch them and stuff them into the mouths of enormous bugs. What can that mean?"

"Poor Hélène! Such nonsense escapes you! The bug, this is the evil talk, the torment and anguish."

"Yes, Madame," Hélène agreed. "That is surely so. But I cry at Colonel Latimer, 'Give me back my mistress, you criminal! You are the one who carried her away!' Very quick, he changes into the criminal Monsieur McCall. He laughs. He say, 'Your mistress? You no longer have one! Come see!' I follow him into a church. There is a body draped in the white pall. 'There is your mistress,' he say. He is laughing. Sometimes he is Monsieur McCall, sometimes Colonel Latimer. Does Madame believe that I am happy she was dead?"

"Happy she was dead?" What a shocking question. And yet such a familiar one. Of course, Rebecca paused before answering. "Certainly not, Hélène! A dream is not a crime, but still this may come to pass. Remember, everything changes here below!"

At that Hélène came forward to the bed and grasped Rebecca's hand, an act of such contrition that it caused Rebecca to smile.

"Madame is wrong to suspect me," Hélène whispered. "I have never loved anyone as I love Madame! But . . . but Monsieur McCall rejoiced, and I rejoiced with him. I ask how Madame died. He tell me that Madame was scalded by a pot of boiling sugar."

At this Hélène pulled free of her mistress's hand and stepped away to pantomime the dream's action. "McCall say, 'Even in death, she want to do the right thing, and she hide her pain. See!' He lifts the pall that covers Madame. I pull it with him. I laugh. I think nothing of Madame. Madame can do nothing. Madame was once a beauty. Now the boiling sugar has burned her body. I saw the exposed heart. Her hands, they are burned, but even in dying, she fashioned sugar into a beautiful white flower. I have never seen anything so lovely! While looking at Madame so peaceful, I remember all of her kindnesses to me. I begin to scream, 'Assassin! You are the one who killed my mistress!'"

Rebecca had heard quite enough and frowned to show her displeasure. Yet Hélène seemed driven to complete the drama. "'No more than you!' McCall shout. He is laughing so hard that I am filled with terror. He say that I have killed my mistress. I am so frightened. Is it true I have killed my mistress? And then I dream that you throw your mosquito net at me. It poisoned the bugs. I carry it towards the harbor. I am filled with horror, afraid of being touched by these monsters. I tell myself the ocean erase everything without a trace! I cry and let the bugs fall in the drain that led to the sea."

Rebecca stared at her open-mouthed and in way of answer raised a hand to tighten the silk collar where it joined at her neck. She could not bring herself to speak.

"Madame believes that that means something?" the girl asked.

"Madame believes that Hélène is capable of silliness at times! Be suspicious of dreaming of bugs."

"Yes, Madame," Hélène said and curtseyed, which, since they were living in a democracy, she had never done before except in a teasing way. However, Rebecca accepted this as a compliment and gave a weak smile. "I love you dearly, Madame," Hélène said. "I love you in this world, and I love you in the next world." Rebecca gave a slight nod and accompanying murmur. "I love you," Hélène repeated and, turning, rushed from the room.

On that same April morning, at approximately the same time the dream was told, Thomerson had made a casual entry in his diary—a list of economies, hardly more, but the last sentence read, "What need have we for a French maid?" Soon after, Hélène looked over his shoulder, read this, and broke into a violent fit.

"You call me that? 'The French maid.' You call me that?" she screamed and snatched up the book.

"Give that to me!" he shouted.

"I will not be called a 'French maid!' Not by you!" she screamed in return and made for the open grate and its blazing fire. And guessing her intentions, Thomerson grabbed for his treasure. Too late. The two of them fought, the woman restraining him, but just barely, for he had grown. No, he was not yet her size, but his anger gave him strength, and he meant to plunge his hands into the flames in which the book was fast disappearing. And all the while the boy yelled, so naturally his mother came from her bedroom across the hall.

"She has burned my diary!" he wailed.

"How dare you destroy a child's property?" his mother raged at the girl. "Have you lost your senses?"

Hélène Burdayron, her own temper still high, threw off her mask. "I fool you all!" she screamed. "I know that McCall plan to murder your husband! He tell me all before the crime. I know, and I am glad!"

Thomerson's mother gave only this stern rejoinder: "Pack your trunks. You shall leave this house immediately."

But as the banks were closed and since his mother must finance the departure, the girl had remained with them until the following day.

Thomerson. The boy had needed her most. From the very beginning she had taken Thomerson under her wing. That is what they said: The mother hen. And on that worst day of days he had seen her there all alone on the floor of the bedroom, seen her rolling in anguish on the carpet, and had offered what comfort he could. He had said something. She did not know what. He had never mentioned that day—not to her, and she did not think to his mother either—for she believed his intent was to protect her. But no, she was "the French maid," nothing more. They had abandoned her—all three. As she'd seen in the dream, they had struck her from the carriage and gone on.

Hélène said as much to Mrs. Patrick. While her mistress waited for the banks to open, Hélène slipped away to see the fortune-teller, where in a great rush of tears, she revealed all that had happened—not just on that day, but in the previous years.

"I am alone," she wailed. "The Captain, he is gone. He leave the children with no father, the wife with no husband. But I, too, am alone. This place is empty. The Captain . . . they say so many fine things. He has done his good deeds everywhere. His noble actions on this earth are for all men to see, but he must live now with the angels. I loved him. I loved my mistress. I love them all. I see now that they do not love me. I have no one in this country. I kill Captain Lawton! I break my mistress's heart!"

At that point Mrs. Patrick took the governess into her arms and assured her it was Dr. McCall who had killed her employer. Then she stroked the governess's hair and continued to listen.

"I agree to what the doctor said. I let the doctor kiss me. He make the plan to leave his wife. I am not fit to be the guardian of the captain's children. Why must I pretend? I am not good. Now, I tell my mistress. I tell her what I know, though this is not something that I know. Only when I see the Captain does not come out of the doctor's office . . . then I know. He is dead. He dies for me. In the dream I have, Madame dies for me. Everyone . . . I love my mistress."

At that point Mrs. Patrick, who also went by the name of Madame Chazzar, had the Swiss girl recite her dream of the previous evening. And after hearing it she whispered: "Love wears many faces, and some of them be very ugly. Listen to me, God's child."

"Yes," the governess whispered in return.

"I will find you a future," Mrs. Patrick said and peered into her dark ball of crystal. "Listen close. There you be. You return to that city of Paris and take your employment in the home of a handsome doctor, but this be a sad man with ailing wife and an unruly rude daughter. Oh, you have trouble enough, but through your loving of the child, you win her troubled heart. 'Tis seen. There. And there, as well." Mrs. Patrick pointed with two quick jabs into the ball, and then clasped her hands above her head. "For three long years you raise this daughter up as your own—for the mother is bedridden, now isn't she? And at the end that poor woman knows nothing, sees nothing, hears nothing except her own sad fancies. But the handsome doctor feels for his wife a wild and hopeless passion, and on her death he keens so you fear he, too, may lose his wits." The fortune-teller lowered her hands and with a gesture beckoned the girl closer. And, wide-eyed, the girl obeyed.

"Hear me now, Hélène. I see the way only as in shadows. 'Tis you, you who must find this future for yourself. But there . . . look there. In the midst of a thunderstorm—that grand weather that lays all heaven's sheets of rain against the windowpane and holds those lightning streaks that fly as arrows of gold through a black, black night—there amongst that boom and clatter, the handsome doctor, don't he put his arms about you? And as the child sleeps on through all calamity, might he not be free to ask you that fine question. 'Be my wife,' he pleads. Of course, you accept the man, for then you may have children of your own and be very happy."

"That!" the girl gasped. "All that is mine?" The two women had withdrawn from fortune's ebony ball and faced each other, one in open supplication, the other in responding confidence.

"Yes, Hélène. Perhaps not 'so, and so then,' not in just such a manner. But I tell you this: in the world of time that comes, you receive far more than your mistress Rebecca can allow."

On the day of his father's death, at the approximate hour of his father's murder, when nobody, not even the police, suspected what had come to pass, the boy heard Hélène rushing up their great central stairway. The governess was sobbing. From his room he heard this and went at once to see what was wrong. He traced the sound to his mother's bedroom. Then he alone, this boy of eleven, saw the young Swiss woman rolling in seeming agony on the rug in front of the fireplace. The grate was empty. No fire burned. Before this altar she was weeping and moaning out: "Oh, my mistress—my mistress!" She had always been devoted to his mother, but such an outburst he had never seen. She rose to her knees and hugged herself, hugged the much-clothed bosoms with folded arms. She looked up beseechingly. Then she fell once more to the floor. He fancied she was taken with cramps or colic and meant to call for help. He went up to her and, kneeling, asked what was wrong. "What must I do to help?" he asked.

Turning half over and seeing him, Hélène experienced a sort of spasm, a brief trembling, and rising to a sitting position, she beseeched him through tears to go away, and when he had not, she clutched at him, brought her arms around his shoulders, pinned him to her, and wept upon his shoulder until the moisture began to seep through the cloth and touch his skin. Then she sprang up and, still sobbing, ran into her own room and locked the door. He knew only that she was having some sort of fit. But on the day of the diary-burning he came to understand the true nature of her crime—of the potential for disaster, the power of a sexual attraction, that hellish attraction—to destroy all within the home's radius. He wonders at it still.

For Thomerson what bitter years have passed since his father's death. Yes, God! The boy knew with certainty that there were wrongs not even eternity could efface. Sister Anna was not present when Hélène confessed her guilt. She was not told and would never be told, for from his mother came a demand for secrecy. She consulted only their lawyer, Mr. Griffen, and also made him swear to tell no one. Only further distress would come from reopening the case. Both son and attorney stood by their promises. For the attorney what hardship could this bring? But for the boy?

Long years later Thomerson stands at the window of his Paris apartment and stares out at the night—at the sparkle and glow of that foreign metropolis. He has grim secrets twisting within. He has fears in place of answers.

He is a grown man now. He is tall and accomplished. He is the most skillful of newspaper men, a confidant of the heroic sculptor Rodin and of the supreme moralist Joseph Conrad. He is a protégé of these and of President Teddy Roosevelt as well. And he hopes soon to prove his true worth as a novelist. This young man Thomerson examines his reflection in the black glass of that window, that Paris-viewed confinement, that apartment shared until the season before with his mother, Rebecca—Rebecca who now sleeps that final sleep and dreams of all that has passed. He holds his father's walking cane and with steady rhythm slaps the tip into the open palm of his free hand. A welt is rising, but the sting lessens.

"What has God wrought?" he whispers aloud.

CHAPTER NINETEEN

Since Abbie lived in New York, she was given the responsibility of getting Hélène onto a ship bound for Europe. She had only her lunch hour, but in the rush to the ticket office, the Swiss girl mentioned that Rebecca had given her no recommendation. Of course, Abbie realized the seriousness of this omission, for such a silence from a past employer could only be construed as displeasure. So Abbie, not understanding the nature of Hélène's removal, assured the girl that the endorsement was waiting for her in Geneva.

Abbie wrote to Rebecca urging her to give such a letter. Despite all that had passed, surely Hélène had possessed at least "everyday virtues." And she reminded Rebecca that Hélène had always professed a deep love of her mistress and an appreciation of the kindness shown to her. Yes, Hélène clearly understood that Rebecca's sorrow was her own, and in the shadow of that sorrow, she would live and die. Now Rebecca must understand that in leaving, Hélène was attempting to do what was best for all concerned.

In response Abbie received a brief note telling her to write such a recommendation herself and mail it on to Switzerland. She might use what excuse she liked for Rebecca's own failure to do so. Abbie did this.

Then came a second letter from Rebecca explaining all that happened when the diary was thrown into the fire. How Hélène confessed to knowledge of the murder and rejoiced in David's death, and how Rebecca was now quite certain the girl had sexual knowledge of Dr. McCall and of many other Charleston men. The governess was a whore.

Of course, Abbie replied at once that she should have been told. Hélène was neither timid nor stupid and capable of buying her own steamship ticket. They were fools to extend such charity. Still, despite the girl's confession to knowledge of David's assassination, Abbie did not think Hélène a prostitute. Being of foreign birth, one could not expect the normal moral sentiments, but a woman free with her favors could not have remained in Rebecca's home for any length of time without discovery.

No, the Swiss girl's actions in that tragedy were due simply to ignorance and inflated vanity, both of which blinded her to the consequences of her actions. And now she apparently confused fiction with reality and considered herself the heroine of one of her novels, a young girl wronged and thus the object of glorious pity. Trite fictions—love lost, love found, love undying— those romances had been the girl's undoing and hence the undoing of them all. Folly unmasked? It was too late to publicly denounce her, to say the governess had knowledge of a plot, and Abbie had already given her a letter of recommendation. However, they must do something.

But, on consideration, Abbie viewed the matter with less anger. The lawyer, Griffen, should not have kept Hélène's confession from the world. Still, in justice to the girl, Abbie doubted Hélène knew at the time McCall made his threat that her silence would lead to David's death. Again, it was only vanity that caused her to boast so to Rebecca. Abbie wrote this to Rebecca, who did not agree and continued to insist that her governess had been an active prostitute—continued to repeat that preposterous notion.

True, though, the girl was a coquette. Abbie had known that from the first moment, from her meeting of the ship—for there, coming down the gangway, was Rebecca and the children, and in tow behind them this peasant girl. Such a one could only flirt coarsely and hence with disastrous results. But Abbie did not share that past insight with her sister, for the belated news would have brought no comfort. That counsel she kept.

Then the governess wrote saying she had been offered employment in America and might return. Abbie told her that would most certainly be a mistake. "Never," she wrote. "Never. Never return to America." America was crowded enough.

The city of New York was certainly crowded enough. Still, Abbie enjoyed living there more than ever. She welcomed that press of anonymous humanity. She strolled in the parks, wandered the museums, and window-shopped for fashion she did not need and could not afford. She simply enjoyed being alone in the midst of many. Not alone exactly. Her daughter Catherine married an accountant, a steady man, and they lived close by. Catherine had a child, a girl she named Abbie, and Abbie took pleasure in Abbie. She loved them all, but it seemed she loved only Rebecca with an absolute completeness.

Men, she told herself, no longer mattered. She would put her face close to the glass and search out every hard-earned line and wrinkle, examine every hair and exalt in the gray ones. She was growing old. She told herself that she no longer cared what a man might see when he looked at her or what a man might feel when he touched her. She was for herself alone. Perhaps, that was true. And perhaps not. Perhaps not.

Oh, a city held so many pleasures. At least once a week she attended either the opera or the theater, for she still found great satisfaction in the grand passions announced therein. What were they? Love lost, love found, love undying. She sat in the midst of strangers and clapped and clapped.

CHAPTER TWENTY

Two years have passed since I made an entry in this book. All this time it has remained packed in my valise. Father had just returned from Washington when I packed it away. Last year I visited Flat Rock and had a lovely time. This year we are not going away. We sold a big chair this morning. It is not the first thing we have had to sell. It seems so strange. We are in "reduced circumstances" for the present. It is horrid to be poor and to keep up appearances. Never mind, we are happy.

I don't think I mentioned that Hélène went home in April. There was some fuss, and she went while I was at school. I told her goodbye, though. We never speak of her.

For Anna, too, Mrs. Patrick had a future. This capable daughter of the Lawtons will, at the age of nineteen, be married to a competent and well-connected physician. They will live in Bucks County, Pennsylvania, and have many happy, healthy children. As any might have predicted, Anna is well suited to this modern world.

CHAPTER TWENTY-ONE

CHARLESTON, MARCH 1894

Colonel Latimer's star had waned, and Rebecca's promised to rise. Though she was not enriched in a monetary sense, the Colonel was brought to the point of death by brain fever—stricken with seeming insanity on the day he arrived at his palatial mountain retreat. Yes, at last the villain was forced to face in nakedness the wrong he had done to David and to David's family.

May God have mercy on the man! In a weak moment Rebecca prayed just that. A mistake. God heard her. Before Christmas her enemy rallied. After ten weeks of paralysis and imbecility, the villain returned to Charleston and managed to walk cautiously about and boast in a very vain manner of his miraculous escape. But all knew his soul was dead and his intelligence quickly following. She took comfort in that fact and waited for justice to be served. Two years passed, and finally Colonel Latimer did drop dead—dropped dead in the midst of a particularly violent rage, one concerning his taxes.

And by the hand of Providence this occurred on what was for Rebecca a holy day—March 13th. The fifth anniversary of David's burial, the fifth anniversary of the seizure of his life's work and property by that evil man, whom her husband, in the generosity that was his second nature, took on as a partner.

Rebecca's vision of the world was clouded over thick with grief. Each day she woke into the frightful nightmare of living alone there in the City of Charleston. Dr. Decatur understood this. She was still in the care of this physician, who seemed to grow smaller and more twisted beneath the burden of his back-turned foot, a foot he had dragged behind him for three score and ten of decreasingly eventful years.

The good doctor sat back in his oaken swivel chair. His office was increasingly cluttered—book-piled and dusty. He saw fewer patients. He read more. Novels, for the most part. "You no longer store up earthly treasures," his friends teased him.

Indeed, the news of Colonel Latimer's passing could serve as lesson not just to one but to the multitudes. What a mess David Lawton had left behind! Latimer had been forced to absorb his partner's personal debt, a debt unconnected to the paper, and then continued to pay the widow's living expenses out of the paper's nonexistent profits, and all the while suffered that hysterical woman's repeated slanders. Decatur knew for certain fact that Rebecca's brother Asa had asked her to cease. He tried in vain to explain the true nature of her situation. And Rebecca's own lawyer, the honorable Mr. Griffen, had done the same, had even threatened to resign if she could not contain herself. And yet she could not. Clearly, her anger at the partner kept David's memory alive—David, the husband for whom the doctor had once, so very long ago, played the cupid. The doctor as matchmaker. The very thought brought forth a pained bark of quiet laughter.

Abbie was concerned. In her letters she now threatened to come south—to rescue Rebecca, to return her to the living. Abbie called her "the hermitess." It was true. Rebecca no longer went visiting, for she could no longer receive visitors. Mrs. Griffen and several others had persisted in their calls, but finally they understood that Rebecca was "not at home." How could she come down to greet them? She had practically no furniture. And she lived in a house of ghosts—a hollow house filled with ghosts. They came to her, whispered, passed on, only to return, and with equal brevity went again. Fleeting apparitions. She wished for more. "Why not speak to me?" she would shout, but only if the servants were well away. At night she was alone. "David? Answer me, David." She did not truly think he was among them, for that had not been in her husband's nature. No, he would be off in heaven waiting for her. David was not a haunter. But the others were. They crowded around her in this hollow house.

She went out seldom. Dr. Decatur came in to see her and insisted still on the blood tonic. She must eat red meat and take long walks. She did neither. She lacked the taste for meat and the strength for walks. Dr. Decatur told her not to read, not to enter into discussions which caused her distress. She must gain weight. She must lie still, stand straight, sleep deep—there was no end to the man. She did not speak to him of ghosts. The ghosts were hers—one ghost, in particular. With the banishment of Hélène, Hamp had come closer.

She felt his presence often, saw haze adrift in the room. She knew he wished somehow to manifest himself.

She had devised a method for him to do just that. She rocked alone in the parlor, just as she once had in the Baton Rouge house. A different house, different rocker, and she no longer a girl. No. Far from it. But still she rocked and waited. This would be the place. At the proper hour Hamp would come to her there.

On his last night among them, Hamp had rocked in the parlor. He wore the black coat he bought in Paris, the coat he would wear on the following day. Rebecca had stood behind him with hands upon his head, stroking the hairs neatly into place. And in the months following his death, she could sense him, sense him behind that rocker. At times she had even felt the pressure of fingertips on her shoulder—though it was she who had once stood behind him. Yet he was there. He shared her life, and so in those terrible months following his death, she wished to move the mirror, shift it on the wall, for perhaps he would be reflected or glimpsed in some way. As the seventh child of a seventh child, she might have that gift to see beyond—and yet she could not. Abbie would notice the mirror moved and ask why. Her mother, too. And if Rebecca answered, they would think her mad, or mad still, or mad again, think her the addled sister, the daughter deranged by grief. She, the younger and weak sister. Not Abbie. Abbie even mourned well.

On that last night before the duel, their brother Hamp had teased Abbie, and she had angrily refused to tell him goodbye. In the end she had touched her lips to his and left without a word. It was Rebecca who bent with some awkwardness before the rocker and whispered, "Come back soon to me." Suddenly he had kissed her—on the lips and more firmly than usual. "I will," he promised.

Did he mean it? Had he returned? Rebecca might take the mirror down and prop it against the wall so that she and the rocker were revealed, and thus she might see Hamp. Or she might glance quickly over her shoulder, but that did not work, Or she might grab at the touching fingers, but that did not work either. No. Better to simply sit rocking and pretend at cross-stitch and pretend to some normal thought. She would do that now. Thirty years had passed, but what was that to the dead, who lived in eternity? She would sit in her hollow house and rock. She had pulled the mirror from the wall and placed it just so against the paneling. She would knit and pass the time in normal thoughts—raising capital, educating her children.

The triumph over Colonel Latimer had been a moral victory only. In the five years since her husband's death, Rebecca had been forced to sell off most of her household furnishings. Stick by stick, they went. An emptying house and two servants only, cook and maid, but through these economies both her children were enrolled in Virginia schools. Both were freed from this blighted state of South Carolina, blighted city of Charleston—she could not bring herself to say blighted house.

Odd, the empty halls and parlors. The great organ wrestled away by four men, taken after dark as if somehow to preserve the illusion of idle wealth. The cupids sold to a Yankee dealer in antiques. The bedsteads sold last of all. Only her bedstead remained. Only her bureau, only her dressing table. The Great Earthquake had treated them far better. Abbie had written to her of that—the house a collapsing shambles, but their possessions for the most part unscarred. But long before, the home of her girlhood had been overrun by vandals, and they had lost so much—lost even the black coat of Paris, the coat she thought would hang forever sacred in that chifforobe of dark walnut. Thirty years? Could so much time have passed?

BATON ROUGE, 1863. THE PAST.

Having camped with their family for three nights in the Asylum for the Deaf and Blind, the two sisters were finally allowed to reenter the city of Baton Rouge. Even when they reached the plank road, it was a rough pitching buggy ride. There, five miles from the town, was the first of the Yankee camps, but nothing remained except charred wood and tents half-consumed by flame and hanging in dreadful abandon. And on the ground were strewn the articles of the soldiers—a brush, a Bible, clothing, letters, and the makings of a dinner. At the next turn was worse, a grave on each side of the road, two fresh bodies, not so much buried as lying in the ditch with the bank pulled over them and the blue of their coats poking out in places. Ahead branches were torn from every tree by the shelling—which they'd been told was the work of the enemy's artillery, the fire their own men had endured. And as they detoured around a fallen tree, Rebecca saw the skeletons of both man and horse, for both had fallen together and gone unburied. The rest she did not see. She shielded her eyes until the site was passed and from then on faced forward with eyes partially averted.

Yet she could hardly ignore the damage done, especially as they entered Baton Rouge. Clearly, the houses of the city had been violated, some even reduced to rubble. But their own still stood. She entered the hall. The portraits of her ancestors were slashed and slashed again, except her mother's portrait, which had been half cut from the frame and lay on the floor. Abbie's beloved piano had vanished, as had the cursed and loved rocker. Her parents' armoires were smashed into kindling, and the missing rugs replaced with the scattered letters and papers of the family and odd bits of their apparel. And in the parlor only one book remained—*Idylls of the King*.

Oddly enough, her guitar still rested in its stand, untouched or at least unscathed. But, of course, nothing else of Rebecca's escaped. On entering her bedroom, the tall mirror squinted back from a thousand broken angles. Here she had smoothed her hair but three short weeks before. Her desk! Not only those treasures given to her by Hamp, but all the trinkets and keepsakes of a lifetime were stolen or smashed. Of course, Hamp saw this, too. No doubt he stood behind her and looked out on all of this . . . with what? Sad or merry eyes? Her precious letters were scattered among the heaps of broken china and rags that had been her clothing—except those items appropriated by the invading troops.

She was told that one brave soldier had placed her velvet bonnet upon his head and the satin cloak with precious fitch collar across his shoulders and gone traipsing through the streets. Yes, the satin cape with the fitch collar, that triangular collar of gleaming black fur, from which her slender neck rose with the iridescence of alabaster, the cape of which Abbie was so jealous. The cape was gone.

And in Hamp's room, she found the chifforobe lying facedown. She and Abbie together pulled it over. One door was completely torn away. Hamp's Paris coat was missing. Yes, that coat of such importance was now on the back of some insolent Yankee footsoldier—unless perhaps he shed it. On entering the city she had seen clothing discarded on all sides, for other vandals had decorated themselves—had come from the houses decked out in finery, mostly women's. Oh, yes, they had frolicked in the streets, until the Southern boys ended that vile debasement and sent the Yankee heroes off to find new amusements—preferably those of hell. Abbie had assured her of this. She had held Rebecca to her, rocked her in those sisterly arms, and whispered in comfort, "What is it? You must tell me."

But Rebecca could not tell her, and they did not find the coat.

What does Hamp wear now? He is beside her. He is here in Charleston. Her trap of mirrors is sprung. She continues to rock, gives nothing away, for she is certain he is lurking just beyond her view—perhaps in his bloody black Paris coat, perhaps in some angel garb of white linen, though she does not think the latter likely. Naked, perhaps. Her secret sharer, naked, but carrying her father's sword cane. The Apollo of Hamp's statue, fig-leafed but carrying the cane. Rebecca has grown so used to the presence of her dead brother that even this notion does not shock her, nor does she wish to share this mad knowledge with her sister Abbie. She will not include this in her weekly letter. Hamp is hers and hers alone—in madness.

Not alone. Not exactly alone.

Since her husband's death, Rebecca had called on Madame Chazzar at least monthly. And to that Gypsy she had poured out at least some portion of her heart and also had her future told—but not to any great satisfaction. The dire predictions continued to come true, and she saw little of the happy promises. Still, she had come to trust the woman who she knew was not a Gypsy but an Irishwoman of perhaps mean origins. They said this in Charleston, but there were few in Charleston whom she trusted on this or any other account. None, in fact.

She had shared much with her fortune-teller. She told of her battles with Colonel Latimer, and, of course, she shared her discovery that Hélène was a prostitute, that she had been taking money from the doctor and from others. Perhaps in their very home Hélène had engaged in outrageous acts of uncleanliness. She thanked God that David had been strong enough to resist that woman. "Thank God," Marie Patrick had echoed. But that was long before, and now Rebecca came to speak of new revelations.

"Madame Chazzar," Rebecca said, "I must throw myself on your mercy." This was a common enough beginning.

"Yes, God's child. Tell me all."

"There is another woman," Rebecca announced.

"Who?"

"She came in the mirror. I placed the mirror against the wainscot, slanted it just so, and then she came. Not the widow of the martyred Hayne—not so ancient as the Revolution. You cannot guess. I am certain. Not even you."

"Who, then? Tell me."

"Hélène. The governess."

"I am not surprised."

"She came unbidden. She is in the mirror. She looked over my shoulder last night. The others have only been suggestions, but she I saw quite plainly. There is a gap between her teeth. Blond hair. I knew it was she."

"And what does she want of you?"

"I asked her. Just as you advised, I asked her. She refused to reply. I lost my temper with her."

"She has a message. Surely the message comes. You must be patient."

"Patient!" She seldom snapped at Madame Chazzar, but Rebecca felt she had been far too patient for far too long.

"There be another," Mrs. Patrick says. Not a question but statement of fact, accompanied by raising her ring-crowned finger.

"No. Only her."

"I mean your brother."

"Hamp? No. Only the whore of a governess."

"He is in the room."

"You know that?"

"You have told me."

"Have I?"

"Yes, my human child, you have."

"He is never there completely. I think to catch him in the mirror. I look quickly. He is in heaven. He watches me. Always. Yet he comes down to the house. He is in the house. He does not watch over me. He watches me."

"Why?"

"I have sinned."

"You have broke a promise."

"I promised never to marry. When he came back from Paris, that first night, he demanded it. 'Promise me you will never marry,' he shouted. 'You will come to Paris.'"

"The two of you, there upon the boulevard," Madame Chazzar whispered.

"Oh, no. Never. I was afraid I might think more of my brother than I did of God, that I would obey my brother, follow him, go to Paris to live and deny all else."

"You could not," the other woman replied quietly.

"On that same night I left my bed, and, kneeling, I asked God not to let me love Hamp so very much, not to let me make this man my earthly idol."

"You would not listen to your brother."

"I had the dictates of my conscience. In ten days he was dead."

"But you did not kill him, Mrs. Lawton."

"I prayed for his death. I went to my knees and prayed, 'Dear God, let my brother die.'"

"Indeed, that is a sin."

"Yes."

"But his will for you was sinful. And that, too, has been forgiven. God forgives our sins, no matter what they be."

"I could not love my brother. Not as he deserved! Do you understand? I could not love him as he needed! And now I will never again hear his voice or see his face on earth. Oh, yes. God has heard me. He has answered all my prayers! Took my brother. Took two more brothers. Took my child. Now He has taken my husband. There is no end to His bountiful goodness! What a fool I was!"

"No," the other woman said. She had risen from her chair and circled to Rebecca's side. She knelt and placed a thick arm about her visitor. Rebecca did not seem to notice, or rather she accepted this embrace as a child might, laying her head in an awkward manner upon the fortune-teller's shoulder.

"I have a new prayer, now. Do you wish to hear it?" At the nod Rebecca went on. "In the next world, please, God, grant me an oblivion of this one. I prayed to you once for my brother's death. That prayer was answered. Why not this one? Dear God, free me from all hurtful knowledge of the past. Yes, I am a sinner, but Christ the Lord had declared that He would not cast out those who approached Him. Grant me please, the peace that passeth all understanding."

"Amen," said Madame Chazzar.

No more than that. She offered no future for Rebecca, who felt somehow cheated. Having confessed to so much she was entitled to a future, but her wait was not so very long.

That same night as she sat before her dressing table and searched this smaller fastened mirror, watched among the shadows of the emptying room, she was rewarded.

"You," said the gap-toothed mirage, "You, Rebecca are the seventh child of a seventh child. What do you need of fortune-tellers? You have the gift of prophecy."

"Cursed gift!" Rebecca shouted back.

"You saw your brother's fate."

"In his eyes. Shining in his eyes!"

"These eyes?" the woman of the mirror asked, and Rebecca saw there not the cursed governess, but the face of her brother. An unblemished laughing face. Rebecca turned from the mirror, and he approached her, not naked as she had feared, not with organ exposed, but dressed in his Paris frockcoat and that coat unbloodied. And rising from the cushion, she, too, was transformed. She was a young woman, dressed in taffeta, and she threw her arms around her wandering brother.

Here, now, on the very night of his arrival home, she has glimpsed the future. "I dreamed of us last night," she told her brother. "Such a dream it was, Hamp. DeQuincey with his opium could not have beheld such sights as you and I were treated to."

"Tell me, Sister. I promise I will not laugh."

"Laugh! How dare you even consider such behavior?"

"Tell me!" And Hamp raised a palm to his lips as if to stifle mirth. She grabbed the hand and pulled it down. And held it still.

"Listen, then. You and I, we two alone, walked through the garden of Paradise. I am quite certain it was Paradise for there were fountains bubbling, and classical statues of white marble, and flowers in such profusion. These surrounded us on every side, and we wandered hand in hand." At this point he gave her hand a squeeze and smiled. "Yes," she continued, "we wandered just so and then stopped before a statue that held a finger to its lips. And you said, 'Did you ever see Fitch's celebrated picture of Eternity?' 'No,' I answered. 'I have never heard of such a picture.' 'Well,' you said, 'I will show it to you. Nothing but that picture can give you an idea of the vastness of this Eternity. Come!' Then I followed you through beautiful alleys, golden buildings on each side, and just this narrow path for us to travel, until you stopped us before an immense crystal wall. You held my hand without speaking, and we watched together. Oh, Hamp! In the crystal, on the other side, forms were moving, always moving! Over all, above, below, beyond, hovered a Something, a Something too great, too awful, and too mysterious for me to comprehend, though I did struggle to make sense of all I saw, and striving still, I awoke!"

Hamp stared at her. In reply to this wonderful dream, he could only direct towards her the gift of his odd and sincere attention. "Well," he said finally, "I am speechless in the face of such a vision."

"Oh, dreams are such a blessing, Hamp."

"This was Fitch's picture of Eternity? Rebecca, who is Fitch?"

"A great artist, I am certain. But his forms were moving, always together, always in a mysterious unison."

"Forms? Could they have been men? Men and women?"

Rebecca struggled to remember. "Why, yes. I do suppose they were, but shapes only behind that crystal screen."

"Brothers and sisters, too?"

"Why, of course," she laughed. "Won't we spend eternity together?"

"Doing something great and awful?" He laughed but on his face was no expression of humor.

"What can it be?" she practically shouted.

"A secret. That is why the statue cautions silence."

"Yes, yes. To be given even that glimpse of what awaits us is enough. I tell you in all truth, I would not care to sleep if I could not dream."

"But this is the dream," her brother said. "Aren't we that? The stuff of dreams. Shouldn't I say, 'Wake now, Sister.'" And he brought a hand to her cheek, touched it barely, and whispered, "Wake."

Then Rebecca reached up and held his hand in hers, and leaning in, she kissed him—a soft, cool, delicate kiss. Then he brought his hand about her waist and sought her lips and pulled her close so that she felt a shudder run through his body and through her own. Then he stepped back slightly but continued to hold her hand.

"Now you know what I have been fighting against," he said.

"But why?" she asked and once more pressed against him and placed her now warm lips on his, at least upon his imagined lips—for he, the brother, was only that, the participant of his sister's dream, and she, too, is imagined. And now the two of them are shifting garments, unbuttoning, unfastening, undoing until they can form their perfect longed-for and dreaded union, move in unison . . . but was that possible? In Heaven? Was there some corporal significance? No. What she prayed for, what she expected to find there in God's enchanted bosom, was simply the end of dreams. What she prayed for was an end of artifice and for the beginning of life. She prayed that she might love her brother and that he might love her.

Awake. Rebecca lay abed and wondered at the scene. On the far wall the three great windows, each running floor to ceiling, glowed like three massive columns. The bent mahogany legs and backs of the bureau and the settee and the dressing table, these shone in distinct curves, and the mirror above the table came as a blank rectangle of shimmering light.

Rebecca realized now that the morning was well advanced and that she was not alone. Someone had thrown open the thick, damask curtains. Someone had let the light in. And this someone, this woman was approaching through the door, which stood open both high and wide. And this woman seemed to float towards her. A figure dressed in black, all in mourning, always mourning. No. Wait. Dressed in blue. All in the blue of midnight. And this blue-shrouded woman took both of Rebecca's hands between her own and held them in firm attachment. And Rebecca studied the high forehead and the halo, rich and reddish, above that alabaster flesh. And then she sought out the dark eyes, sparkling eyes encased in a more weary flesh, eyes that spoke of sorrow—and of something else, perhaps—spoke of some profound trust, some common, if sorrow-filled confidence, that she had come to share, some fearless intimacy that might stretch on even into eternity.

"So," her sister Abbie said, "I am here to bring you back among the living."

"Yes," Rebecca said. "I am forgiven."

"For what?"

"A secret. I must tell you, Sister. I must tell you now."

AN AFTERWORD

The apartment Thomerson Lawton shared with his mother, Rebecca, was in a neighborhood like many others of Paris. An unsteady line of two- and three-story houses crowded against the street—masonry houses, similar and gray, but judging from the abutting wall, theirs boasted a garden. And he did then think of Charleston. Not to compare, as he might have, this portion of an enduring city with that recalcitrant town. Rather, he experienced that odd rush of emotion which may accompany some indefinite remembrance.

Thomerson was a big man. He was large-boned and athletic like his father, David, and like his father, he wore a broad mustache that accented, as a window sill might, his deep-set eyes and high forehead. Yet the visitor knew he was not his father, who once accomplished all things to perfection. On this day, son Thomerson struggled hard with the latchkey and with bent shoulder heaved open the great oaken door, and they entered upon a flagstone entry.

Thomerson and his mother had only the bottom floor, but that space was well occupied with upholstered sofa and divans with many cushions and portraits and a great mahogany wardrobe and exhibiting cabinets and bookcases —entire walls of books, except for that wall where glass-paned doors opened wide onto the garden. The year was 1907, and the month was June. The wisteria came late to this city and contained itself while here in the Old World. No, none of that wild, aggressive sauntering about the rooftops. This was not Charleston. And yet the smell of those spilling blossoms and the smoke of Thomerson's cigar returned the visitor there for one violent moment of regret.

"Mother," Thomerson called out, and from the recesses of the house came the rustle of movement, and in the far doorway appeared a very small woman dressed all in black satin, the black of eternal mourning. And their visitor at once felt a sense of inferiority. Yes, in Rebecca Lawton's bearing he recognized already that assumption of entitlement which came so naturally to her generation. He could not say exactly what Thomerson's view on her might be. Oh, that he loved her, of that there was no question, even doted on her to a degree that might border on the unhealthy. Yet in preparation for this meeting, he had referred to her as "exquisitely absurd" and even as a "vain and silly child."

"She never recovered from her seventeenth year," he had explained. "She was the most beautiful belle in all of Baton Rouge and quite the essayist as well."

This ancient belle moved towards the visitor—the black satin dress of ample skirts, the black lace and silver hair and the harmonious, restrained movement of those dainty alabaster hands, the sparkling eyes which looked upon one with such surprising intensity. In response to an introduction she breathed out a welcome and directed him to a chair. She mentioned Charleston, of course, but only briefly. They had acquaintances and even memories to share but not so very many, for the visitor did not use his given name of Patrick, nor the taken name of Spencer either. Quite obviously she did not recognize him from that earlier time, and even if she did, she would not know he was Mrs. Patrick's son, the fortune-teller's son, which was just as well. She would think him privy to her secrets, which he was.

Then they complimented him on his publications, both of his novels and the slim biographies of Lanier and Poe. The novels had been moderate successes, but he had not mentioned the other works to Thomerson and was surprised he even knew of them. And he was even further surprised when she announced, "Your services to our family will be greatly appreciated."

"Madame?" he questioned.

Only then did Thomerson explain that they wished him to attempt a life story of their beloved and heroic David Lawton. A publisher was interested. Modest funds were available. These would tide him over until the royalties began—"the future riches."

Of course, he protested at once, saying that though flattered, he was not the one to undertake such. "Mrs. Lawton, your son should write that history," he said, and added with some honesty, "Naturally, I am familiar with your husband's life and am certain the subject is deserving of full treatment. But your son has not only the talent but a ready-made knowledge at his disposal."

"No, no. My son is quite busy enough with the living of his own life, a life which in the end will match my husband's in accomplishment and honor."

"Oh, Mother, please," Thomerson laughed—though in fact he appeared to agree with her completely. Then he bowed to the visitor and saying, "My friend, excuse me for a moment," he left the room.

At once there passed across Rebecca Lawton's face a curious relaxation—a mellowness. She smiled faintly at the visitor. "The point, Monsieur, is that you are not a stranger to us. You, as a Southerner, must understand that like all fine natures, my son is a being of strange contradictions, which the trials of life have not yet reconciled in him. With me it is a little different. I have survived my trials. But then men are more complex than women, more concerned with that inner self. Have you not found that to be true?"

"Madame," he said with a quiet laugh, "I have never thought to dwell on my inner self." In part he lied. At times he had done little else.

"Ah," she responded. "That is very wrong. We all should reflect upon the manner of being we are. Of course, we are sinners and require God's forgiveness. But we are all romantics as well, and as such, suffer from that most profound discord—the separation between the lowly impulses of nature and the lofty idealism of feeling. Monsieur, how do we forgive ourselves? Monsieur, is that not the question?"

Of course, he agreed that was a question of importance, agreed with an aging child who sat on the chair's edge, the heels of her patent leather boots floating three inches above the carpet. No, not a child, for she was doll-like in that pose and in the porcelain serenity of her face. And there came the constant smell of the wisteria, that distant blue curtain against which the bees threw themselves.

Rescued. Thomerson appeared once more, and the conversation went speedily in the direction of how the visitor might go about the grand task of writing David Lawton's biography. Then the small woman led him by the hand into the library, where, in addition to more books, he was confronted by the wide and ornately spooled desk they shared and by numerous plain and sturdy filing cabinets—these containing, as he was quickly shown, thousands upon thousands of items relating to the life of David Lawton. Letters, diaries, newspaper clippings, even the account books and memorandums of professional and domestic nature.

What then? At such a point he could hardly confess his true identity or even suggest that on some deep, dark level he might harbor them ill will. Perhaps they did, at least, understand that he was not of their class. Perhaps they thought to win him over and hence to win over an indifferent world. To justify, to prove themselves somehow.

Still, how odd their choice. In his own meager way he, too, had courted Hélène, and he, with a single misplaced word, had begun the ruin of all their lives, a ruin he then completed with his cowardly anonymous notes. Ruined? No. Changed their lives. The death of David Lawton had changed their lives immeasurably. Was he truly to blame? No. He was only a small instrument of colossal fate. Only in his failure to win the girl did his part stretch beyond the minor, and that of importance only to him—and only to him as he was then—young and infatuated. No, he lied to himself. He loved Hélène, truly loved her. He lied. He was to blame. Or was he?.

Could David Lawton have been his father? He saw no resemblance between himself and this man Thomerson. Perhaps in heaven—perhaps heaven was a place of answers. For some answers he could wait that long.

Would this free him? Perhaps. Did he truly see the Lawtons' story? Did he see anything? What would he be attempting? To tell a dream? But how? How did one convey the dream sensation, the commingling of absurdity, surprise, and bewilderment of the struggle, the notion of being captured by the incredible, of having beneath our feet no firm ground?

He nodded his consent to Thomerson. And thus, they stood in that Paris apartment before this great horde of family archives, this grand accumulation of words upon paper—of truths waiting to be unleashed.

"My friend," said Thomerson, "here is where you begin."

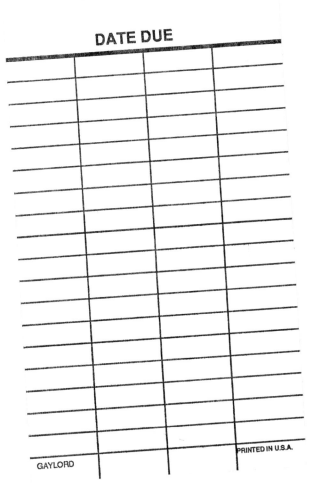

DATE DUE